Hannah At Thirty-Five, Or How To Survive Divorce

Hannah At Thirty-Five, Or How To Survive Divorce

ANABEL DONALD

HODDER AND STOUGHTON
LONDON SYDNEY AUCKLAND TORONTO

British Library Cataloguing in Publication Data
Donald, Anabel
   Hannah at thirty-five, or how to survive divorce
   1. Divorce   2. Divorcee
   I. Title
   306.89   HQ814

ISBN 0 340 34441 5

Copyright © 1984 by Anabel Donald. First printed 1984. All rights reserved. No part of this publication may be reproduced or transmitted in any form or by any means, electronic or mechanical, including photocopy, recording, or any information storage and retrieval system, without permission in writing from the publisher. Printed in Great Britain for Hodder and Stoughton Limited, Mill Road, Dunton Green, Sevenoaks, Kent by Biddles Limited, Guildford and King's Lynn. Typeset by Hewer Text Composition Services, Edinburgh.

Hodder and Stoughton Editorial Office: 47 Bedford Square, London WC1B 3DP.

1

Hannah Dodgson wasn't stupid. Far from it. She had distinguished herself as an undergraduate at Oxford and gone on to write a doctoral thesis, the definitive assessment of the poetry of William Casterton, an Elizabethan poet so minor that only Hannah and a PhD student at the university of Uppsala even noted his existence. The thesis was published in Britain and America and languished unopened on library shelves throughout the English-speaking world.

But in real life Hannah had major problems.

She had married the wrong man.

She totally lacked self-confidence.

She assumed that everyone meant well.

She looked for the good in each situation and shut her eyes to unpleasant facts.

In consequence, she awoke on her thirty-fifth birthday about to find out that her husband Brian had left her for an older woman.

She was alone in their house – except for the two spaniels, Whisky and Soda, living mementoes of Brian's country gentleman phase. Brian was away on a business trip. She didn't ask, but she assumed he had a girl with him. He had been a professional footballer. Too old to play with his previous mastery, he had retired three years before. Retirement didn't suit him. He'd been a golden boy all his life – mother's darling, hero of the Midlands town he came from, hero of England – and took the companionship of adoring women for granted. Many of his post-football ventures into business had been disastrous; only success with women remained as a public reflection of his own estimation of himself.

Brian was conceited; he was not nearly so smart as he thought he was. He was useless at handling money; selfish, immature, socially ambitious without any of the social skills needed for success, and he limped slightly from a bad knee injury.

He was also charming, glib and an excellent lover. He was well co-ordinated, physically strong, good at saying what women wanted to hear, a convincing liar and apparently immune from boredom. He was a tolerant and affectionate father to his two children, whom he insisted on sending to smart boarding-schools. He was generous.

Hannah loved him, but she didn't look too closely. Hannah was a loving person. She loved her two children, the two spaniel dogs, her parents (and loving the Crester-Fyfes was a task that would have daunted St Francis of Assisi); she loved several of her friends, she loved some of the nuns who had taught her at school, and she cried for two hours when Elvis Presley died.

Loving she was, but not entirely devoid of sense. She knew that all was not well in her marriage. For one thing Brian was seldom at home, for another thing he slept with her only when he was drunk, and for a third thing he often absent-mindedly called her Marjorie.

Hannah assumed that Brian was having a long-standing affair with Marjorie, whom she imagined as nineteen, nubile, blonde and silly. Hannah herself was dark, tall and decidedly heavy – even in her slimmest days she was big. She went in and out where women generally went in and out, but more so than most. The Victorians would have admired her looks.

So on her birthday morning Hannah was sitting in the pine country-house-type kitchen (Brian's choice – a contemporary of the spaniels), clutching together the fragments of the ideal marriage her mother and the nuns had told her about. A large house; dogs; children; lots of friends; charity work; warm hospitality; a real Catholic home.

The children were nearly always away at boarding-school, true. She had stopped doing all but the most rudimentary housework, to deter Brian from bringing home his louts of friends to drink and shout and paw her and show off, true. The charity work she did mostly consisted of talking to other middle-class women, true; but still . . .

Hannah sipped coffee, opened birthday cards from her

children and made plans for the day. She was lunching with Bibi – lovely.

She deliberately refused to wonder why she had not heard from Brian. He should have been back from a business trip to the Midlands at least two days ago. He hadn't rung – not unusual – but surely he wouldn't ignore her birthday.

If only she had a job. But that wouldn't please Brian. He wanted her at home, like his cosy, cooking, houseproud mother.

The doorbell rang and the two spaniels immediately burst into a crescendo of hysterical barking. The woman standing on the doorstep was well into her forties, but she was standing no nonsense from passing years; her hair was dyed courageous red, her bust surged outwards like a flying buttress and expensive stockings drew attention to the fact that she had kept her ankles. Hannah had never had any ankles to keep – her legs simply terminated in a narrower expanse of flesh that turned under to form feet.

"I'm Marjorie. May I come in? I think we should talk."

Hannah obligingly let her in – she was always obliging – and gave her black coffee. "What good ankles you have," she said.

Marjorie looked puzzled. Then, as she saw Hannah was serious, she was flattered. "My legs have always been good," she said proudly. There was a faint Welsh intonation to her voice.

"Not common, in Wales," reflected Hannah. "Very few Welshwomen have good legs."

"What, pray, do you have against the Welsh?"

"Nothing," said Hannah. "Unless one of them is just going to tell me she's taking my husband."

When Hannah arrived at Bibi's for lunch she didn't, at first, tell her about Brian. Bibi was too full of her own news – she'd been to an infertility clinic and she wanted Hannah to hear the latest moves in her campaign to get pregnant. Bibi's flat, like Bibi, was much smarter than Hannah. Bibi was a successful interior decorator and her flat was even now in the process of total renovation. It had been decorated for the last six months in high tech style; now hard-edged furniture in primary colours was stacked forlornly in the middle of the long main room while two workmen silently papered the walls with hand-painted pastel designs of birds and flowers, and Bibi pattered on about her latest doctor. "He's small and bald and *very* understanding, and his internal examination doesn't hurt a *bit*." Hannah rolled an embarrassed eye in the workmen's direction but they were concentrating on the wishy-washy paper.

It was impossible to confide in Bibi with an audience – and, besides, while Hannah kept the news about Brian to herself it seemed less real. Then they moved into the kitchen and Hannah watched thin, elegant, impatient Bibi flitting about looking for Hannah's birthday present. For the first few years of their friendship (they met at school) Hannah had been the better-looking one. Bibi's face was comical, cramped, like a monkey, with gleaming alert little eyes, while Hannah had clear features and thick dark hair. But now Hannah was unkempt and over-weight, and Bibi was still her metallic, well-presented self.

"Here it is! Here it is!" Bibi tweaked an envelope from behind accumulated postcards on the memory board beside her gleaming, mud-coloured, slimline wall phone. "Happy, happy birthday! Open it now, I want to talk to you about it!"

Hannah tore open the envelope and stared at the embossed card inside. "It's a year's membership for this marvellous new fitness centre that's opened in Hampstead High Street. I've joined too and I want you to come with me this afternoon to one of those classes where you grunt and heave and become incredibly fit, like Jane Fonda..."

"Brian's leaving me for another woman," blurted Hannah and began to cry. With little noises of sympathy Bibi hugged her close until the tears slackened to a trickle; then she asked, "Is it anyone I know?"

Hannah described Marjorie and her visit while Bibi snorted in astonishment and sympathy.

"Did this Marjorie woman tell you what arrangements Brian was going to make for you and the children?"

Hannah nodded in misery. Marjorie had explained carefully what she had decided. Clearly the Welshwoman was both well-off and practical, if not bossy. Hannah's children were to continue at their present schools, paid for by Brian. The house in Hampstead was to be sold and half the money given to Hannah to buy a place to live for herself and the children.

"Will he pay you maintenance?"

"She says it's better for me if he doesn't, so I can be independent. Mind you I've always wanted to work. It was Brian who didn't want a working wife."

"A working ex-wife being clearly different," said Bibi. "Are you going to take it lying down?"

"What's the option?"

"Get a good solicitor and take Brian to the cleaners."

"It's not worth it – Brian never has any spare money."

"You're too good to be true, Hannah. Don't you even feel bitter?"

Hannah gazed blankly at Bibi's hand-painted kitchen blind. She didn't feel anything. I must be in shock, she thought. "Why? He probably left me because I'm too fat. I should have stuck to the diet."

"Which one?" Bibi had supported Hannah through every fad diet known to medical science and several known only to beauty editors of fashion magazines. "Weight has nothing to do with it. You're big, but gorgeous."

"You never liked him much," said Hannah, remembering that Brian had often told her how undesirable he found Bibi. "That scrawny bitch," he had called her.

Meanwhile Bibi was remembering Brian's tendency to pounce on her in dark corners.

"Don't you think I should fight for my marriage?" said Hannah wistfully. The heroic role always appealed to her, especially if it involved self-sacrifice and difficulty. "What about Karen and John?"

Bibi clicked her tongue impatiently. "The children will be all right, they're much tougher than you think. Do you imagine this Marjorie woman is going to give in easily? And do you honestly think you have a marriage to save? You've been unhappy for years."

"No I haven't," defended Hannah automatically.

"Yes you have. You look a mess and your house is a tip. Most of the time you live in a dream, eating Mars bars and being nice to people. And you read all the time, non-stop. Even when you walk the dogs you have a book in your hand."

"I like reading," defended Hannah again, conscious that Bibi was right. Her reading had become addictive. In the early days of marriage Brian had laughed when he found her with a book in her hand, and teased her about it; sometimes he took it away, put it down and kissed her. Then the arguments started and he sneered at her. "You know all about books and nowt about life, that's what Manny says." Manny was the boss at Brian's football club.

Certainly Hannah found books safer than life; you could always put them down.

"And Brian's been unhappy too," continued Bibi. "He's never at home, is he?"

"No," admitted Hannah. "Bibi, Marjorie said something odd. She said I was too nice. How can you lose a husband by being too nice? I don't understand." Large tears filled her clear brown eyes.

"You're too unselfish. You protect other people too much. You should shout and throw things. You have to fight, Hannah."

"I don't want to. I want to be nice to people. I want to be happy."

"It hasn't worked," said Bibi ruthlessly. "Start telling the truth for a change. Get a solicitor. Fight for what you want. Otherwise, Hannah, you're going to go under."

"Go under where?"

"Under everything. Sunk without trace. I remember you when you used to be funny and original."

"Aren't I still?"

"No," said Bibi. "You're like wet newspaper, soggy. You pretend you don't matter and that everything's all right."

Hannah looked at Bibi, appalled. "You sound as if you hate me."

"Not you. Just what you do to yourself. Being a long-suffering calf will only get you to the knacker's yard." Bibi's Mexican silver bracelets tinkled irritably. "*Fight*, Hannah!"

The fifteen-minute drive back to her own house took Hannah two hours. She could not bring herself to go back. She had an instinctive dread of returning, she knew it would hurt. The house had too many associations, and all those associations were now silted under Marjorie's visit. Hannah could hear the Welsh tones. "Brian needs a firm hand" – just like a nanny, though she was probably right.

At first Hannah sat in her little battered Renault just round the corner from Bibi's flat, in a smart cul-de-sac. That was unfair on the spaniels who, confined to the back, snarled and yapped at passers-by. Hannah started the car and drove to the place where she usually walked the dogs. It was a large stretch of scrubby grass surrounded by stunted trees, with the blasted, deserted air of non-smart parks in London. She groped under the seat for a book to read, then, impatient with herself for exactly fulfilling Bibi's observations, went without reading matter.

The dogs, ebullient and mindless, ran in circles and chased the flocks of seagulls that rose briefly in contemptuous acknowledgment of their presence, then settled back as the whirlwinds passed. It was a warm, bright, early summer day. Normally Hannah would have lain in the sun starting work on her tan – she had thick, good skin that tanned evenly to a warm biscuit colour – but today she huddled into her clothes and tried not to suffer.

She felt bewildered. Marjorie could have been talking about another person, this Hannah she was describing who would buy a cheaper house and get a job and have care and control of her children. And who was the Brian who wanted to do the right thing, of course, and see as much of the kiddies as possible? It wasn't the Brian Hannah had married. "My husband," said Hannah to the seagulls and they waddled apart on the muddy grass to let her through. The dogs gambolled eagerly round a pile of litter. Kentucky Fried Chicken litter. Hannah, vainly attempting to wrest chicken bones from Whisky and Soda (ridiculous names for dogs but Brian had thought them the Right Thing), remembered the first ever time she had eaten Kentucky Fried Chicken – in the late Sixties, in America, on their honeymoon. Brian and she had never heard of Colonel Sanders (no loss) and they had sat at a drive-in movie – romance of Brian's childhood, he was captivated by America – and eaten fried chicken.

Vainly shouting, "Whisky, Soda, drop it! No!", Hannah began to cry for her marriage.

Hannah went to see her parents next day. Normally she would have worried about upsetting them; now she was too hurt and bewildered to care.

They had lived in a small, rose-covered cottage near Didcot since her father's retirement from the Consular Service. Reginald Crester-Fyfe did the garden; his wife Jane kept the house. They drank gin and tonic and talked about England going to the dogs. He was a church-warden. She, inconveniently Catholic, had to content herself with working tirelessly for the Conservative Party. There were copies of *Country Life* in the lavatory and Reginald had a room to himself, called the den, the walls lined by old school photographs, that Jane cleaned only twice a week.

"This is a surprise," said Reginald nervously, greeting Hannah with the garden gate between them. He had been good-looking and was still extremely vain, training his few remaining hairs in improbable patterns over his bald, tanned scalp. "Did you have a good birthday?"

Hannah came straight to the point. "Brian and I are getting a divorce."

"Oh." Her father's well-manicured hands flew to the silk cravat he always wore to disguise the scrawniness of his neck.

"Can I come into the garden?"

He still stood with the low gate between them barring her entry. An inarticulate man, he was casting about for words. He felt more for Hannah than his undemonstrative nature had ever let her guess. She had long ceased to expect anything more than formality from him. Now he wanted to protect her from her mother's tactless suggestions and criticisms, he wanted to smooth the frown from her face. But he also noticed how middleaged she looked, and it worried him. He adjusted his cravat. "I'm very sorry, Hannah," he said. "You'd better tell your mother."

"You've let yourself go, that's what it is," said Jane Crester-Fyfe. "Give it another try, darling. Lose a stone and have your hair done, and we'll go shopping for some nice new clothes. Drink your tea."

Hannah's mother hadn't let herself go. She kept husband, house and self under a frigid discipline – her body was as firmly corseted as Marjorie's, without the Welshwoman's promise of wholesome and enthusiastic sensuality when the abundant flesh was released. Jane never liked to be seen without the armour of clothes and make-up. She emerged from her room at seven-thirty each morning fully turned out for the day and Reginald hadn't seen her undressed for years. Not that he specially wanted to. He slept happily in his den.

"I don't want to give it another try," said Hannah. "It's no good. Brian's quite right."

Reginald cleared his throat awkwardly from behind the *Daily Telegraph*. "I think I'll just pop upstairs to my den. Come and see me before you go, Annie."

Jane frowned at this endearment – she didn't approve of pet names. "Now your father's gone," she said, as they both watched his cavalry twills and well-polished shoes retreating up the stairs, "I can talk to you openly. Remember your faith, Hannah. Divorce isn't allowed, you know. Not unless you pay lots of money for an annulment."

"I don't believe in any of that," said Hannah.

"You don't believe in God?" said Jane, nonplussed, not so much by the content of Hannah's observation as by its bad form. "Poor darling. You'll feel better soon."

Up in the den, Reginald sat at a clumsy, scarred, roll-top desk inherited from his father, a country vicar. He was shaking from Hannah's news. Apart from anything else, the idea of divorce forced him to consider his own marriage. R. F. G. Crester-Fyfe, faded in sepia, grinned at him engagingly from the cricket eleven, the tennis six, the house prefects' group. Reginald studied his younger self intently, but the handsome, slightly dreamy face held no messages.

What on earth, he thought, would Hannah do now? And would she expect him to help? He didn't have much cash to spare . . . and Jane kept the household accounts . . . she wouldn't be prepared to do much. Frankly, she had never liked Hannah. The Crester-Fyfe family was hardly a success, he thought wryly. But he had looked forward to Hannah's birth.

Reginald and Jane had produced her after much discussion ten years after their marriage. Reginald was hewing out an undistinguished career in a lowly branch of the Foreign Service, a consul in lesser-known overseas postings, enjoying the entertaining (with entertainment allowance) and the stature of representing His Majesty abroad. He had spent an uneventful war in South America preserving a British presence, and, apart from the general chilliness of home life with Jane, he was enjoying day-to-day living. But then he looked at himself in the mirror one morning and saw how far his hair had receded, noticed the lines around his eyes. True, he had a hangover which made him look worse. But, all the same, it was enough to make him listen seriously when Jane suggested a baby.

Jane wasn't maternal, and she didn't enjoy sex, though she knew it was her feminine duty to pretend to. But she knew that at twenty-eight she was getting on. Most wives of her age had completed their families and were on to the stage of worrying about nannies and schools. Pain loomed large in her life; she dreaded childbirth; but she knew that, socially, she had to have a child, and she closed her eyes firmly to the unpleasantness she would have to go through to get one.

She didn't want to lose Reginald, either. She had noticed his eyes straying to the young secretaries sent out from England, noticed the loudness of his laughter when he talked to them and his eagerness to help them in and out of cars. She could do no more to make herself attractive to him. She was already dieted, permed, made-up, dressed and scented for him. She knew his deep conventionality. If she once produced his son then he would be sure to be loyal to her.

So she dusted her contraceptive diaphragm with talcum powder, wrapped it in tissue paper and packed it away in its neat little box, and their once-weekly sexual encounter took on a pleasing raffishness – because who knew when their son would be conceived?

But it wasn't a son, it was Hannah, and Jane had such a painful birth that she decided immediately to have no more children. That being so, it was unfortunate that she didn't like Hannah. A small baby was messy – a Spanish-Indian maid looked after Hannah until she was two. Reginald used to sneak into the nursery and play with Hannah as much as he could – he found her enchanting – but when Jane realised how fond he was of his daughter she set about preventing him from seeing the child. She wasn't clear in her own mind why – a combination of jealousy that he would rather be with Hannah than with her and rage with Hannah for making Jane feel such unladylike things for her own child.

The Crester-Fyfes finished their tour in Uruguay and came home. For six years Reginald was at the Foreign Office in London. All allowances were cut, gin cost UK prices; there was no money to spare for servants, so Jane tucked away in a little rented house in Surrey, had to look after Hannah herself.

She had to look after Hannah and she did, but Jane resented Hannah too much to enjoy it. She wasn't a boy; she wasn't pretty; Reginald talked baby-talk to her and called her Annie (stupid name!); and even at three or four she was disconcertingly intelligent. She peered at Jane from behind her thick dark fringe, eyes detached, and, as Jane thought, critical. Even as a very small girl Hannah could remember being wary of her mother, trying to behave well – but good behaviour was a movable feast in Jane's calendar and Hannah never managed to attain it.

Everything about her irritates me, thought Jane looking at Hannah now. No wonder he's divorcing her. She was torn between the mortification of having a divorced daughter and the satisfying feeling that Hannah was getting what she had always deserved from her sloppy, dreamy, intellectual ways. "I never liked that man," said Jane. "You should have married someone of our sort. And you should never have gone to that university. I told your father at the time. Too much education is bad for girls. It gives them ideas."

"I'll work it out, Mother," said Hannah. "I wanted you to be the first to know, so you don't hear it from anyone else. And I wondered if you could have the children to stay a while next holidays – I'll probably be moving then."

"Where are you moving to?"

"Somewhere cheap," said Hannah. "Can you have the children for a while?"

Jane looked put-upon and virtuous. "I can't refuse," she said. "Besides, Karen is old enough to be a help in the house." Hannah's mood lightened momentarily at the prospect of the epic battle that would certainly ensue if Jane tried to get Karen to do housework.

"I must get back to London," she said. "I'm going to a solicitor this afternoon."

On the way back to London Hannah made an important decision. In the future she would speak her mind. She was still smarting from the frustration of dealing with her mother; all the replies she could have made were ringing in her head. She remembered Bibi's exhortation, "Fight, Hannah!" Words were the only weapons she knew; words and thoughts. All her life had been spent saying what other people wanted to hear, and suppressing her thoughts and opinions because they were different. She had tried to be nice, and it hadn't worked. She wasn't even very good at playing the social game; she never got the tone quite right. Now the tone could go hang. She'd say what she wanted when she wanted, with nothing to lose.

The solicitor was recommended to her by an acquaintance who had been through a divorce. "So sympathetic," she had said.

His office was on the second floor of a tall dusty building off Fleet Street; when Hannah arrived, precisely on time for her appointment at three o'clock, she had to wait for ten minutes while the solicitor negotiated and re-negotiated the order for tea.

"A doughnut, I think. No – fruit cake. The kind with cherries in it. No, a doughnut. With icing."

The girl, a bleached blonde who was probably still in her teens but looked more experienced than Edith Piaf, set off down the stairs.

"No, wait! Jinni! Fruit cake after all."

The solicitor, short, fat and closely suited, looked like an educated pig. He was also younger than Hannah. "Pendlebury," he said briskly, gripping her hand.

"Dodgson," said Hannah. "I had an appointment for three o'clock and it's ten past now."

"Ha-ha-ha," he laughed. "Had to get the tea order straight, first things first and all that. I always eat my tea about this time."

"So do I," said Hannah, "and if you're going to be eating during my appointment I want a doughnut. With icing."

He looked at her in horrified disbelief. "Ullo-ullo-ullo," he said. "I hope we're not going to be difficult."

"*I'm* not," said Hannah, "if I can have a doughnut. With icing, please."

After five seconds of his company Hannah suspected Pendlebury was a fool. After half an hour of it she was convinced. Not even the doughnut was comforting her.

"So you've never – ah – actually worked?"

"Not since my marriage," said Hannah. The room they were in, narrow, long and piled with papers, reminded her of a bedroom she had had in a London flat her parents had rented on one of their leaves. They were always short of money so their London flats were shabby boxes with a good address. Hannah thought wistfully of the space and familiarity of her present house, so soon to be sold.

"And you've been married – ah – "

"Fourteen years." Fourteen years ago today, she thought but did not say. It was the happiest time of her life. Hannah had never met anyone like Brian before. He was totally unintellectual, uninhibited. He desired her, and said so. He made love to her decisively and tenderly, giving her immense pleasure. She saw his conceit as self-assurance, his Midlands manners as masculine directness. She didn't care about the difference in their backgrounds, about his accent, his vocabulary, the way he ate.

He proposed marriage three weeks after their first meeting. Her parents were appalled. The idea of her marrying a man of his class! A professional footballer! "No gentleman plays football," said Jane. "And his parents! What can I tell my friends?" Hannah just nodded, not listening. "Why do you have to rush into it so?" protested Jane. Because I love him, thought Hannah. Because he makes me happy. She reflected very little and a month after his proposal, they were married.

Brian had wanted the wedding on her birthday; passionately in love with her, haunting her presence, standing in the rain outside the London flat waiting for her to return, telephoning her at all hours – he wanted only to please her.

But one of the sets of parents had objected to the date – both sets had objected to most things, above all to the marriage itself – and then the Press found out about their plans, so date and place had to be changed.

Hannah didn't want any reporters and Brian, publicity mad under normal circumstances, was besotted enough with her to agree. The ceremony itself would have been depressing for Hannah if Brian hadn't been there lending the glow of his physical charm to the cavernous church. A strange priest with a speech impediment, the Low-Church Dodgsons all suspicion and rectitude, the Crester-Fyfes acutely embarrassed (embarrassment being the strongest emotion they thought it appropriate to show) and Hannah and Brian totally absorbed in each other.

They were right when they said it wouldn't work, thought Hannah. His friends. Her friends. The football manager and coach. Both families. They had been right, it hadn't worked, but she wouldn't go back and not marry Brian. Parts of the years before the children – two brief years – had been so startlingly, radiantly, suffusingly happy.

"I've been married for fourteen years," repeated Hannah. "You've written that down twice already."

"All right, all right, little lady. Don't get upset. All in good time."

"Apparently not," said Hannah. "Not at this rate. All I want you to do is tell me if you can help me or not."

"I should think so," said Pendlebury with professional glee. "We'll make him pay for his bit of fun. You have no income of your own – have you ever been employed?"

"I taught part-time while I worked on my doctorate, and I was offered a full-time job in America."

Hannah remembered the triumph she had felt when the talent-scout from Berkeley offered her an Assistant Professorship. She was only twenty-one, with a year's work on the doctorate already behind her, firmly established as one of the most promising graduate students of her generation. Another year's supervision by her tutor and then she could finish the thesis anywhere she chose – and the American invited her to Berkeley. The deal was struck over an expensive lunch in Oxford. It was a blustery January day; Hannah's worn dufflecoat flapped open as she walked up the hill towards the centre of the town. She looked at herself reflected in shop windows, long black-stockinged legs, Sixties' skirt, wild hair – I'm a success, she thought, I'm really an Assistant Professor.

But then she met Brian.

"Little chance of employment in the present economic conditions," the solicitor said scribbling furiously.

"I've got an excellent degree from Oxford," said Hannah.

"In English Literature. Perfectly useless, if I may say so, after fifteen years out of the labour market. You can't type, I hope?"

"Only with two fingers."

"There you are then. We'll adopt the position you're unemployable. He's taken the best years of your life – "

"I do hope not."

"And we'll make sure he keeps you and the poor little kiddies in the style to which you're accustomed."

"You think I'll get custody, then?"

"Sure to. You don't drink, take drugs, or cohabit with someone other than your husband?"

"I'm by myself when Brian's away. Except for the two spaniels."

"Excellent." The pig-solicitor was writing furiously. "Judges like dogs. There are you with a perfectly happy home, two children, dogs and a lovely house – no extreme political views?"

"No," said Hannah, "I don't have many political views at all. I do help with the Conservative Bring and Buy Sale."

"Even better. That's not a political view, it's a social service. What would you say were your husband's assets?"

Hannah pondered. "He's still goodlooking in a fleshy way; he's got bright blue eyes, a little like Paul Newman's, and lots of fair hair. His body's terrific – he's just under six feet and he has well shaped legs, sturdy thighs – "

"That's not what I meant," gobbled the pig-solicitor. "Money. I meant money."

"Oh, did you? Well, I might as well finish describing Brian," said Hannah. "He's got clean-lined buttocks that stick out, blip – " she outlined the contours with her hand – "and a muscular chest. His arms aren't bad, either. His knees have taken a battering but he hardly limps at all . . ."

"Dear lady," said the solicitor with evident patience, "I'm hardly the person to listen to all this."

"I don't see why not," said Hannah. "I'm paying for your time."

"But I'm not interested," he yelped, dreading more intimate revelations.

"That's life, though, isn't it," reasoned Hannah. "I don't want to listen to you calling me 'dear lady'; you don't want to listen to my descriptions of my future ex-husband. But if I have to do the one I don't see why you shouldn't have to do the other."

"Social convention dictates..." began the hapless solicitor.

"I've stopped caring about social convention," said Hannah.

"Dates and places," said Pendlebury hastily changing the subject. "You'll have to get me dates and places of your husband's adultery. He's not going to contest the divorce, is he? Splendid. Then all we're arguing about is money. Don't worry, Mrs Dodgson. I'm on your side in this difficult time."

"That's what's worrying me," said Hannah.

Something had to be done about the children and Hannah knew Brian would leave it to her. Early in their marriage she had found out that he had a strong sense of the distinction between men's work and women's work. Some things, like making decisions, shouting for clean socks, getting drunk, men did; other things, like changing nappies, getting hysterical, telling children their parents were about to divorce, women did. At first it was irksome. After a time, feeling his loss of interest in her, she found his attitude to her female role comforting. She took it as a part of his attitude to their relationship, as a sign that Brian thought of her as feminine in a special way.

Rattling down the M4 towards her son's prep school – chosen by Brian because all her titled friend Caroline's non-Catholic relatives went there, and that made it smart – half her mind concentrating on driving the dilapidated Renault, Hannah practised sentences to herself. "Daddy and I . . .", "John darling, we haven't been happy for some time . . .". Their hollowness echoed in her ears. I sound like my mother, she thought with shock.

John's headmaster, an amiable ex-army officer with lashless green eyes and a nervous laugh, was politely surprised at Hannah's arrival; his perpetual smile faltered and dimmed when Hannah told him about the divorce. "I say," he said uncomfortably, "what can I say?"

"Nothing," said Hannah, not unkindly. "But I'd like to speak to John about it."

"Of course. Dash it – of course." Behind the stock phrases he was really upset. "He'll be out in his garden, I expect. Do you know the way?"

Hannah knew the way. She crossed the sunlit rose garden with Whisky and Soda gambolling at her heels. From the cricket pitch she could hear the familiar summer sounds of bat, ball and hectoring coach.

Only John was in the gardens, working alone. The gardens were essentially a publicity manoeuvre designed to impress prospective parents looking round the school, and make them feel that their eight year old, instead of crying for Mummy, would be busily occupied on his own little patch of earth. Most boys spurned them – it was a games and cramming school, and the pupils played games with demonic intensity, or else were taken again and again through the hoops they would be required to negotiate for Common Entrance: but John had taken to the idea of a garden with passion and his wellingtoned figure could be seen well into the dusk when other outdoor activities had ceased, tilling and rearranging and weeding his garden.

He looked up as his mother approached and the dogs hurled themselves on him, barking furiously. His broad Midlands face, so like Brian's in feature but so like Hannah's in dreamy expression, lit up with pleasure. He was much closer to his mother than his father. "I've taken over another three gardens," he said proudly, and bent to greet the dogs, burying his head in their wriggling bodies. "Smythe-Patterson left last term and I took his over . . . Why are you here, Mummy?"

Hannah told him. His body seemed to shrink and shrivel. "Is it my fault?"

"Why should it be?" Hannah took his hand. It was damp, chilly and touchingly small.

"I don't know . . . Do you mind, Mummy? Are you very upset? Doesn't Daddy like us any more?"

This is intolerable, thought Hannah. "Of course Daddy still likes me – and he loves you just as much, you'll see."

Eventually John was comforted: a walk with the dogs, Hannah

explaining that he'd stay at the same school, their new house would be near the old one, telling him silly jokes. His goodbye kiss was affectionate, and his expression wise, as he confided, "Most of the boys' parents in my form are divorced, you know. They've survived."

Karen was much harder to deal with, as Hannah expected. Her sharp questions searched out the weaknesses in the detailed arrangements for the break-up. "So you don't know where Daddy is now and you don't know where we'll live but it'll be cheap and grotty and you'll get some rubbish job." Hannah looked coolly at her and Karen looked as coolly back. Tall for her age, slender, dark, at thirteen with full make-up she looked like a startling young adult.

"I don't know why they allow you to dress like that at school," said Hannah. "I never bought you a pink ra-ra skirt, surely."

Karen sighed. "It's the weekend, Mummy, we can wear home clothes, and I borrowed the skirt from Charlotte St Leger, all right? Can we get back to the point, please?"

"We've been through all your objections already. Unless you've anything new to say, we'll leave it there."

Karen drummed her heels impatiently against the glazed chintz of the headmistress's sofa. "You won't want to take me with you. You don't like me."

"Sometimes I don't like you," said Hannah, "mostly when you sneer at me. But I always love you."

"That's double-talk," said Karen, but she was relieved. "Have you told John?"

"Yes."

"I might have known you'd tell him first, he's the favourite, goody-goody John. What's Daddy's new woman like?"

Hannah described her. "Yuck," said Karen. "Sounds really boring and old. He might as well have stayed with you."

Halfway back to London, rattling and jolting along the middle lane, pushing the Renault far faster than it ought to go, Hannah hated Brian. She thought of John's beseeching face, of Karen's accusing stare, and saw them as embodiments of Brian's weakness. Brian, too, tried to appeal to Hannah's protectiveness and then blamed her if things went wrong. When husbands left, thought Hannah, children were supposed to be a comfort. You took them away into a corner and huddled close to them for warmth. But she didn't feel like that, she felt separated from them. When she looked at both of them she saw half-Brian, and she didn't want half-Brian.

He can't just *go*, she thought, anger welling up and tasting metallic in her mouth. How could he walk out after fourteen years and refuse to see her or even speak to her? His solicitor had been adamant on the phone that morning. "My client feels it would be in nobody's interest to have a meeting now." Hannah didn't even know Marjorie's last name, so she couldn't track Brian down through her. But surely, surely if he'd see her, they could try again? The prospect of the months ahead, the weary drag – money, loneliness, houses, loneliness, settlement, loneliness, children, job – if only Brian took it back. That's all it needed, a few words from him.

"I hate him, I hate him," she said aloud and ground her teeth despairingly. The bitterness in her mouth turned to nausea and she pulled the car to a stop on the hard shoulder, scrambled out and felt the vomit force its way up her throat and between her teeth. It tasted sweet and, faintly, of baked beans.

Even absorbed in her physical misery she puzzled over this. She never ate baked beans. She lay on her side on the scrubby grass that banked the hard shoulder, a discreet distance from the vomit, utterly miserable. Ten yards away cars and lorries hurtled past. She imagined their occupants discussing her. Should they stop? Was she injured?

"Internal bleeding," she said, inaudible above the swish and rumble of the cars. "I'm bleeding internally and it's all Brian's fault."

After a while lying there she savoured the forced inactivity between the unwelcome things she had just done and the further unwelcome things she had to do. Until she felt less sick she couldn't move and the simplicity of the fact was a great comfort. It removed guilt, responsibility and self-reproach. She drank in the diesel fumes from the massive lorries that rumbled past, heaving and shaking the ground beneath her. She could almost feel the atoms bombarding each other.

Previously, she had thought most physics fanciful; earth was earth, not surging particles. But now her marriage like the solid ground itself was shifting and crumbling and even atomic theory was plausible.

"Stop feeling sorry for yourself," said Bibi sharply. Hannah clutched a mug of coffee and surveyed her own cluttered kitchen with some satisfaction. "At least I don't feel so sick now," she said. "The motorway police were kind. You've no idea how miserable I felt, Bibi."

"So you keep telling me."

Hannah's eyes filled with tears. She had settled into comfortable gloom and Bibi, summoned by the motorway police to look after her, was refusing to play the role of sympathetic friend.

"But he won't even talk to me. And this morning his solicitor said he's put the house on the market."

"You don't like the house, remember? Too big, ugly proportions, impossible to keep clean, pretentious, too much room for Brian's friends to stay . . ."

"Did I say all that?"

"Frequently. Incessantly."

"But I know it. It's familiar. How can I get a house and fit it out and live in it by myself? I can't," wailed Hannah, "I just can't. And I'll have to be cheerful for the children, it'll be awful for them. I wish they'd never been born."

The words relieved her as she spoke them – often previously felt, never acknowledged, appalling. And particularly appalling to Bibi, she remembered with a lurch of the heart, as Bibi's face crumpled into sobs.

"Don't say that, Hannah, not when I want a baby so much. You don't know how lucky you are. All you've lost is a man. They're two a penny. The only reason you don't have strings of them waiting for you is your manner. 'Don't fancy me, I'm just a pile of old clothes and blubber.' That's how you behave. If you snapped out of it . . . But look at me. I've been trying to get pregnant for ages, and no sign at all. There must be something terribly wrong with me. I'd give anything for two children."

Hannah sat beside her on the pine bench and hugged her

close. "Oh, Bibi, I'm sorry I upset you. Tell me what happened last time you went to the clinic." And in comforting Bibi she forgot herself.

Next morning a young man arrived from the estate agent's. He was very very young, covered in spots, unable to live up to his pin-striped suit; he looked at the house with scorn. Hannah had refused to give it more than a cursory cleaning; it was a tiny, futile revenge, a thumbing the nose at Brian who had spent so much time raging at her over the standard of her housekeeping. The spaniels tried to bite the youth and he nearly decapitated himself on a clothesline.

"The property market's in the doldrums," he said gloomily, and took his departure.

Her mood of self-pity gave way to rage; rage at herself for being so stupid. How could she have gone so long without lifting a finger to help herself? Why had she not insisted on getting a job? How had she let their marriage rot away without even talking to Brian about her feelings? All those nights she had sat, angry, waiting for him to come home – why hadn't she shouted, wept, let him see her humiliation, her sense of loss? He wasn't unkind; imperceptive, insensitive, but not unkind. Reluctantly, Hannah saw how thoroughly she had imbibed her mother's teaching. Grin and bear it, don't expect too much, all men are beasts, don't let him see he's hurt you. A woman's place is in the right.

Beginning, dimly, to see what she had done wrong when it was too late to set it right, Hannah warned herself against future cowardice and self-deception and set about finding a job. Her solicitor had been right. It was going to be exceptionally difficult, if not downright impossible. Wherever she applied the answer was always the same; even teaching jobs, which she had always conceitedly imagined she could snap up for the taking. No training, no experience.

Failing a job at least she could find out about her rights to state benefit. She went to a social security office to get a Single Parent's Allowance form. The office was a vast room in a dingy building. Row upon row of chairs, some occupied by bedraggled people, faced the interview counter. Overhead was a large displayed number – 77. Underneath it was a box of similar numbers, the top one being 102.

Presumably if you wanted to speak to one of the people behind the counter you took a number and waited in turn. But she didn't want to speak to them – she just wanted the form. Look as she might, she couldn't see any forms displayed. So she went up and spoke to a woman behind the counter.

"Excuse me, where do I find forms to apply for a Single Parent's Allowance?"

The woman, grey of skin and virulent pink of cardigan, aged somewhere between thirty and sixty, didn't look up. "Number seventy-eight," she droned.

Hannah repeated her question.

The woman repeated her drone.

Hannah repeated her question.

An old man clutching number seventy-eight sat down in the chair.

"Take a number and wait your turn," droned the woman.

"Are you a person or a machine?" said Hannah conversationally.

"Take a number and wait your turn."

"Bloody sit down, can't you?" hissed the old man. "You lot think you can barge in anywhere and take what you want."

Hannah took number one hundred and ten and sat down. Two hours later her number came up. She sat down in the chair facing the pink cardigan.

"Excuse me, where do I find forms to apply for a Single Parent's Allowance?"

Wordlessly, the woman leant under the desk and produced the form.

"Why don't you put a pile of these forms in a box somewhere so people can just take them without waiting?" Hannah asked politely.

The woman stared at her with blank eyes. "That is not our procedure."

"Couldn't you make it your procedure?"

"We're understaffed."

Later that day Hannah wrote letters. She resigned from the Catholic Marriage Guidance Council (regretfully – counselling was interesting – perhaps she should have taken some of her own advice). She resigned from the Friends of St Saviour's Hospital, from the Parish Committee, from the Board of Governors of a local Catholic school. She collected the myriad unpaid bills together, bundled them in an envelope and addressed them to Brian's solicitor.

Then she took Whisky and Soda for a long walk through the dusty evening streets, the breeze stale but welcome on her face. Finally, she posted the letters. It was a symbolic action as much as a practical one. She felt like a liner setting out on a long voyage, loosening one by one the ropes that bound her to shore.

2

"So how much extra do you get for the children now Brian's hopped it?" Bibi asked, avid with curiosity. One of her great strengths as a friend was her interest in the small practical details of other people's lives.

"Three quid or so, but we have to be separated for thirteen weeks first."

"So what are you going to live on?"

"I'll have to get a job, that's all there is to it."

"But you've tried and tried. What does that solicitor think you'll get from Brian?"

"Something like a third of his income, but I won't take it. Money for the children yes, but not for me. I've got to stand on my own feet for once."

"Three million people are out of work, and some of them can do useful things – you must realise you don't have much chance, Hannah. You're being noble again."

"I'm not. What kind of existence do you think it would be for me being a pensioned ex-wife?"

"You'll marry again."

"That's what the solicitor kept saying, eyeing me up and down."

"Judges look at you, you know, to decide how marriageable you are."

"That's a very subjective approach. It must depend so much on the taste of the judge. Of course," reflected Hannah, "the entire English legal system depends ultimately on the taste of the judge."

Undiverted by abstract speculation, Bibi pursued more practical lines. "Come to that," she said thoughtfully, "you could marry a judge. I've heard they like beating people and you're nice and fleshy. You'd look splendid in a corset and suspenders."

"It's lousy not being qualified for anything," said Hannah.

"You'll have to pull strings, that's all there is to it. Have you tried Caroline?"

"No," said Hannah. "I can't even bear to think of Caroline at the moment. She was with me when I first met Brian and I wonder if she wasn't half the reason he married me."

It had been an unseasonably hot day in October. Hannah was glowing with health and good spirits, bubbling over with confidence now she had a job in America; Caroline (a school friend) wanted her company at a men's wear exhibition at Olympia. "It's this funny little PR job I'm doing at the moment," said Caroline. "Too sweet, really. I just chat people up. You come and chat them up, too."

It was one of her uncle's companies she was working for, fortunately, as Caroline made no attempt to adapt herself in any way to the demands of the job. Dressed in tweed skirt, twin-set and pearls, Lady Caroline Parkhurst-Maine made the conversation she knew to assorted rag trade dealers who thought she was talking a foreign language. Hannah, in black tights, minidress and flowing hair, looked more congruous but felt more out of place. Caroline never felt out of place. If she noticed disharmony between her and her surroundings she assumed the surroundings were at fault.

Towards the end of the afternoon everyone had drunk a great deal. Hannah and Caroline wandered towards a stand they had not yet visited, Don Juan Modes. It seemed more lively than most; a crowd had gathered. Hannah pushed her way to the front of it and saw Brian.

He was beautiful. That was her first thought. Despite the electric blue silk suit he was wearing, presumably for advertising purposes, he glowed with physical charm. He caught her eye and held it. Dazed and lecherous, Hannah introduced Caroline and Brian's attention immediately shifted to her. He scrutinised her body closely. Visibly regretful, he turned back to Hannah, and as clearly as if he had said it she understood that if he could have fancied Caroline, he would, but as he couldn't her friend would do.

When she knew him better she understood even more. Caroline's title was magic for Brian: it was a badge of fame, of membership of an inner circle. He had absolutely no understanding of the complex and subtle English class system. He thought there was only one upper class, a kind of grab-bag of famous, rich and titled people: he wanted to belong to it. He believed he should belong to it, by right of his popular success as a footballer, because he appeared in TV advertisements.

He found upper-class people attractive and exciting. He included Hannah in this class because she was a friend of Caroline's. Every so often during the course of their marriage he made attempts to enter this charmed world which existed only in his imagination.

But it hadn't been only what he imagined to be her class that attracted him, thought Hannah. Physically, she was his type. He loved big women. Sophia Loren, Shelley Winters, Diana Dors – and Hannah.

"You're not listening, Hannah," said Bibi impatiently. "If you really won't try Caroline, at least have lunch with Nicholas. He'll know somebody who can help. I'll fix it up."

"Are you sure?" said Hannah doubtfully. She had never got on particularly well with Bibi's husband, a director in an advertising agency. "Couldn't I just come for a drink at your flat?"

"Much better without me. He'll feel protective towards you."

The restaurant, quiet, smart, extraordinarily expensive, was just filling up as Hannah was shown to the table. Nicholas wasn't there yet. In ten minutes he arrived, making a royal progress through the room to show how many people he knew. He was over forty but still had a thatch of fair hair which he wore too long; his suit was extremely expensive.

"Ah! Hannah!" he said with an air of discovery which would have been exaggerated for Cortez sighting the Pacific. "What are you thinking?"

"I was thinking that your suit must have cost at least a hundred weeks of Single Parent's Allowance," said Hannah.

His smile faded and she could see the same look dawning as had dawned in the solicitor's eyes.

"No, I'm not going to be difficult," said Hannah. "It's just that I'm telling the truth now. Hasn't Bibi told you?"

They looked at the menu. "How can they charge three pounds for a plate of Irish stew?" said Hannah.

"You're not bitter, are you, Hannah?" said Nicholas nervously.

"No," said Hannah. "I'm not bitter. I just don't understand it. Why would anyone pay three pounds for a plate of Irish stew?"

"Most companies get it off tax," said Nicholas.

"But if they didn't get it off tax the government would get the tax, and they could spend it on something better than Irish stew. Or they could spend it on something worse," said Hannah, being strictly fair.

"What sort of job do you want?" Nicholas obviously preferred to talk business rather than economic theory.

"Any job. The trouble is I'm unqualified. I also don't have any manual skills – I can't draw or make things."

"So what have you to offer?"

"I'm very intelligent," said Hannah.

"Of course you are, my dear, and pretty too," said Nicholas a bottle of wine later, squeezing her knee.

"You're squeezing my knee," said Hannah.

He took his hand away as if it had been burnt. "Just a friendly gesture."

"I didn't think you fancied me," pursued Hannah implacably.

"Well I – of course I – "

"Actually I don't think you do fancy me much," said Hannah. "It's just that I'm available."

"So Nicholas couldn't suggest anything?" said Bibi next day.

"Not a thing," lied Hannah, valuing Bibi's friendship more than truth.

"Men are useless," said Bibi, acknowledging what Hannah knew and she knew but neither of them was mentioning. "*I'll have to put my mind to it.*"

Brian's solicitor rang. Could she please make sure the house was in order when prospective clients came to view?

This fully deserved slur on her housekeeping enraged Hannah and she became even more determined to clean nothing; at the same time she wanted the house to sell for a good price. She resolved to find a cleaning firm and send the bill to Brian. The first company she tried said they would send a man round right away to give her an estimate. Next day she called them again and they said they would send a man round right away. She waited an hour and called them again.

This time it was a different voice. "I'm sorry but we won't be able to send anyone for at least a week. We're understaffed."

"Why didn't the other person I spoke to tell me that at first?"

"I expect he didn't want to disappoint you. Business is booming at the moment; we've far more work than we can handle."

"So why don't you take on more staff?"

"Then we'll have too many when business is slack."

I'm sure that's rotten business practice, thought Hannah briefly; she put it out of her mind and went on through the Yellow Pages. Two days later she reached Zabriskie, the Polish Cleaner.

"Yes," said the Pakistani or Indian voice. "We clean houses. When shall I come and give an estimate?"

"Right away, please," said Hannah. She then went to have a bath secure in the knowledge no one would come.

Twenty minutes later the doorbell rang. The spaniels burst into their usual cacophony of noise and Hannah struggled into an old towelling dressing-gown of Brian's, shrugging off the pang of nostalgia it gave her.

A small, dark Indian stood on the doorstep smiling. "Here I am. Zabriskie Cleaners, at your service."

"Isn't that a Polish name?" said Hannah.

"I bought the name legally," said the Indian proudly. "With cash money. I am Mr Patel, at your service, Mrs Dodgson. May I take a look round your charming house?" Hannah trailed after him, watching his disapproving face. "Oh dear dear, this house needs cleaning badly. I will put it in excellent condition for just forty pounds."

"Will you really?" said Hannah. "How soon?" (The earliest date she had been offered by other cleaners was three weeks.)

"This afternoon, I will start," said Patel. "Finish tomorrow. OK?"

"OK," said Hannah.

"This Indian is amazingly efficient," she said to Bibi.

"That's probably why the British working man hates them

so much," said Bibi. "I phoned to say I've got you a job interview at twelve o'clock this morning."

"Bibi, you angel!" Hannah's whole body was suffused with delight. "A real job? What doing?"

"It's this funny little private school in Autumn Road, near you. St Ethelberta's, it's called. Angela Graham's daughter goes there."

"The batty daughter? Is it a batty school?"

"Not entirely," said Bibi cautiously. "They're looking for someone part-time to teach Latin, English and History. And help with Games."

"Gosh," said Hannah. "Is that all?"

St Ethelberta's was a large, shabby Hampstead villa, tucked away behind dusty rhododendrons between a bridge academy and an abortion clinic. The sign said, "Private School for Young Ladies 11–18. Headmistress: Miss Beatrice Thirkettle, MACantab."

A school secretary answered the bell. She was a cheerful woman in her forties with a powerful squint, or possibly a glass eye. She exuded a strong smell of peppermints. "Miss Thirkettle will see you now," she said. "Speak clearly – she's a little hard of hearing."

It was not surprising Miss Thirkettle was hard of hearing, thought Hannah peering at the headmistress through the dim green light that struggled through the rhododendrons, it was surprising she hadn't retired. The old woman must have been at least seventy-five; short, solid, in a tweed skirt that had long lost any semblance of shape, and a twin-set.

"Howjado?" said Miss Thirkettle in a brusque croak. "Speak up – I'm deaf. You are Hannah Dodgson and you went to school where?"

Hannah recited her education and qualifications.

"Done any teaching?"

"None at all. But I need a job, badly. I'm just getting a divorce – "

"Younger woman, I suppose?"

"Older woman, actually. She has money."

"At least his values are sound," said Miss Thirkettle. "Not taken in by an empty-headed young trollop. Don't mention a divorce to the girls – we have a high moral tone here."

There was a pause. Hannah looked out of the window at a group of twelve-year-olds playing in the front garden. Miss Thirkettle nodded towards them. "Mostly Arabs and Pakistani Moslems, ja see. They like single-sex education. Not easy keeping St Ethelberta's above water. Break even point for budget, one hundred and two pupils. Legal maximum, one hundred and five pupils. We don't pay Burnham, but we don't ask for much in the way of experience. Just keep your eyes on them – don't turn your back – and keep two pages ahead in the textbook."

"Are you giving me the job?" said Hannah. The headmistress had lapsed into abstraction.

"Start on Monday," said Miss Thirkettle. "Whatja want to be called? Married name or maiden name?"

Hannah paused. She didn't want Brian's name; still less did she want her father's.

"I just want to be called Hannah," she said slowly.

"Don't be whimsical and odd," snapped Miss Thirkettle. "That's something a woman alone has to watch for."

"I've made up my mind," said Hannah. "Miss Hannah, Mrs Hannah or Ms Hannah."

"Mrs Hannah," said the headmistress, "since you've got two children. As I said, start on Monday. Arrive at half-past eight and the deputy headmistress will give you a timetable. Mrs Fanshawe, her name is. Bloody useless woman but the parents like her. Get details of pay from the school secretary. She doesn't drink, by the way, she just likes peppermints."

Hannah's house looked distinctly better after Mr Patel's ministrations; three silent women in saris scrubbed, polished, vacuumed. Mr Patel came to collect his cheque.

"Sure you wouldn't prefer cash?" Hannah suggested tactfully.

"Certainly not, dear lady. My business is all strictly above board. I welcome inspection from the Inland Revenue at any time." He looked so sly as he said this that Hannah assumed he had other fiddles in progress.

"Lots of work about, I suppose," she said politely, remembering her telephone conversation with the other cleaning firm.

"Unfortunately not," he said with a graphic, deprecating gesture of his delicate dusky hands. "I have some problems in that direction. Mr Zabriskie lost most of his customers towards the end – unreliable, I'm afraid, like so many Middle Europeans. They're very emotional, you know."

"Really."

"I'm afraid so. Fine musicians, often, but they're not *steady*. That's what you need in a cleaner, steadiness. Not emotionalism."

"I'm sure you're right," said Hannah, a little stunned. He finished his tea and left Hannah to the first of her prospective purchasers.

On Friday the pimply youth from the estate agent's rang to say that Brian had received an offer he was prepared to accept, and did Hannah agree.

Hannah agreed.

She now knew she had about twenty-five thousand pounds to find herself and the children somewhere to live in the London area – in the St Ethelberta's area, come to that.

"You could try a houseboat," said Bibi.

"Ha ha," said Hannah hollowly. "I've worked out how much my pay will be from the school. It's only part-time, so they don't pay holidays. Counting the Single Parent's Allowance and Family Allowance, I'll have two hundred pounds a month after tax."

Bibi gulped. "Have some more brandy."

On Monday at eight o'clock Hannah was toiling through light drizzle round the local park eating a yoghourt and exercising the dogs at the same time. They would be left alone for the whole morning, and the least she could do, she thought throwing sticks for them to chase, was take them for a brisk early run. The spaniels, unused to such hours, ignorant of Hannah's good intentions, were suspicious and trailed unresponsively at her heels letting sticks fall where they might. Their intransigence seemed to Hannah a bad omen, and she was already apprehensive about her first day at school.

The rhododendrons outside St Ethelberta's were, perversely, gleaming in the sun as she arrived. The school secretary showed her up the dark narrow stairs lit only by the straggly beams penetrating a heavy Victorian stained glass window. One of the doors off the landing sported a large notice: GIRLS PLEASE KNOCK AND WAIT. The school secretary, as yet still unidentified by name, pointed it out to Hannah. "The staff-room. Go in and wait. Mrs Fanshawe *should* be in any time now, and she'll attend to you. I hope," she concluded darkly, one of her eyes meeting Hannah's in a meaningful stare, the other swivelling west.

The staff-room was empty of people but the scent of school dinners past hung heavily in the air, with an overtone of stale cigarette smoke. The room was uncompromisingly square and furnished with sagging armchairs, battered upright chairs and a much-scarred long wooden table; green linoleum covered the floor. In a corner a gas-ring stood surrounded by cracked mugs in various stages of coffee and tea encrustation, next to a sink where a tap dripped.

Still no member of staff appeared.

Ten minutes later Hannah was terrified. She was still alone and she had worked out from the information on the staff noticeboard that the first lesson began at five past nine, when she would presumably be expected to teach Latin, History – or English. Or even, conceivably, Games. She patted the tennis shoes in her plastic bag for reassurance.

An extremely good-looking girl in her mid-twenties came in. "Oh Lord," she said with Australian good humour, "if you're the new teacher and you're hoping for help from La Fanshawe, forget it. I'm Lorene Taylor and I teach Games, part-time."

"What do you do the rest of the time?"

"Train. I'm a marathon runner."

"I need my timetable," said Hannah, too apprehensive for social chit-chat.

"Easy enough. Just look at the master timetable on the board here. First Latin, then History with the Upper Four, then English with the Lower Four."

"What class will the Latin be with?"

"There's only one Latin class," said Lorene. "Any of the girls who want to do Latin proceed at their own pace. One or two of them are sitting O level next week, I expect you should concentrate on them."

"O level?" Hannah's own Latin had been weak O level standard in the long-ago days at the convent of Mary Immaculate.

"Don't worry about it. Just bluff. That's what everyone else does," said Lorene peeling off her track suit and revealing a pair of extremely long brown legs clad in tiny white towelling shorts. Hannah averted her eyes, trying not to imagine her own legs in those shorts, trying not to feel jealous of the girl, blonde, healthy, young, who had her mistakes still to make. It was uncomfortable being a beginner at Hannah's age.

In the next five minutes while Assembly went on downstairs the staff-room rapidly filled up. A dumpy, middle-aged woman with pale eyes and dust-coloured, lank hair, nodded to Hannah and made herself tea, then produced a lemon from a capacious shopping bag and began slicing it. From below, a piano thumped and the quavering strains of Jerusalem were occasionally recognisable. "I'm Angela Richardson," said the dumpy woman, squeezing lemon into her tea with, Hannah thought, unnecessary viciousness. "I teach Science and I run the Guide group. I enjoy working with girls, and I hope you will too. We have good girls here." Her voice was thin, reedy, with an undertone of complaint.

The four other women who appeared ranged in age from thirty to sixty and Hannah was too tense to listen when they introduced themselves. She did notice, however, that there was no sign of Mrs Fanshawe.

Assembly ended and the girls dispersed to their classrooms. Lorene led Hannah to a small room on the third floor where six girls of assorted ages waited. "This is Mrs Hannah, your new teacher," she said brightly, and left Hannah alone.

Break at eleven was a welcome relief, though Hannah dreaded the staff-room. She had met too many new people that day; the girls were not entirely convinced that she would manage to teach them – neither was she – and her hair, set in heated rollers that morning in a gesture towards appearing efficient, was beginning to fall out of curl and cling to her sweaty neck. She stood on the landing outside the staff room and a wave of hatred for Brian swept over her. How *could* he walk out and leave her to this, how *could* he? Working in this ridiculous school for peanuts, all because he wanted to live with a joke of a woman called Marjorie.

That night Hannah couldn't sleep. She paced up and down the empty rooms where Brian had, latterly, hardly been and where she had only half-tried to please him. But his loss seemed irreparable. Her whole life, as she saw it, had been balanced on their relationship. The idea of being a self-reliant single woman was all very well: the reality, after the first day of an underpaid job for which she was only marginally qualified and totally ill-prepared, was dreary in the extreme. And it wasn't any good saying she hated Brian. That felt even more lonely. It was easier to pretend she understood – easier, but only half-true.

Walking restlessly from room to room, Hannah tried to get from Whisky and Soda the reassurance that she was loved, talking to them, rubbing their ears. They were perplexed spaniels; they knew food, exercise, they knew barking at the postman. They didn't know what Hannah felt as she wandered round the house kicking the walls.

Towards midnight, as she was munching through her third bowl of Shredded Wheat, her stomach already telling her that the second had been mistake enough, the telephone rang.

"Mummy . . . ? It's John."

"Where are you?" said Hannah, her mind flooded with disaster images – John run away, John kidnapped, John ill.

"I'm in the head man's study."

"At this hour? Is something wrong?"

"I couldn't sleep. I was worried about you. You didn't write . . ."

"John, are you supposed to be in bed?"

"*Of course* I am," he said, bewildered at her naivety. "They'd never let me ring you up in the middle of the night. I didn't get your letter today."

"Did you get one yesterday?"

"Yes."

"That's it then. I write every other day, you know that."

"I was worried," he said stubbornly. "I don't know how you are."

"I'm fine," said Hannah, lying personfully. "I had my first day at my new job, and it's great fun."

"Is it really?" She could hear the weight lifting from his shoulders in the far-off study. "What's the job?"

"I'm teaching – English, Latin and History. And some Games."

"Gosh, I didn't know you could teach Games. What is it? Cricket?"

"I'll tell you on Sunday."

"Do I still have a leave-out?"

"Of course you do. Why ever not?"

"I don't know. Everything's changing so much."

Hear hear, thought Hannah. This was too true to be dwelt on. "We'll have stew and apple pie for lunch."

"Karen doesn't like apple pie."

"She can have ice cream. Off you go to bed now, John. I'll tell you all about my new job on Sunday."

When she replaced the receiver, she felt different. Still bruised and hurt, but the hard core of rebellious self-destructiveness was melting. One more mouthful of soggy Shredded Wheat finally dispersed it and she pushed the bowl away. John's insecurity and his attempt to protect her drew her attention outwards from herself. She wrote two letters she had been putting off, to clients at the Catholic Marriage Guidance Council, explaining why she wouldn't be seeing them any more.

Work day succeeded work day and Hannah grew accustomed to St Ethelberta's. She began to look forward to the lessons, planning strategies for each subject and each class. Somewhere in her, competence was stirring.

She had always liked schools; she thought of the two she attended as oases in the arid stretches of life with her parents. Even going to school for the first time had been an unalloyed pleasure. Five-year-old Hannah was a trial to her mother; Jane Crester-Fyfe, cleaning, polishing, hectoring, criticising, was an agony to her daughter. The Crester-Fyfes pretended to discuss what school Hannah would attend. Five was rather too young for boarding-school, Reginald protested, and for once had his way. Hannah would stay at home. "Education's a waste of time for a girl, in any case," said Jane. "The council school is *quite* good enough," and so Hannah was despatched to join forty-two other Surrey five-year-olds in a draughty pre-fab classroom.

The harassed teacher quickly realised that the serious little girl with the unbecoming fringe, already reading any book she saw, could be left alone. Day after day Hannah sat in the corner of the classroom with sole responsibility for the school hamster, a lethargic beast that spent most of its time asleep. She was milk monitor, leader of the choir and easily the best in her class at hop-scotch. Cannily, she invited none of her friends home for Jane to patronise. She knew the ropes, she was popular. The smell of wellington boots, lavatories, chalk – even thirty years later they were whiffs of remembered happiness as she bustled through St Ethelberta's, grossly underpaid but at least employed.

And the school was never dull, though often exhausting. It was a higgledy-piggledy, contingent place, held together by Miss Thirkettle's determination and Mrs Fanshawe's self-interest. The senior mistress, as Mrs Fanshawe liked to be called, was a slim willowy woman full of conscious grace. She was the only teacher on the staff who hadn't been to Oxford or Cambridge – except, of course, for Lorene Taylor – and her qualifications were a secret from the staff, who gossiped and speculated about her endlessly. She was a very pretty woman in a soft, pastel way; she had large, apparently limpid, blue eyes and a neat little cupid's bow mouth, and delicate brown hair fluffed becomingly and deliberately about her face. She was a measured person; she thought carefully before she spoke, she was only malicious to people who couldn't or wouldn't answer back, and she had a gushing attentive manner with parents, rich or well-connected girls.

She owned a share in the school; how large a share no one knew, but it must have been substantial. Her aunt had been co-founder of the school, with Miss Thirkettle; and the head-mistress so clearly disliked and despised her second-in-command that it must be more than simple respect for her aunt that kept Mrs Fanshawe employed.

Mrs Fanshawe taught sewing. In other schools it would have been home economics, but all she knew was embroidery and so the girls embroidered. Some became very good at it. The apparent incongruity of a senior mistress teaching such a peripheral subject was grasped and overcome by Mrs Fanshawe in a typically adroit fashion. She read girls' characters by their prowess in, and attitude towards, fine stitching.

Hannah, astonished, listened to these semi-mystical character interpretations at break, when Mrs Fanshawe came to break – usually she was too ill to come to school or too fatigued to climb the stairs to the staff room, so the cook brought her a tray with her special china cup in the sewing room. "Of course, Shakira is a darling. B-l-a-c-k, of course, but an exquisite needle-woman; precise, modest, reliable. *She'll* make one of her own people an excellent wife. But Maria is *quite* another kettle of fish. Over-anxious. Blood-stains all over her sampler. I mean, what can one say?"

By her own account Mrs Fanshawe was a devoted mother and she often repeated sanctimonious little conversations she had had with Camilla (sixteen) and Thomas (fifteen). When she learnt Hannah's situation, she took to giving her knowing glances and sighing heavily whenever husbands or children were mentioned. This was galling to Hannah, particularly since she was abnormally sensitive to such references and didn't want Mrs Fanshawe's sympathy.

The rest of the staff were either congenial or comprehensible. Miss Thirkettle's Oxbridge hiring policy meant that the teachers were fundamentally intelligent, though several were eccentric or incompetent or both. Angela Richardson, the Science mistress, had apparently been a brilliant undergraduate (weren't we all, thought Hannah) with a great future in biochemistry (surely a contradiction in terms, commented the historian) until her nervous breakdown, just before finals. She took her examinations in a closed ward of the local mental hospital, still managing a good second class degree. She now bumbled from cult to cult and was currently an enthusiastic scientologist. But through it all she retained a belief in the value of Guiding.

"Don't think much of the movement myself," Miss Thirkettle said to Hannah as they passed each other on the stairs after lunch, nodding her head towards a Guide meeting in progress. "Why put peculiar clothes on to do the washing-up and be kind and thoughtful? Doesn't make sense."

"Why make the girls wear uniform to come to school?" countered Hannah.

"Easy to spot 'em if they solicit in the lunch hour," said Miss Thirkettle.

One evening Jane Crester-Fyfe rang. "I'll be in town tomorrow. Let's lunch together."

"I can't," said Hannah. She was tired after a day at school, her feet hurt from formal shoes and she had just returned from walking the dogs through the cold late-June drizzle to read a long, detailed letter from her solicitor.

Jane waited for Hannah to explain her answer. Hannah stood reading the letter. She was in the drawing-room, a gloomy room now that its long windows were bedewed and obscured by rain and grime. Solitary Hannah never used it but sat in the kitchen – warmer, friendlier, less Brian's – instead.

"Why can't you lunch with me?" pursued her mother.

"Because I'm working."

"Working? Do you have a job?"

"Yes," said Hannah. Her mother sighed. Hannah blew the dust off Brian's Bang & Olufsen stereo system. It was ranged on custom-built shelves with row upon row of records and cassettes. He had bought it four years ago and it had spoken eloquently to him of success. Now it spoke eloquently to Hannah of Brian, and the small gesture of dusting it seemed an affectionate tribute to him. Sometimes she hated him. Sometimes she felt his loss with anguish. At other times, like now, she missed an understood and loved companion.

She knew him. Together they had enjoyed so many things, and the loss of that sharing was almost as painful as the loss of her perfect marriage dream, and Hannah wondered how long the pain would last. The stereo's gleaming silver knobs jutted at her, round and firm as a pin-up's nipples. Hannah resented most of Brian's extravagances, but the stereo had been bought after consultation with her and on her advice. Several Sunday mornings had been spent in harmony; he brought her breakfast in bed (one of his best treats – the toast was never soggy), and then they both read through technical magazines looking for the best buy. Brian admired Hannah's skill at absorbing, understanding and summarising written material, and he had a naive respect for the written word. Eventually she reported that Bang & Olufsen was the best buy – so he had bought the equipment Hannah was now gazing at.

"Hannah, my patience is nearly at an end," said Jane. "Are you still there?"

"Yes," said Hannah. "I won't be able to have lunch. How are you?"

"Very well, thank you. I wanted to have a talk about Mother."

"Is she ill?"

"She's just the same. But your aunt needs a rest from looking after her and we thought it might take your mind off your own problems."

Hannah liked her aunt Anne. She'd stayed with her often during school holidays. But at the moment . . . "That's out of the question," she said decidedly. "You must see that. I'm house-hunting at present, quite apart from my job. Did Anne suggest you ask me?"

"No," said Jane. "It was my idea."

"Why don't you go?" said Hannah, knowing that Jane found the care of her senile mother highly distasteful but no longer feeling obliged to join in her attempt to disguise it.

"You know your father doesn't like me going away," said Jane. "He can't look after himself."

Hannah said nothing. She wondered why her parents clung together so much when they liked each other so little.

"Is there something the matter, Hannah?" said her mother sharply. "Your manner is most odd."

"I've decided to tell the truth," said Hannah.

"What an extraordinary thing to say, 'decided'. Didn't I bring you up always to tell the truth?"

"Not exactly. You tried to teach me manners as well."

"But politeness isn't *untruth*, it's just respecting other people's feelings."

"I've respected other people's feelings so much I've lost my own."

"I can see it's not much use continuing this conversation. I hope you're feeling better soon." Click, went the receiver, and Hannah went to feed the dogs.

The following Saturday Hannah went to Bibi's for supper. She remembered the evidences of redecoration from her catastrophic birthday lunch; but she wasn't prepared for bird and flower prints, soft pastel greens, twittering and rustling in all seven rooms and two bathrooms. The decor should have been restful, but to Hannah's eye it had taken on a febrile intensity that reflected Bibi's own recent edginess.

Nicholas was at a conference in Frankfurt and Bibi had something on her mind but, typically, talked about everything else first. Hannah knew better than to try and rush her, so she said as little as possible about the flat and ate steadily through her own food and Bibi's.

"Is it very hard work at that school?"

"No. I like it."

"But not for the rest of your life?"

"Not on the money they're paying. Not anyway."

"So what are you going to do? Look for a man?"

"No," said Hannah. "I'm going to convalesce. Take time, heal, get better, recover. Ameliorate myself."

"Recover from what? Brian?"

"Self-delusion."

Bibi laughed. "That'll be the day. You're a terrible dreamer, Hannah." She was sitting cross-legged on the sofa, her long legs spindle-thin in faded jeans, cropped hair spiky. "The biggest sucker in the Upper Third, you were, and if anything you've got worse."

Hannah smiled. "I'm changing that."

"You'll see. It'll be another dream. St Teresa of Avila, Reverend Mother, that beefy prefect – "

"She wasn't beefy," protested Hannah.

"She was, she went on to Physical Education college. Then Buddy Holly and Elvis Presley, and lastly Brian, the amazing footballer, media personality and great lover. So who will we put in his place?"

Hannah was hurt by her tone but she could see Bibi was

upset. "Tell me how the pregnancy clinic is going," she said.

Bibi grimaced. "That's the trouble. It's Nicholas. He won't agree to a post-coital investigation."

"What's that?"

"They take a sample of sperm from my vagina after we've had intercourse," said Bibi. Her sexual vocabulary was normally colloquial if not earthy, but where babies were concerned she talked like a textbook.

"How soon after?"

"As soon as I can get to the clinic. We don't have to have sex there, if that's what you mean. I could understand that putting him off."

"Can't you just go to the clinic without telling him?"

"But that means we have to have sex during clinic hours, and he just won't." Hannah was about to speak, but Bibi interrupted irritably. "And don't suggest seducing him, because I've tried all that. I've tried everything I know." At this awesome prospect – Bibi was renowned for sexual experience and inventiveness – Hannah fell silent.

"And he wants a baby, I know he does. He still thinks about little Nicky." Nicholas' first wife and small son had drowned in a boating accident some years before he married Bibi. "He really wants a baby," she insisted, losing credibility with every repetition, "he does, I know he does. Hannah, what do you suppose is wrong?"

"Does he give a reason for refusing?"

Bibi spread her hands in a hopeless gesture. "We don't talk about it much."

This was inconceivable to Hannah. Nicholas and Bibi talked to each other incessantly and they were very close. He hadn't always been faithful to her – one night stands far from home were his line, or so Hannah had heard through Brian – but Bibi apparently knew, or cared, nothing of this. Nicholas was devoted to her, possessive of her. Whether he himself wanted children or not, Hannah was sure that he wanted what Bibi wanted. He liked her happy.

"I feel so unloved," said Bibi. "I've gone through all the tests – some of them are very painful – and he won't do this one thing for me."

Hannah could offer no solution, only attention and sympathy. For her, conceiving children had been easy. She saw Bibi's quest as uncomfortable and probably futile.

Bibi blew her nose and wiped away incipient tears. Her monkey face was haggard. With a growing sense of unease, Hannah remembered other occasions lately when Bibi had broken down in tears – most uncharacteristic. "Is everything else all right between you and Nicholas?"

Bibi brushed the question aside. "Don't fuss about me, Hannah, you've got enough on your plate as it is."

Hannah expected a call from Brian's parents. She had expected it ever since her birthday. Marie Dodgson had always disliked her. No woman would ever have been good enough for Brian, and Hannah especially was not good enough. She was a blue-stocking (one of the few points of agreement between Mrs Crester-Fyfe and Mrs Dodgson was that education was wasted on girls), she didn't clean the house, and though she could hardly credit it, Marie suspected her of criticising Brian.

Marie had wanted a very different type of girl for her boy; a pretty girl, perhaps even a model, a girl who knew how to present herself, submissive and malleable, open to a mother-in-law's suggestions and advice, a girl who would be impressed by the Dodgsons' respectability and Walter's position as a clerk in the Town Hall.

So when the telephone call finally came and Hannah heard the flat Midlands' vowels, she expected her mother-in-law to gloat. But she was tentative, her normal over-loud voice muted and trembly. "That you Hannah?" Awkward pause. "This true what I read in the papers?"

"About Brian?" Hannah was surprised. Marie was clearly on a fishing expedition, so Brian couldn't have told her about Marjorie.

"You've heard we're getting a divorce, I suppose."

"Where is Brian now?"

"I don't know exactly. With Marjorie, the woman he's going to marry – but I haven't got his address."

"Nor have I." Neither spoke. The telephone line hummed with a loss they would not share.

"You and me haven't always seen eye to eye," said Marie with audible effort, "but I can't say I think he's doing the right thing. I don't hold with divorce. And I daresay you did your best to be a good wife to him."

"It was half my fault," said Hannah.

"You can't say fairer than that. Do you want me to take the kiddies off your hands in the holidays?"

"Please," said Hannah, remembering her own mother's grudging reluctance to be of practical help. "Can I let you know when?"

"And how are you placed for money? My boy can be thoughtless, I know. Walter asked me specially to tell you, if you're hard up, let us know. We've got something put away for a rainy day."

Walter was a silent man who went his own way with an amiable determination Hannah admired. He wasn't a doting father to Brian; if anything, he preferred his other sons, Keith and Colin, both doing well in the Trustee Savings Bank. He kept pigeons at the bottom of the long, narrow garden of their semi-detached.

"We're getting money sorted out. Don't worry about it, Marie."

"My regards to your Mum."

"I'll pass them on next time I see her."

"Why isn't she with you? A girl needs her mother at a time like this."

"We don't get on specially well."

"I know you've had your differences, but surely . . . oh well, you'll know your own business best."

Marie's call set Hannah off-balance. It was ten o'clock in the morning of a non-school week day. At twelve o'clock she had an appointment to look at a possible house; two hours stretched, disturbingly empty, in front of her.

She began to sweep the kitchen floor, bare feet cool on the quarry tiles. Brian's treatment of his mother was puzzling her. She had thought she understood him – even his abrupt departure had shocked but not surprised her. But now it seemed he had left not only a wife but also a mother, and she felt sorry for Marie.

The floor swept, she turned on the radio. Jimmy Young and a politician distinguished only by his Christian name exchanged compliments and then gave way to a self-pitying country and western wail by a singer who had lost her "mayan".

"You and me both," said Hannah to the singer, "but at least you get paid for saying so." She had become abnormally sensitive about references to family, marriage, weddings, wives, husbands, lovers; they pressed on her failure bruise. Unfortunately for Hannah, it was June 1981 and Britain was gripped by royal wedding fever; Lady Diana Spencer and her fairytale romance were everywhere.

The Times was usually a safe refuge with its catalogue of business failures and far-away wars, but it let Hannah down today. The fashion pages were devoted to wedding dresses; home news had an item on one-parent families; foreign news included an assessment of Nancy Reagan's contribution to her husband's career; and tucked away in the sports section, in an article on the English soccer team for the coming season, lurked Brian. "England will once again miss the thrusting skills of Brian Dodgson."

So do I, thought Hannah ruefully, half-amused, half-upset.

She arrived at 93 Crimea Road just before the appointed time. It was end-of-terrace, opposite the gas works and next to an expanse of waste land that was ripe for development as a rubbish tip. The house looked cramped and dingy, though it bore no obvious signs of neglect, and Hannah nearly didn't bother to go in. But she saw a woman's face looking at her from behind the lace curtains.

The woman answered the door. She was about fifty, bone-thin and swamped by a sack-like flowered overall, with a pasty face and a nervous twitch in her hands. The hall smelt of damp and cats. "Yes?" she said peering at Hannah with the flicker of a hope that someone promising or pleasant might knock on the door.

"Mrs Harris?"

"Yes?" She showed no sign of understanding and didn't step back to let Hannah in.

"Didn't the estate agent tell you I was coming?"

"Estate agent?"

Oh really, thought Hannah exasperated, she must be half-witted. "I've come to see the house."

"The house?"

"Your house," said Hannah with patience honed by dealing with Felicity Wakefield, moron of St Ethelberta's. "Your house is for sale, isn't it? Can I come inside and look round?"

"It's not convenient," said the woman helplessly, and shut the door.

Hannah spoke through the letter-box. "Mrs Harris, is your house for sale?" She removed her mouth from the letter-box and replaced it with an eye. Mrs Harris had retreated down the hall and was shaking uncontrollably. Hannah spoke through the letter-box again. "I'm sorry, please don't be upset. There's obviously been a misunderstanding. I'll tell the estate agent to fix another time."

"Oh, don't do that," called the woman. "No, wait, don't go away." She opened the door and beckoned Hannah in with jerky sweeps of her arm. "It's my husband, you see," she said leading her into a tiny, poky front room, over-full of shiny vinyl furniture. "It's probably my husband. I didn't really think – well, I suppose I did. He doesn't like illness, you see. Do sit down."

Hannah perched on the edge of the sofa and looked around her. Every surface was covered in a film of dust, but the woman herself was scrupulously clean. As if reading her mind, Mrs Harris tugged a duster from the pocket of her overall and started wiping the beige tiled fireplace in unco-ordinated jerks. "The house isn't as clean as I'd like," she said so quietly that Hannah had to guess at her words. "I didn't expect you. My husband's put the house on the market without letting me know."

Hannah sensed that to show surprise would be insulting. "Difficult for you," she said.

"Well, they can be difficult, can't they? Men, I mean. Not like us. You can't rely on them, really, can you? They don't see things like we do, they don't think of their duty to people."

"I don't know," said Hannah, both because she thought the generalisation too sweeping to be valid and because she could see that Mrs Harris was quite indifferent to her opinion.

The woman went sweeping on as if some release button had

been pressed. "It wasn't too bad at first when they told me at the hospital, multiple sclerosis, they said – MS for short, you may have heard of it – you may never get better, they said, the course of the disease can't be predicted, they said. And for two weeks or so Steve was nice as pie, helped me with the cleaning and the cooking, though heaven knows he's all thumbs and he just moved the dirt around and he never wiped the kitchen surfaces after he did the washing up, it got on my nerves, but men are like that, aren't they, and it was the thought that counted. He drove me to the clinic for treatment and he took me out twice, we went to the cinema, the telly isn't the same is it? But my shaking annoyed him, I could see it did, I think he thought I was putting it on. I don't know, really. Then one day he left, went round to his sister's and didn't come back. He wrote me a letter and said he was sorry but he didn't like doctors and illness and why didn't I go to live with Sharon and Christine in Australia. They're my daughters you see and married to nice boys but why should they have to look after me when I'm ill? It's not right, it's no way to spend your life, looking after an invalid, and I won't let them do it. They're young, they've got kiddies, they write me lovely letters and send photographs, it's like Paradise out there from what they tell me. Sun all the time, and beaches, you wouldn't believe the beaches. So Steve said I should go out there and I thought he meant he'd come with me, that's what I thought at first, I've always wanted to go to Australia to live, I mean I've only got the two daughters and I've never seen my own grandchildren, I've got four now and never seen even one. Steve's a bit close with his money you see, what you'd call careful, and he doesn't like abroad. We went to Guernsey once, I wanted to go to the Costa Brava but Steve said it was common and anyway Guernsey was cheaper because we stayed with my cousin, and he didn't even like Guernsey, he missed England. So when he said about Australia I was beside myself with joy as you can imagine, you look a sympathetic kind of a person Mrs – "

"Hannah."

"Well Mrs Hannah I thought he'd had a change of heart on account of my illness and was making an effort to please me. But then he wrote in his letter about living with his sister and me going to Chrissie and Sharon turn and turn about and I realised what he meant and it wasn't right. But now I don't know what to do," she concluded and subsided into a chair, holding her left wrist with her right hand to stop it shaking.

"Australia sounds lovely," said Hannah. "Couldn't you go and live there by yourself? You're alone here, aren't you?"

"I don't think the Immigration authorities would let me in," said Mrs Harris. "I don't have any money you see and I'd just be a burden to the State. I thought about that. I'm no fool, I got my Matric. you know, I could have gone to college, I thought of training as a teacher. I do like little ones. I'd have enjoyed that. Ever so pleased I was when I got the results of my exams, and my dad was so proud. I'm glad he didn't live to see me like this."

Hannah was torn between sympathy and irritation. The woman's plight was a grim one but there was nothing that she, Hannah, could do about it and this impotence was aggravating. It was also evident that she would have to pay a high emotional price to go round the house, which she was beginning to see as a possible place for her to live.

"At least the children will be a comfort," said Caroline earnestly. "Do try the kipper pâté, it's excellent here." Hannah settled for kipper pâté and white wine and wondered how soon she could escape Caroline's clutches. She was an old friend; in her own way as close as Bibi. Hannah often met her in the round of Catholic good works and they enjoyed each other's company, probably because each found the other a refreshing change from her usual social circle. But just at the moment Hannah wanted to spend as little time as possible with her. Not only was she a reminder of Hannah's first meeting with Brian, but she was a convinced Catholic who didn't believe in divorce. She was also well-bred, well-married, well-off and insensitive.

"Why are we here?" asked Hannah, looking round the pretentious wine bar. "Is this place new?"

"It's run by a cousin of mine."

"Everything in England is run by a cousin of yours," said Hannah with unmistakable sharpness. Even Caroline caught her tone and looked up enquiringly. She was a pleasant-looking woman with smooth, milky white skin and thick, fine, blonde hair just touched with grey. Her features – delicate arched nose, firm chin, small piercing eyes – were family features; when Hannah had gone to stay with her at the castle as a schoolgirl she had looked at the portraits of bygone dukes and duchesses and thought that Caroline's looks were on loan, to be passed on to future aristocrats. She had done this work thoroughly; she had married the second son of an earl and produced five children, the youngest of whom was still in the nursery.

"That sounds cross," she observed. "What's biting you, Hannah?"

"It's not your fault. My situation makes me cross," said Hannah.

Caroline gave a deep sigh and leant towards her. "That's what I wanted to talk to you about," she said. "Hannah, have you thought about this divorce? Are you *sure*? Remember what the Church teaches us."

"I lost my faith years ago," said Hannah. The traditional formulation seemed appropriate when talking to Caroline: it was also a more or less accurate description. Her faith had seeped away. Gradually, she had stopped going to confession; then missed Sunday mass; and by the time the children were old enough to go to church, she didn't take them. The whole structure of ritual and theology seemed a fairy tale, remote.

Caroline smiled with a nun's knowing sweetness. "Oh, that can't be. Once a Catholic – you know the saying. Hannah, I feel responsible for you in a way. You remember when you arrived at the convent, Sister Bernadette asked me to look after you? I took that responsibility very, very seriously."

You certainly did, thought Hannah, remembering the numerous occasions when Caroline had informed on her for her own good; remembering also the smell, wax, incense, floor-polish, musty clothing, of the front hall of the convent where she had hugged her parents dutifully and then been engulfed by the starched, rustling formality of the nuns. Tubby eleven-year-old Caroline, the sash of her gym-slip marking where her waist should have been, stood confidently behind Sister Bernadette and fixed Hannah with the serious gaze of a junior prefect. Junior prefects were usually at least thirteen, but they had made an exception in Caroline's case. She was an unusually well-behaved little girl and her father was one of the premier dukes of England: the mistress of discipline's voice softened like butter on the stove when she spoke of her. "Of course Caroline . . . Our dear Caroline . . ."

"The woman's a fearful snob," Bibi had whispered, "but Caroline's all right, she can't help being a Lady and frightfully pi, we just have to show mercy."

"Let's talk about something else," said Hannah as the food and drink arrived. "How are your children?"

"Fighting fit. All away at school except Podge, and it's only a matter of time before we can get rid of Nanny, I'm counting the minutes. It's like Pass the Parcel, you see. Nanny's past retiring age anyway and she'll probably stay with whoever she retires with, and I'm praying and praying it won't be me, I can't stand her. She won't let us throw away old socks, she will insist on darning them, and she's so bad at it the children all have blisters."

As usual when Caroline recounted her tales of woe, Hannah immediately identified with the person she was complaining about. "Your nanny is a nice old thing," she said.

Caroline raised her eyebrows. Hannah was being even more obstructive than she had expected. It's all her pride, she thought, her stupid pride. I could help if only she'd let me. "I'm trying to help you, Hannah," she said.

"I know," said Hannah, "but let's leave it for the moment, shall we?"

"I understand. You want to paddle your own canoe. I like doing that, too."

Ah, thought Hannah, but in your case it's not a canoe, it's a quinquereme; five banks of oars manned by the Establishment, all pulling for Caroline.

3

It was nearly four on a Friday afternoon and Hannah was supervising prep in the Assembly Hall at St Ethelberta's. Sixty junior girls, who would have been playing rounders if it weren't for the rain, shuffled uneasily in their seats. Hannah was keeping them more or less silent by pure strength of will. She enjoyed being a teacher; she sat watching the clock tick round feeling the satisfaction of a week's work done.

She was looking forward to the evening. She and Bibi were to inspect 93 Crimea Road. After seeing countless other flats and houses, Mrs Harris's was the only one to appeal to Hannah at all. But she couldn't decide if that was just perversity on her part; perhaps by choosing the gas works and the rubbish tip as neighbours she was choosing a reproach to Brian, to her parents, to the world.

"Nonsense," said Bibi briskly when Hannah expressed these ideas to her as they left the house after clinging goodbyes from Mrs Harris. "It has distinct possibilities, and Lord knows it's cheap. I'm surprised you can get a hovel at that price. The gas works has clean, elegant lines and industrial townscapes are perfectly all right. Besides, think how central – just five minutes from me and not much more from your school. There's an excellent butcher just round the corner."

Hannah took these meanderings with a basin of salt, but still she could see Bibi was in favour. She herself was hesitating. The prospect of making a decision, of choosing the house and going to settle in it with the children by herself, was really terrifying. She pushed the terror down and spoke bracingly to herself of freedom and independence, but the fear was still there. By herself, who would she be?

It wasn't an easy question to answer. For some time she had hidden behind the uneasy compromise of her marriage with Brian; but now, with no restrictions on her freedom but the children and lack of money, what would she do? What could she do? Indecisive as ever, not having Brian to hide behind, she saw she was latching on to Bibi. But she had to make the decisions, she had to decorate the house, she had to shape the life she would lead, earning her own living, by herself.

She and Bibi went back to drink wine, watch Hannah's television and gossip. By tacit consent neither mentioned Nicholas.

"You're a fool not to use Caroline's contacts," said Bibi. "She could get you a job with an MP or something – she's so good at pulling strings."

"I know, but I'd prefer to trot along quietly in my own way. Besides, Caroline's favours are so constricting. One always has to do something peculiarly inconvenient in return."

"Just don't turn into a hermit, Hannah."

"I'll show you I'm not a hermit. I'll take you out to dinner."

"At a real restaurant?" teased Bibi. "I was looking forward to our usual scrambled eggs and baked beans with the dogs watching every mouthful."

"Italian or Indian?"

"Italian. Indian makes me dreadfully ill."

"Since when? It never used to."

"Since the last few months."

So Hannah rang the local Italian restaurant, but the manager was reluctant to accept her booking. "We are very full," he protested. "You wouldn't like it. Not a good atmosphere."

"You've never tried to put me off before, Marcello. What are you getting at?"

"Perhaps later – at 9.30, we will have a table."

"Brian's there, isn't he? Is that it?"

"No no," said Marcello, but he might just as well have said "yes yes". "You are mistaken . . . I will have a nice table for you at 9.30. Please. Believe me."

"What's the matter?" said Bibi. "You've gone white. What is it, Hannah?"

"Brian's at the restaurant – probably with Marjorie. Marcello as good as said so."

"OK, then, we'll go to another Italian restaurant. Pass me over the Yellow Pages, I'll find one."

Hannah was very shaken. Not being able to see Brian had

been frustrating, but it had also relieved the emotional pressure. Now she didn't know what to do, what to think. Her first instinct was to do the considerate, tactful thing and keep away. Next she realised that she would be considering other people only, not herself. She wanted to see him, to tell him everything she had been storing up ever since he left.

"Are you sure it's wise?" was all Bibi said when Hannah told her.

"I don't know if it's wise. I just can't not see him now I've got the chance."

"Then we'd better get a move on."

"I want to do my face."

"No time. It'll be dark, anyway."

The old Renault wouldn't start. The motor turned over, rattled, refused to catch fire, again and again. Hannah felt tears of frustration pricking her eyes. Whisky and Soda, wriggling on the window seat overlooking the road, howled and yelped in indignation at being left behind. It had started to drizzle.

"Come on, let's walk," said Bibi when the battery finally died. "We'll get there in ten minutes if we hurry."

They scurried along, half-running, Bibi finding it painful going in paper-thin court shoes. Hannah, driven by rage at the car, the dogs, and Brian, strode well ahead.

Breathless, Hannah turned the corner into the cobbled courtyard where the restaurant stood, light pouring from its windows. All around were the shuttered doors of silent garages; the sound of chatter and laughter, the clink of plates, was loud in the back-street hush.

Bibi caught her up. "Are you going to make a scene, Hannah?" she gasped between deep breaths.

"Possibly."

"Wait till he comes outside, then. Keep it out of the restaurant."

"Why?"

"Because then they'll let us have our dinner afterwards."

Now she was there, Hannah couldn't bring herself to look inside. Instead, she wandered down side streets looking for Brian's car; when she found it she gazed at it helplessly. She had believed yet not believed that she would see him, but the dully gleaming Porsche with its leather covered steering wheel, Brian's driving gloves casually on the seat, an unfamiliar woman's scarf in the back, all brought home to her the reality of her loss.

She walked slowly back to stand peering through the lighted windows. Bibi stood beside her reading the menu.

"Good, *tagliatelle alla crema*," she observed, and then pointed to a table in the corner. "There he is, Hannah."

"It's our table," said Hannah. "The one we always had for anniversaries and special occasions. You'd think he'd at least have the decency to choose another table." She was deeply upset. In the warm, flattering light Marjorie looked years younger and provokingly happy, smiling at Brian who was sitting with his back to the window.

"I bet he's saying the same things to her that he used to say to me."

"Probably," said Bibi. "Men usually stick to one line of chat and they're all corny unless you're on the receiving end. Come on, Hannah. Let's walk to the High Street and get a taxi to my car, then we can drive to another restaurant. What do you say?"

Hannah was almost persuaded. She felt miserable and abandoned, no longer angry.

They turned to leave as the door of the restaurant opened and Marjorie came out followed by cashmere-overcoated Brian. Without thinking, Hannah ran up to him and stood close to him, ignoring Marjorie completely. She forgot her presence. She looked into Brian's eyes, almost on a level with hers. Tears started to trickle down her cheeks.

"Don't cry. Oh, don't cry," he said, his hand grasping her wrist. It was partly selfishness, she knew – crying women disturbed him – but his tenderness wrecked her composure, took her back and back like a hall of mirrors to other moments they had stood together while he begged her not to cry. She stood helplessly, all fight drained out of her, tears rolling down her face. "I knew it wouldn't help, seeing you," he said, and the self-righteous self-pity fired her again.

"That may be true for you," she said, "but what about me? Don't I have any say in it?"

"This isn't going to help," he said. "Bibi, you're a sensible girl. Tell her this isn't going to help."

"On the contrary," said Bibi, "I think it's only fair. You told her what you thought of her by leaving. Now she's got the chance to reply."

"Interfering bitch," muttered Brian, feeling surrounded. "Come on Marjorie, let's go."

"Please wait," said Hannah. "Let me talk to you, Brian. We have to make arrangements about the children's sports days—"

"I'll tell the solicitor," said Brian, edging past her.

"Please listen, Brian, you never listen."

"I don't like hysterical women."

"And I don't like you," shouted Hannah suddenly, losing her temper. "I absolutely *hate you! I hate you!*"

Brian was hurrying away from her down the street, limping slightly in his haste; she remembered nursing him after the repeated unsuccessful operations on his knee, and her emotions were torn. She scurried along the slippery cobbles after him. "Talk to me, Brian, please talk to me."

"If you hate me, why should I? You hate me. That's all right then, finish." He smirked, pleased with his argument, and she knew he would stick to it now no matter what she said. He always clung to one idea at a time.

Hannah held his arm, close enough now to smell the characteristic Brian smell of after-shave, cigars and sweat. She could hear Marjorie approaching behind her.

"Get the Porsche, Marj," Brian called. Hannah couldn't believe it. His precious cars, the Porsches changed every three years at enormous cost to the Dodgson budget, that Hannah was never under any circumstances whatever allowed to drive. But he was prepared to let Marjorie drive one. Hannah, still crying, was pierced by a jealous rage more acute than anything she had yet felt for Marjorie. Brian stood still in her grasp with heavy male passivity, waiting for the hysterical, emotional woman to tire of making her demands and leave him alone. His expression reminded her of the times when she had so nearly accused him of having affairs with woman after woman, beginning after Karen was born.

"You screwed that girl in Edinburgh, didn't you?" she said. "The one who kept ringing up."

"That was fifteen years ago," said Brian blankly.

"Thirteen years ago. Just after Karen was born."

"What does that matter now?"

"Because she was the first."

He looked at her in astonishment. "You must be joking."

"You mean there were others before her?"

"Leave it out, Hannah. This is stupid. It's nothing to do with you any more. For God's sake, keep your voice down."

A small crowd had gathered; two couples from the restaurant who recognised Brian, a passer-by watching because others were watching, Bibi well back in the shadows wondering whether to intervene. The Porsche nosed its way slowly along the road towards them.

"Why do you let her drive?" Hannah was feeling desperate. Her minutes with Brian were ebbing away.

"She's a good driver," he said.

"So am I," said Hannah.

"You're not bad, just careless," said Brian impatiently. "Do we have to stand in the rain discussing your driving? And why do you look such a mess, Hannah? Get rid of those mucky old jeans, they make you look even fatter than you are. And what are you doing walking round the streets at night?"

"I'm walking round the streets because the bloody Renault wouldn't start," said Hannah crying again. Brian pulled away from her and hopped into the car, which started to move.

Hannah, rain trickling down her neck into her already sodden sweater, saw Marjorie and Brian, warm, dry, triumphant, and it was too much for her to bear. She ran beside the car for a few steps and then heaved herself on to the bonnet and lay across the windscreen, blocking Marjorie's view. The car stopped immediately; Hannah began to slide off and clutched the windscreen wipers to save herself. They pulled away in her hands.

Brian's face crumpled in fury and he thumped on the inside of the windscreen. "Get your maulers off my car," he yelled.

"The car, the car, what about me?" shouted Hannah. "I sweated blood for those cars! I lived in old jeans to buy your sodding cars, told lies to tradesmen about how their cheques were in the post when they never were – "

"Bloody amazing," shouted Brian. "I never saw you doing a hand's turn to earn money. You couldn't even keep the house clean – and get off the bonnet, you fat cow, you'll dent it!"

"Right," said Hannah, thumping the bonnet with her fists,

convulsed with rage and tears. "I'll dent your car, see if I don't." She stood precariously balanced on the sloping bonnet and jumped with all her weight, again and again. Brian made a low, stricken, moaning noise.

"Take care, dear," called Marjorie. "You could have a nasty fall."

Hannah felt a surge of euphoria as the car rocked beneath her; she scrambled over the roof and stamped on the airfoil attachment at the back. It stood firm. With a flash of inspiration, she grabbed the house keys from her back pocket and scored ever-widening circles on the paintwork. "Paid for by bank managers, driven by over-age footballers, wrecked by ex-wives!" crowed Hannah.

Bibi and Hannah sat in the Italian restaurant. Hannah had almost stopped crying; occasionally a tear would escape from her swollen eyelids and trickle down her cheek, but the convulsive sobbing was over and she was eating the odd mouthful of the food Bibi had ordered for her.

"Thank you for getting rid of those people," said Hannah. When finally the battered Porsche had limped away, Bibi had dispersed the fascinated audience by a prodigious feat of tact and eased Hannah into the restaurant against Marcello's resistance. Crying women were not good for business.

"Thank you for standing up for yourself," said Bibi. "It warmed my heart to see it."

"You weren't embarrassed?"

"Not in the least. My favourite bit was when the windscreen wipers came off in your hand."

"I liked jumping on the bonnet."

"That looked fun, too. Like an event in "It's a Knockout". You've a good, strong, systematic style when it comes to car-wrecking."

"Perhaps I shouldn't have kicked the side-lights." Hannah was beginning to smile as the humour of the scene dawned on her.

"Did you hurt your feet?"

"I don't think so." Hannah leant back in her chair, her sweater steaming gently in the dry air, limbs heavy in the aftermath of effort. "I don't think I've hurt myself at all. I feel much better. Wasn't it odd of Marjorie not to say anything except that about me hurting myself?"

"She behaved very well, I thought. Composed and cool. Mind you, there wasn't much else for her to do."

"Considering that she's in the winner's enclosure, you mean?" said Hannah, reading Bibi's mind.

"And, of course, she's got the maturity," Bibi observed. "On a clear day she could watch fifty receding behind her."

"As old as *that*?" gloated Hannah. "Surely not." But Bibi's bitchery was comforting, and intended to be.

At break time on Monday the staff room at St Ethelberta's was in ferment. Mrs Fanshawe had changed the Games duty roster again; again, in her own favour. "She's only taking Games three times this whole term," complained Angela Richardson, knitting feverishly, "and I'm to do it fifteen times. Fifteen times. Is that fair? I ask you, is that fair?"

"Good for your varicose veins," said Lorene Taylor unsympathetically. She was doing sideways exercises for her hamstrings and taking up an inordinate amount of the small space available for the staff to sit and drink coffee. Lorene felt the others didn't show the proper enthusiasm for outdoor sport. Hannah eyed the Australian's extended brown legs; in their length and fineness they looked more animal than human.

"I wonder if there's a species called a Taylor gazelle," said Hannah.

"I wouldn't be so smug if I were you," said Angela crossly; she didn't understand Hannah's remark so she assumed it was critical of her. "La Fanshawe had you down for an extra duty as well."

"It's outrageous," said Sarah Austin crisply. She was the historian, a brisk all-girls-together woman in her early thirties who always wore Jaeger skirts and a scarf knotted tastefully somewhere under her right ear. "I think it's outrageous and so does Jeff. He absolutely choked on his g. and t. yesterday when I told him the latest Fanshawe story. He thinks we should do something about it."

"Trust a man to say that," grumbled Angela. "What does your precious Jeff suggest we do?"

"Why don't we just ask her to explain it to us?" said Hannah.

"She's downstairs in the sewing room, isn't she? Let's ask her to come up and explain the system of allotting duties. All duties, not just Games ones."

"She won't fall for anything as simple as that," said Lorene, now standing up and placing the palms of her hands flat on the floor. "You can try, but you won't get anywhere. Selfishness incarnate, La Fanshawe."

Hannah's mind drifted away from staff-room politics. Since Brian's departure, in her effort to recover emotional balance she found it very difficult to concentrate on anything except herself. Now she was reflecting on her attack on Brian's car. It became more and more satisfying, in retrospect. She didn't regret it, didn't feel embarrassed or foolish now she was calmer; she did wish she'd been more thorough. Surely a truly liberated Hannah would have immobilised the car, even finally destroyed it. It seemed particularly frustrating that the headlights with their narcissistic little covers should have gone unmolested.

And Brian had been silenced. She had expected him to fight back, to hit her perhaps, to restrain her certainly. But he had been too stricken for that. Perhaps she had inflicted on him just a small part of the shock and pain he had left with her, perhaps he was now sharing her suffering. There could be no possible virtue in bearing it all herself, taking it away to live with the children and fester in disputes over custody and maintenance. "Are you alone now, Mrs Dodgson?" "Well, not to say alone. I live with two children and two dogs, and there's my *pain* of course."

"Don't you think so, Hannah?" Sarah Austin appealed for agreement. "The school's filthy. Chewing-gum everywhere. Those cleaners just aren't doing the job properly – they're some wretched contract firm La Fanshawe insisted on bringing in. Honestly, our working conditions are *awful*!" Her Doris Day face was bright-cheeked with indignation, and waves of her Dior scent (a present from Jeff bought at Schiphol on his last business trip) mingled with the traditional cabbage odour and the powerful though hygienic smell emanated by Lorene.

"I don't think we should complain, though," protested Angela. "She's even worse if you complain. Don't involve me in any way, not in the slightest, not in the least, I disclaim any association with a complaint." She was working herself up into a paroxysm of agitation. Her grubby grey sweater rose and fell alarmingly over her disorganised bosom and she began to pant.

"OK, OK," said Sarah good-naturedly. "Have a Valium."

Just after eleven that night Hannah plugged in the electric kettle to make her bedtime cup of tea. There was a small crackling noise and the kitchen lights went out. She looked for a torch in vain, then lit a candle and inspected the fuse board in the basement, which was also in darkness. Sure enough, the wire was burnt through. She went upstairs again and switched off the kettle – that was what Brian had done last time it happened. She then hunted, again in vain, for fuse wire, finding that Brian had taken his tool kit. Possibly, thought Hannah bitchily remembering Marjorie's armour-plated corseting, for use as an extra-marital aid.

Down in the basement once more, she took a sound fuse and replaced it in the kitchen circuit. There was a sizzle and a pop; that had fused too.

Her first instinct was to go to bed and forget the whole thing. Then she remembered the freezer. It was full. She could see a time coming when she would need the food.

The dogs were sound asleep on their sag-bags and could not be induced to go for a walk, so Hannah set out alone in the car in search of fuse wire. She tried two Pakistani corner shops: one had just shut, the other was innocent of fuse wire though the proprietor pressed a royal wedding tin of biscuits on her as a substitute.

"You do not like biscuits?"

"I don't want any at the moment."

"You don't want the royal wedding?" he said incredulously. "Such a pretty lady, Lady Diana."

"I want fuse wire," said Hannah, and set off to drive home. The Renault was making a suspicious ker-plunk ker-plunk ker-plunkety plunk noise and the night was chilly for July, with a strong breeze blowing. A moon straggled through the swaying trees and illuminated a stray drunk sleeping, or possibly choking, in the gutter. By now she was near Bibi's; several lights were on in the flat. They're bound to have fuse wire, she thought, and stopped the car.

After three buzzes on the entryphone with a wait between

each, Nicholas answered and let her in. She went up in the lift and pushed open the unlatched door of the flat. The hall was empty apart from the wild-life writhing on the wallpaper. "It's me, Hannah," she called. "Can I use the phone?"

"Go ahead," called Nicholas from a bathroom. Wondering where Bibi was, Hannah called the police and told them about the drunk in the gutter. When she finished Nicholas appeared, padding along the corridor, his bare feet silent in the deep carpet. He was wearing a short towelling dressing-gown; his hair was wet, plastered to his head, and there were drops of water still glistening on his surprisingly muscled chest. For the first time in the eight years she had known him, Hannah saw him as a man, not just Bibi's husband. She stepped back and clutched together the open neck of her shirt. The top button was missing and her defensive action drew attention to her breasts.

He stared at her breasts and she stared at him staring. He was a bulky man, over six feet, well muscled and overweight with a slight paunch clearly visible under the black towelling. Hannah forced her gaze to drop no lower than his waist in search of bulges.

"Where's Bibi?" she squeaked; coughed, cleared her throat, tried again. "Is Bibi away?"

"At her mother's," he said briefly. "Come and have a drink."

"Yes. Well," said Hannah appalled and delighted by the wave of lust that was engulfing her. What a pity, what a pity that it was Nicholas. Not only was he married to Bibi, but she didn't even like him. "I can't stop. I wanted to borrow some fuse wire."

"Plenty in the kitchen junk drawer," he said, waiting for her to walk past him to the kitchen. As he was standing in the middle of the hall she would thus have to brush past him.

"Could you get it for me?"

He laughed. "I thought you were the independent one. Going to look after yourself." He was teasing, but sharply.

"Please, Nicholas. My freezer will warm up if I don't mend the fuse soon."

"You could replace it with one of the other fuses," he pointed out.

"I tried. The fuse blew again."

"You'll have to find the fault in the circuit. Do you want me to come over and mend it for you?"

"No thanks. I can manage."

Nicholas laughed without amusement. "You're getting on well without a man, is that it? Don't you ever feel lonely?"

"Yes," said Hannah. "But not for you." Every inch of her body tingled and her imagination presented her with vivid, not to say lurid, pictures of herself and Nicholas coupling on the carpet, in the bath, standing up in the kitchen, on the dining-table – would it take the weight? – on the canopied four-poster bed...

He laughed like a seducer in a play and put his arms round her. He didn't feel impotent. Hannah wondered at Bibi's difficulties in getting a sperm sample, she let him press her body close to his, she allowed herself to lean her head on his chest and imagine nothing but the moment. Brian had last made love to her six months ago, and it had not been a successful occasion. He had gone to sleep – or passed out, hard to tell – half-way through. Nicholas at least was sober and interested.

Time to stop, she thought; pushed him away firmly and asked, "Do you fancy Lady Diana?"

"What?" said Nicholas, thrown off his stride.

"The man in your corner shop tried to sell me royal wedding biscuits," said Hannah nipping past him to the kitchen and fuse wire. "I just wondered if you thought Lady Diana was attractive."

"Easy to package and sell," said Nicholas, the advertising man stirring within him. Then he remembered his present enterprise. "You're just trying to change the subject."

"On no account am I going to have sex with you," said Hannah, rummaging through the drawer.

"Why?" said Nicholas. He had adopted an Erroll Flynn posture, arms akimbo, head thrown back. Half-amused, half-randy, Hannah thought the pose rather suited him. "Three reasons. I don't want to upset Bibi; I don't like you much; and..."

"Liking has nothing to do with it," said Nicholas with an air of worldly wisdom. Pause. "What is it about me that you don't like?"

"And thirdly, I'm not taking the pill any more."

"Don't worry – " he began, then broke off abruptly.

Hannah found the fuse wire and closed the drawer. "Goodbye, Nicholas, and thanks."

I'm attractive, I'm attractive, thought Hannah as the car started first go. I'm attractive, my car starts. She drove past the gutter where the tramp had once lain. He had gone. I'm attractive, my car starts, and I help tramps, thought Hannah, and I'll mend the fuse. Good.

The Lower Fifth classroom was at the top of the school building in a sloping attic that would have been a servants' dormitory in the days when one family waited on by half a dozen servants lived where a hundred and one girls and a dozen or so staff now worked. The classroom was a treasured Lower Fifth privilege: it was up its own little flight of stairs and few staff bothered to investigate what was going on there out of lesson time. Lower Fifth girls were fifteen, a liberated age old enough to be contemptuous of authority and young enough not to worry about exams. By the Upper Fifth even the motley crew that attended St Ethelberta's had settled down to working for the end of year O levels.

Hannah enjoyed teaching the Lower Fifth. It was fantastically ill-assorted even by St Ethelberta's eclectic standards. Miss Thirkettle's admission policy was simple: if a parent or guardian could afford to pay the fees, and a child wasn't actually dangerous, then she was in and it was up to the staff to make the best of her. For parents it was a school of last resort. So in the Lower Fifth Felicity Wakefield, the stupidest girl in the school, as English as the Badminton Horse Trials, sat next to Kimia Panahizadi, an exotic and brilliant Iranian. Two English punks who had been expelled from most of the top boarding-schools, three pleasant Pakistanis who giggled behind their hands and whisked their coarse, shiny pony tails of raven hair, three other Iranians – all chattered and squealed and banged the desks, made friendships and broke them, and, occasionally, paid attention.

It was a dull overcast day and the long room with its tiny windows sweltered in the humidity. Someone's cassette recorder pumped out the simple rhythms of a reissued Beatles song and Hannah felt youth run through her veins like amphetamine. It was like wearing a mini-skirt again.

But teacher Hannah took control. "Come on, everyone. English lesson. Get off those desks; books out; poems today."

"Please let's hear the end of this track, Mrs Hannah," begged Felicity. "I don't like poetry. I don't understand it." She was an undersized girl, slender, with pale skin and dark circles under her eyes. She had a perpetually strained expression. She was the dunce of the family: her parents were doctors, her elder brother was at Cambridge, her elder sister doing well in the Sixth Form at St Paul's. She was always tagging behind, anxiously trying to understand, to keep up. She laughed at most remarks in case they held a wit or point she could not see; she watched faces intently to catch a clue from her companions' expressions. The school was a haven for her. She worshipped Miss Thirkettle and ran errands for her whenever she could. Hannah always longed to smooth the worry lines from her forehead and explain that intelligence wasn't everything – wasn't, in the long run, much at all.

"I saw the Beatles once. At a concert in London. I touched Paul McCartney," said Hannah. The girls scrambled over the old scarred desks that over-filled the room and settled happily, expecting a time-wasting discussion of Hannah's youth. "Tell us about it, Mrs Hannah."

"When we've finished *Ode to a Nightingale*."

"That's blackmail," said Kimia.

"Yes," agreed Hannah, and they grinned at each other.

"What's a nightingale?" said Shakira, the Kenyan Asian whose embroidery Mrs Fanshawe so much admired.

"A bird that sings at night. I don't think they have them in Africa."

"Yes they do," said Felicity, pleased with her scrap of information. "When I was in Rhodesia some birds sang all night."

"Zimbabwe," said Kimia.

"What?" Felicity looked alarmed.

"That's interesting, Felicity," said Hannah. "Those birds probably weren't nightingales, though. Did you know that Rhodesia has a new name now? It's called Zimbabwe."

"What's an Ode?" asked one of the pink-haired punks. She

was called Cheese in recognition of her extraordinarily toothy smile.

"I gave you notes on that yesterday," said Hannah.

"Yeah, well, see, Mrs Hannah, I was away yesterday. My mother got married."

"Oh, good," said Hannah. "Do you like the man she's marrying?"

"Not a lot. I'll get used to him, I suppose, and he's bought me a video for the telly in my bedroom. Wants me to keep out of their way, I reckon. Not that I'm in that much."

"Where do you go?"

"Round the clubs, mostly."

The Muslim girls were shocked. "Does your mother not mind?"

"Doesn't bloody care, does she?"

"Page 72," said Hannah. "*Ode to a Nightingale*, by John Keats. He lived very near here. About a hundred and sixty years ago he was sitting in his garden in Hampstead and he heard the song of a nightingale."

"He wouldn't bloody hear it now," said Cheese. "Not with the traffic; the bird wouldn't have a chance."

"Please don't swear, Cheese. Miss Thirkettle doesn't like it."

"I like birds," said Felicity.

"Good," said Hannah. "Kimia, read the first verse."

Brian was going to Karen's sports day, his solicitor said, so would Hannah please attend John's? How fortunate, he added, that both events were scheduled for the same date; the arrangement would look perfectly natural.

Immediately, perversely, she disagreed with Brian's decision, though she would herself have chosen to go to John's. Why should it be up to Brian? Then she remembered the Porsche and felt reconciled. Besides, it was easier to leave Karen to Brian for the time being – she preferred her father – and for John's school, Hannah could make less of an effort. Karen wanted a smart mother and though Hannah could never be smart she tried to appear at Karen's school looking presentable. This entailed getting her hair done, buying new clothes or putting new outfits together using old clothes, and hoovering the inside of her car. She would then have to talk to the parents that Karen approved of – deeply boring to Hannah, but rich or famous or both. In that, Karen was just like Brian, though in a daughter Hannah found the characteristic pitiable. In Brian it had frightened her; it was such an obvious sign of his vulnerability and his lack of self-reliance.

John, on the other hand, was much less demanding. Lots of food, the dogs and a happy, attentive mother; that was all he wanted.

Hannah expected rain. It always rained, in her experience, on sports days. Not decisive downpours that the event could be cancelled for; intermittent showers or steady drizzle. And, sure enough, it was drizzling as Hannah drove from London. But as she turned up the long and bumpy drive to John's school the sun emerged from behind the clouds and touched the scene with gold.

Most parents had already arrived and the clearing by the front door was filled with expensive cars and assured voices, Caroline's kind of voice, never lowered in public because anyone was welcome to hear what its owner thought. The few uncollected boys hovered, eyes anxiously fixed on the drive. Hannah saw John and called to him. He ran beside the car, directing it in a useless and at times positively dangerous fashion. "Oh smashing you brought the dogs, did you remember the sausage rolls, I'm in the finals of most of the track events I bet I win some of them, hello Whisky, hello Soda, Mummy don't they look funny clipped, why did you clip them?"

"Summer," said Hannah. "They're hot." She stopped the car and let John into the front seat beside her. She could smell school soap and John; through the window, cut grass and the delicate breath of Harrods cosmetic counters. She hugged him close, savouring the touch of his smooth, beloved skin, and nuzzled into his neck playfully. People were fanning out over the lawns and picking their way through flower-beds, heavily laden with hampers and bottles like a clichéd, anti-private education television documentary. Ironic that Brian had been so insistent on private education, and boarding education at that; Hannah would have settled for a comprehensive school if she could have kept the children at home.

She had loved them passionately as babies. She breast-fed

them, shocking her mother – "I know everything's back to nature nowadays, Hannah, but *really* it can't be hygienic. You can *sterilise* bottles. Much much better" – and annoying Brian – "If you're feeding kids you'll be tied to them all the time, you won't be able to come out with me. Besides your tits will end up round your knees." But she had stuck to the decision and didn't regret it. Her breasts were still above her waist, and the memories of cuddling, bathing, powdering, feeding the children were entirely happy ones.

Hannah and John picnicked in a comparatively deserted corner of the grounds by an old cricket pavilion. The dogs hunted noisily through the rhododendron bushes and skirmished with a red setter from a neighbouring picnic group.

"When are we going to Italy this year?" asked John when they had finished all they wanted to eat.

Hannah was astonished. Every summer the Dodgsons went to a beach hotel some eighty miles from Rome. Now she thought it obvious that they wouldn't go. It was not obvious to John.

"Because I need to get my flip-flops," said John. "I like getting my flip-flops."

"We won't be going to Italy."

John's face flushed and set into a stubborn grimace. "Not going to Italy? But it was our family holiday."

A family holiday. Yes, Hannah had often used the expression. Knowing her marriage wasn't a sound one, though not admitting the idea to herself in case the house of cards whirled and scattered away, Hannah had buttressed herself and the children with family rituals – and the holiday in Italy which, latterly, Brian had squirmed so violently to get out of, had been the most important. The children enjoyed it; Hannah had tried to enjoy it till she was exhausted with the effort. Now at least she wouldn't have to go through the days with Brian showing off, playing football at the beach, and the nights with Brian showing off at restaurants or night clubs. Last year she had suspected he spent most of his afternoons with the girl who worked on the reception desk. She was a nice girl, about twenty-five, dark, slender, speaking lurching, flamboyant English, kind to children. Probably very kind to Brian behind shutters closed against the baking August sun. Hannah had stayed alone on the beach, reading till her eyes ached and she could hardly turn her head for the stiffness of her neck, knowing and not knowing all she wanted to say to him.

But the Dodgson family holiday was an event Hannah had built up into a stick for her own back, and now John, innocently, was irritating her by parroting her own opinions when they were no longer appropriate.

"You and Karen will go to Grandmother Dodgson for a week or two; you'll stay in London with me for a while; and you'll probably go to Daddy."

"But I'll still need my flip-flops. For the summer holidays. I need flip-flops."

"Then we'll get them," said Hannah, ruffled by his insistence, and John turned a sulky back to her.

It was unreasonable to expect him not to be upset by his parents' divorce. Hannah knew that, and she looked ahead with apprehension to all the events she had so carefully shaped into family occasions. The beginning of the holidays. Christmas. The children's birthdays. They would have to be restructured to include Brian and to include Hannah, but separately.

The afternoon wore on; Hannah sat on a rug on the bonnet of her car, waved to John whenever he appeared, cheered him when he won his three races, and chatted to various people she knew. Her resolve only to tell the truth was proving surprisingly useful in social situations; instead of trying to please she now spoke only when she had something to say. When a conversation died naturally she allowed it to. From time to time she could hear her mother's voice inside her head – "*Say* something can't you Hannah, don't just sit there like a lump – if you can't be pretty at least be friendly, be polite." All her adult life she had felt personally responsible for the happiness and enjoyment of those in her company; had felt especially inadequate with people like these, the green wellington boot and Range Rover set. She could think of nothing to say that would interest them, and little they said interested her. The effort to disguise her yawns made her jaw crack. Yet she knew that both her parents and Brian wanted her to be a success with them, such a success that she was asked to dinner, to lunch, to stay; such a success that she became "and Mrs Brian Dodgson" in the caption to photographs in the *Tatler* and *Vogue*. At last she could abandon the futile pretence that she could or would adapt herself to these aliens; or even that she, the alien, could adapt herself to these normal people. Whichever way round it was, she wasn't going to try any more.

Now it didn't matter, she discovered a knack for it. She was chatting without strain to a genial red-head called Rosabelle Trench about her son Charley's prospects of getting into Eton (dim, in Hannah's view, though she wasn't saying so) when Caroline turned up, and the new socially adept Hannah greeted her warmly.

"You do look a lot better," said Caroline kissing her, "but why don't you do something to your hair? I'll take you to my chap, if you like. Hello, Rosabelle, have you recovered from last night yet?" (To Hannah) "We were at the Pigotts' for dinner, you were well out of it, talk about a disaster! You know they used to have a nice Italian couple but then the man left to start a brasserie in Covent Garden, so they kept the wife who does this absolutely marvellous ironing and sewing, then they hired a very *odd* pair of young men from Hong Kong in tighter trousers than houseboys usually wear, and the soup was cold – it wasn't meant to be, I know it's summer but Adrienne has no idea about food and I think it was oxtail with gallons of cheap wine in it, so we suspected something was wrong, didn't we Rosabelle, when we had cold oxtail soup. Then Adrienne rang and rang for Sebastian to take away the plates but nothing happened and so we all talked away valiantly, didn't we Rosabelle, because it wasn't as if most of the people there even *knew* the Pigotts, you know how they are about asking famous strangers. Finally, there was a ghoulish scream from the kitchen and Sebastian staggered in with blood pouring from a knife wound in his cheek."

"Caroline was marvellous," said Rosabelle. "She took control and stopped the bleeding and when the other houseboy ran in brandishing a carving knife she spoke to him firmly and took the knife away."

"Still the head girl," said Hannah, amused. "What was it, a lovers' quarrel?"

"Something like that. It ruined our dinner, at any rate, and it must have cost the poor Pigotts a fortune – they took us all out."

"What happened to the Hong Kong men?"

"Sacked, of course."

"How sad," said Hannah.

"Yes, wasn't it? Poor Adrienne, she'd gone to so much trouble."

"I don't mean the dinner party was sad. I mean the fight and the sacking."

"You can't have servants carving each other up all over the place," said Caroline. "Anyway, I've got useful information for you, about that woman Brian's gone off with."

Rosabelle Trench began making tactful departure noises. Caroline hardly waited till she had gone.

"About Marjorie – "

Hannah felt sick. She didn't want to hear, yet she couldn't forego the chance to find out. "What are you doing here, Caroline?" she temporised.

"Keeping my cousin William company and laying on the grub. His wife's away. Look, never mind that . . ."

"Does he have a son here?"

"Stop changing the subject. You have to know some time, and the sooner the better. It'll affect your divorce settlement, I should think – you'll have to instruct your solicitor."

"What about?"

"Marjorie has pots of money. She's the chorus-girl that Peter Cleveland married twenty years ago. There was a lot of fuss about it at the time – the gossip people took it up in a big way. His parents didn't like it, but there wasn't much they could do, he was over forty and sane in every other respect."

"I should hope not," said Hannah. "What in the world was it to do with them?"

"You have such odd opinions. Of *course* it had to do with them. He was their *son*."

"If he wanted to marry a chorus-girl surely it was up to him?"

"You never understand the simplest things. I don't know why everyone says you're so clever," said Caroline resentfully. "Do you want to listen or not?"

"I'll listen."

"He died last year and left her everything – all the money he made on the stock market (he was Cleveland and Cleveland, you know, the brokers) and all the money he'd inherited too. They didn't have children. She lives in a flat in Eaton Square and there's a place in Wales, I think; somewhere peculiar like Swansea."

"You mean somewhere normal people don't have a place," said Hannah helpfully.

"Exactly," said Caroline, grateful for this ready understanding of the conventions. She did not expect it of Hannah, nor did she suspect irony or even sarcasm. "And now you know who she is and where she lives, you can find Brian whenever you like."

Hannah could imagine herself driving round and round Eaton Square in the early hours of the morning, getting tangled up in the one-way system, looking for lighted windows – or worse, unlighted windows – in Marjorie's flat.

"It's good news, Hannah, if you've really decided to divorce," said Caroline, suddenly anxious at Hannah's crushed expression. A scatter of applause greeted a javelin throw: Hannah joined in automatically.

Caroline, bulky in a green padded waistcoat, heaved herself on to the bonnet of the car. The afternoon sun was full on their faces and, even perplexed, Caroline's forehead was as fresh as a child's. Hannah looked for traces of ageing on her face but found few; patches of milky skin reddened by the wind, fine lines around the eyes, but substantially the same face Hannah had first known.

"I didn't mean to upset you," she said earnestly. "I thought you'd decided your marriage was over. I wanted to help. You wouldn't let me help with a job so I thought this would be useful. I care about you, Hannah. I know you despise me for not being intellectual, but I do have my advantages and I understand things like money and settlements. You live in a world of your own where that sort of thing doesn't matter, but I live in a world where they do matter and I know a lot about them. And if there's something I don't know, then I find out about it."

"I don't despise you," said Hannah. "Far from it. You make me feel out of touch."

"I know it's a hard time for you," Caroline went on, "but it's so important that you think clearly and I don't think you are. If

Brian marries Marjorie Cleveland he's going to have money. Even if she makes sure he doesn't see most of it, he'll still be far better off than you are because he won't have any expenses. So make sure your solicitor is well informed." She waved and blew a kiss to her youngest child Podge, who was striding determinedly in the direction of Hannah's car with a uniformed nanny in hot pursuit. "I brought Podge along today because Nanny does so love coming here. The head boy used to be one of hers."

Greeting Nanny was easy, but Hannah was tentative with Podge, as she could not remember which sex the child was. It was nearly as broad as it was tall, dressed in jeans and a red sweat shirt, its shining head of blonde curls short enough for a male child and becoming enough for a female one.

"Hello, Podge!"

"Hello," said the child in an ambivalent, clear treble.

"Are you having fun?"

"Yes, thank you."

"Have you seen my son John?"

"Yes, he won lots of races. Nanny told me." Nanny smiled and nodded as if to say nothing escaped her censorious, anachronistic gaze.

"Do you want to win races when you go to school?"

"No. I want to ride," said Podge. "Daddy says I can go hunting next year."

"Won't you feel sorry for the fox?" said Hannah.

"Come with Nanny," said Nanny repressively, before Hannah (whom she disliked) could express even more radical views. Child and nurse stumped away and it was the moment for Hannah to make some appreciative comment. She could think of none that were not sex-specific. But she wanted to be generous to Caroline who was being generous to her.

"Podge is a smashing child," she ventured. "So lively."

"Gerald dotes on her. They go riding together for hours."

With this information Hannah could safely expatiate on the beauty and charm of girl-child Podge, and she did. "How's Gerald?" she concluded, reminded of his existence by his wife's reference to him. He was a curiously insubstantial personality, an officer in a Guards regiment whom Hannah remembered as a red tunic surmounted by a moustache, a man of few ideas and rigid opinions, much in demand for shooting-parties as a tireless and preternaturally skilful bird-slaughterer.

"In Ulster," said Caroline. "Keep him in your prayers until next week."

"I don't have any prayers," said Hannah, "but if I did he'd be in them." What strange sense of duty, she wondered, impelled Gerald Brompton to risk his life on the drab, insoluble Irish question? Or did he merely enjoy danger?

"I took it to heart, what you said about me praying," Caroline said.

"I don't remember."

"Bibi told me. She said you said I probably only prayed for the upper classes."

"I hate 'she said you said I said'," said Hannah.

"Women wouldn't have anything to say without it. So Gerald says. Anyhow, about my prayers, I went through them carefully for a week and you were probably right, though I include servants, of course, and hairdressers and priests and things; people I meet in the normal way. And Gerald's regiment."

"Do you pray for the regiment by name?"

"No, by rank," said Caroline seriously. "But I want to tell you my latest idea. I listen to Radio Two most weekday afternoons, and there's a request programme. I pray for the people who write in for requests. I write their names down and I pray for them next day."

"So they not only hear their Barry Manilow record but also get a leg-up on the way to Heaven."

"I can't be sure of that. But I do my best. And how can we estimate the power of prayer?"

They gazed at each other through the invisible barrier of Caroline's belief. The world was still a simple place for Caroline, thought Hannah, though not an easy one: the Catholic faith was guilt-inducing and tirelessly demanding.

The weekend passed quickly; John, still muttering about flip-flops, was back at school. Hannah was apprehensive about what Nicholas might have told Bibi; he was capable of working his rejection up into a scenario which starred him as irresistible stud and herself as sex-starved divorcee. She was also, more realistically (she and Bibi would certainly adjust and shrug their way back to ease with each other), worried about Nicholas's remark to her. She had protested she might get pregnant. He had said, "Don't worry . . ." It could have been "Don't worry I've got a packet of Durex handy" – but if it had been why did he stop so abruptly? It had started like a sentence announcing something more permanent – possibly sterility from natural causes, or a vasectomy.

Impossible, though, to mention any of this to Bibi. She would say nothing until she could speak to Nicholas alone. He wasn't a good liar and she'd find out the truth without much difficulty. Resolutely, she refused to consider what she would do then. Time enough to worry when it happened. She was busy enough with surveyors, solicitors, her job, writing to the children, walking the dogs. And, of course, her memories of Brian.

4

In August Karen, John and the spaniels went to stay with Brian's parents. Hannah deposited them on to the train north with a sense of relief. She wouldn't have to see the Dodgsons for another two weeks, when she went to fetch the children. Until then she was free to supervise the builders in her new house, picking her way precariously through piles of rubble and joining them in ceaseless cups of tea, and to organise the packing-cases in the old house.

Packing was an agonising task. She had not imagined anything so mundane could be so painful. Brian, with his characteristic generosity and laziness, had said he would leave all the decisions to her. So she labelled the tea-chests BRIAN and HANNAH and dealt out the accumulated possessions of their life together like a canasta hand. At first she lingered over each object, trying to make constructive decisions. But that was unendurable. So many of the things held memories, all involving either a painful contrast with the present stage of their relationship or a reminder of the warning signs, the writing on the wall available for her to see if only she'd had the sense to look. Gradually her decisions grew more and more arbitrary. Most of their things were, in any case, Brian's choice; so she gave him everything that she had no definite claim to. The HANNAH cases became a white elephant stall of rusty fish slices and hideous china animals the children had bought as presents, of threadbare towels and early Elvis Presley records (though, of course, Brian would take the expensive stereo system).

What a terrible wife I was, she thought, surveying this flotsam of fourteen years' housekeeping. Her self-esteem, still precarious, wobbled and sank.

It was late August in London and the city weltered in a dusty tarmacadamed heat. All her friends had gone away. Bibi and Nicholas were at someone's villa in Corfu, Caroline and Gerald had taken the five little Bromptons to stay with Grandmama in Gloucestershire. The television programmes were repeats of repeats and the builders went on holiday. Hannah munched her way morosely through take-away meals, grew fatter and fatter, and didn't wash her hair. She was running out of cash; the school didn't pay in the holidays and she had spent most of her state money on clothes for the children. When she was down to her last few pounds she stopped eating take-away meals and ate bread, jam and tea instead.

Olivia Cummin's telephone call interrupted this self-indulgent orgy, and Hannah resented it. She wished Olivia would go away and leave her alone. But Olivia was not easily brushed off. She was a Jewish-American girl who had been at Oxford doing a post-graduate degree with Hannah; a bundle of neuroses and energy, always grumbling about her physical appearance and her imaginary illnesses. She was obsessively devoted to her husband, a long blond English streak of misery who was eminent in his academic field (an abstruse brand of economics) and seldom spoke.

Olivia was paranoid so her friends were often enemies, but she was remorseless in keeping up acquaintanceships and Hannah found her amusing in small doses. On the occasion of this telephone call Olivia was gloating under the guise of sympathy. "I saw about your – marital problems. In the newspaper."

"Sports pages?" said Hannah, flustered by opposing emotions. She wanted to ask what the paper had said, but she knew the information would upset her.

"In the gossip column, actually," said Olivia. "Listen, I'm giving a little dinner party, just twelve people, there's this lovely man you should meet – or maybe you know him, Nigel Barraclough, he was at Balliol, such a clever shrink and very successful in New York now . . ."

"Why aren't you in New York?"

"Well, as you know, we live there, but D. just loves England, he had to come to see his father and the countryside, so here we are in a little rented apartment near Park Lane. Eight o'clock tomorrow night, here's the address – have you got a pencil?"

Hannah took down the address, still undecided. "I don't know, Olivia," she said.

"Are you free or aren't you?"

"I'm free," said Hannah, "but I think I don't want to come to dinner with you."

Olivia gasped. "That's not like you, to be so hurtful."

"OK, Olivia, I'll come."

This self-assertion invigorated Hannah. For years Olivia had made blunt, self-concerned and often insulting remarks to unretaliating friends; feeling like a worm that had not only turned but revolved with pirouettes, Hannah set about choosing something to wear.

This was very difficult. She was a great deal fatter now than she had been a year ago, which was the last time she had bought new clothes. Anything with a fitted waist was out. She looked disconsolately at the pile of dowdy tents large enough to cover her and rejected them all. Poor dear Hannah was going to put a good face on it. She did remember Nigel Barraclough; a mere acquaintance, tall, good-looking, hardworking as all medical students had to be. She had never known him well enough to be disillusioned. A dowdy tent was not good enough.

But equally, she had no money for new clothes. She scrambled with difficulty into the dusty attic and fetched down the clothes she had stored there in black rubbish bags. Most of them were not only too small and outdated, but also hideous. Why was it, thought Hannah ruefully, that she could always see the inadvisability of wearing certain clothes about six months after she bought them? Why couldn't she see at the time, when she tried them on in the shop?

One dress was possible. An embroidered genuine Afghan ethnic number, it had always been arty-crafty. Hannah looked at it, remembering; it had been so unusual when a boyfriend had brought it back from Afghanistan for her in 1966, long before everyone wore them and they were selling in the Portobello Road. It was really brightly coloured, huge squares of blue and red and heavy embroidery on the hem. When Hannah was two stone lighter it had suited her. Now she managed to squeeze into it and didn't look entirely unpleasant, though she did look middleaged and as if she crocheted her own cushion-covers.

She took it off and held the material between her fingers, remembering. For a year it had been her favourite dress, worn only on special occasions. Brian had liked it because Caroline told him it was smart. He went very much by what Caroline said because she had a title. She had worn it for the first dinner party she and Brian had ever given.

The dinner party was a catastrophe of such dimensions that even fourteen years later Hannah couldn't think of it without blushing. Just after their wedding Brian announced that he wanted to buy a flat in London. Knowing that he was under contract to a Midlands club, Hannah had presumed that they would be living near his work, especially when she realised that he had to attend for training matches every day except Sunday and sometimes Monday.

But Brian lived at home during the week, in the same room that he had occupied since he was a child, and his mother looked after him. He wanted no change in these arrangements. What he envisioned was a flat in London where Hannah would miraculously create a social life in which, eventually, Brian would take a prominent place.

Hannah tried to explain that she wanted to be with him and that she was naturally an unsocial being, but Brian didn't listen. "It's easier for you to be in London. You still have to finish your work at Oxford, don't you? How long will that be?"

"Only another year. I don't have to see my supervisor much."

"Well then, you can be in London. Have your smart friends over. Get about a bit. You'll be a top footballer's wife, you know."

So Hannah tried to make the tiny flat off the Cromwell Road into the sort of place Brian imagined a top footballer should live in. At that point in their marriage there was still some spare money: Brian's Porsche cost a bit to insure and run, and his clothes were expensive, but after they paid for a lease on the flat they had over a thousand pounds to spend on decorating and furnishing.

It was the beginning of the football season and Brian was busy, so Hannah was in charge. She co-opted Bibi who produced an archetypal smart 1960s flat, white, stark, with angular furniture of steel and glass. Long-limbed Hannah was always bruising herself on the sharp edges of frequent tables, but Brian was pleased with the flat and spent every spare moment buying oddments and embellishments for it.

Two months after it was completed he wanted to give a dinner party for Manny Lofthouse. Manny was the most important person in Brian's life apart from Hannah, or perhaps including Hannah. He was the manager of Brian's football club; Brian talked about him all the time and quoted his opinions, but Hannah had never met him, and when Brian announced his plans for a dinner party she could not imagine who else to ask.

"Does he have a wife?"

"Not any more. They're divorced. It really broke him up. She was a difficult bitch."

"Oh," said Hannah sympathetically in her capacity as loyal non-bitch, and after a suitable pause returned to practicalities. "Does he have a girl-friend, then?"

"Not in London. He'll be in London by himself."

"What sort of people would he like? Which of my friends?" At that point Hannah still had a very wide circle of friends from school and Oxford days, though she seldom invited them for formal meals.

"Make up your own mind," said Brian impatiently. He hated to be tied down to details. "Ask Caroline and that man of hers. Ask Bibi. Ask anyone you like." He was equally non-committal about the sort of food Manny Lofthouse enjoyed. "Just arrange it, Hannah. Don't bother me."

So once more Bibi was pressed into service, and between them she and Hannah planned a menu. Pâté from Harrods, lamb casserole with French provincial overtones, cooked by Bibi, special chocolate mousse with orange peel and brandy, made by Hannah. White wine with the pâté, red wine with the casserole, and expensive liqueurs with the coffee and cream. After much thought, Hannah abandoned the idea of finding a woman Manny's generation and settled for Bibi with her current man, Caroline and Gerald – they were to be married soon after – and a pleasant twenty-five-year-old woman called Angela, whom Hannah frequently met at early mass in Brompton Oratory (Hannah was still an assiduous churchgoer.) Angela was a football fan and she came from somewhere in the North; she wasn't especially attractive to look at, but Hannah told herself that Manny Lofthouse would probably appreciate sterling worth – having once suffered at the hands of the bitch wife whom Hannah imagined as busty, brassy and mink-coated.

As soon as he arrived she saw her mistake. A burly fifty-year-old in a brown toupee of horse-hair consistency, squeezed into an expensive, flashy suit like one of Brian's worst, he had a fleshy red face and he breathed whisky fumes. He arrived at half-past seven though the invitation was for eight.

Brian was still in a bath heavily scented with Musk for Men, drinking a vodka martini. Hannah was panicking in the kitchen, though thanks to Bibi's efforts that afternoon everything was ready and the smart smoked glass table was laid in its little recess at the end of the living-room, laden with the odds and ends of silver that Crester-Fyfe great-aunts had produced as wedding presents. Brian and Mick Jagger, more or less together, were singing about Jumping Jack Flash.

Hannah had got ready with care; her Afghan dress, silver earrings, her hair curled into a leonine mass, and strappy tart's shoes. Manny looked at her breasts, guffawed, and said, "If you're Anna I can see two good reasons why the lad married you."

"I'm Hannah," said Hannah.

"That's what I said," said Manny, and stared at her. She saw deep hostility in his little red eyes. This man hates me because of my class, she thought, because I'm young and because I've taken his lad away.

For half an hour Manny drank whisky and followed Hannah about, touching her wherever and whenever he could. Hannah removed chocolate mints from their wrappers, laid them on little silver dishes, opened the red wine bottles to let them breathe, tidied up the bathroom once Brian had left it, put out guest towels, arranged the invitations on the mantelpiece so the dates of the old ones didn't show (a subterfuge Brian thought clever and she thought shabby) and tried to talk to Manny. He conversed mainly in grunts, though from time to time he would bellow to Brian, "All right, lad?" and Brian would bellow back, "Bloody right, Manny!"

Hannah could see the evening was unlikely to succeed. Manny was a football team playing an away fixture, and he was going to teach the home team who was boss.

The other guests arrived, the dinner wore on, Manny said

little and poked his knife and fork irritably at the food, refusing to eat it.

"Phew," said Bibi expressively to Hannah as they met briefly in the kitchen with piles of dirty plates.

"Thanks," said Hannah. Bibi had papered over the social cracks with a skilful flow of inconsequential burble.

Hannah leant against the sink and started to cry.

"Come on," said Bibi bracingly. "It's not as bad as that."

"Yes it is," wept Hannah. "He's laughing at me. All the food and the napkins and everything – he's sneering at them."

"Does it matter?" Bibi darted about the kitchen doing domestic things, looking like a dragonfly, her stick-thin arms and legs emerging from a bright green shift that only just covered her bottom.

It was Brian's disloyalty that hurt her, though she made no attempt to explain to Bibi. It had been his choice to invite Manny, he had told her nothing useful about what he was like and how to entertain him – and now he was taking Manny's side. Hannah knew it. Each time Manny made a sneering remark about fancy food or fiddly little knives, Brian smiled in conspiratorial agreement, and his eyes slid away from Hannah's appealing looks.

At a decent interval after dinner everyone but Manny left and he and Brian settled down to serious drinking. Hannah did the washing-up alone, feeling martyred, then she went to bed, a small defiant rudeness that gave her only brief satisfaction. She intended to wait up for Brian but finally, exhausted, fell asleep.

Next morning Brian, in the throes of a hangover, wouldn't talk about the party. It had gone perfectly well; would have gone better if Hannah hadn't been so stuffy and unable to take a joke. What did she mean, why had he ignored her? He'd done nothing of the kind.

Looking back on it from the perspective of fourteen years, Hannah saw herself insecure, over-sensitive, clinging, unable to tell Brian that she felt unloved, fussing over apparently nothing; once more paying a high price for following her mother's advice and not giving herself away to a man.

She had no spare cash to have her hair done for Olivia's party. It was shoulder length and ragged. She washed it, dried it in tiny plaits to produce a crimped effect, put on enough make-up to make it seem as if she had tried, looked at herself in the misty hall mirror with background lighting and her eyes half-closed, and told herself bracingly that even at her worst she looked better than Olivia. This lifted her spirits fractionally, but after the dusty bus journey (the Renault wouldn't start, even after three hundred yards of pushing) she looked at herself again in an ormolu mirror in the luxurious foyer of Olivia's rented flat and she saw herself overweight, badly dressed and manless.

Olivia's flat, designer-decorated for the mid-Atlantic market, appealed to Hannah immediately. It was complete: fully, indeed excessively furnished, unlike Hannah's bare-boarded and desolate house. But Olivia, startlingly renovated with her hair straight and a new pair of improbable breasts, was scornful.

"Not my taste, of course," she said, indicating the decor with a sweep of scarlet nails and cigarette.

"You haven't given up smoking yet," observed Hannah.

"No. My therapist feels it's better not to put me to the test any more ways right now. I've only just recovered from post-natal depression, you know."

"Have you had another baby?" Olivia's first, and as far as Hannah knew only, child was about four.

"No, I don't want to risk poor Rachel going through the tortures of sibling rivalry I had to endure. My therapist told me I had the worst childhood he'd ever had to treat." Olivia had been in analysis with the same man since she was nine and Hannah imagined them locked in step going from the lesser darkness of Olivia's unconscious to the greater darkness of death without any intermission of light or happiness in between.

Olivia gripped Hannah painfully by the arm and drew her into a corner, away from the chattering guests. Most of them were familiar to Hannah, and unappealing. "Have you heard about Paul?"

Hannah racked her brains. "Do you mean Paul Standish from Christ Church? Isn't he writing TV movies in California?"

"He killed himself," said Olivia.

"Oh." There was no possible response. Hannah had never liked the man but now was not the moment to emphasise this, and she found it difficult to concentrate on anything besides

Olivia's new breasts which peered at her triumphantly through a thin silk camisole top.

"And I don't want you to mention it," pursued Olivia. "You know how sensitive D. is."

"No," said Hannah.

Olivia looked at her blankly.

"I don't think Derek is specially sensitive," explained Hannah. Olivia clicked her tongue impatiently. "*Of course* D. is sensitive," she insisted. "Death frightens him and he doesn't like to hear about it."

"The same was probably true of Paul Standish," pointed out Hannah, and she glanced across the deep pile carpet to where sensitive Derek Cummin leant against the wall with his customary self-satisfied expression, deep in discussion of Japanese restaurants with a bespectacled, fortyish man who was something important in a Swiss bank.

"And one other thing," said Olivia, this time uncomfortably. "Please don't mention divorce."

"Does that frighten D., too?" said Hannah, wishing treacherous tears hadn't come to her eyes.

"It frightens me," said Olivia. "I don't want to give him ideas."

"I won't volunteer information," said Hannah, "but I won't lie, and if it comes up in conversation, I'll talk about it."

Olivia gave her an assessing stare. "Are you going to cause trouble, Hannah?"

"Not deliberately," said Hannah.

"If I'd known you were in this sort of mood I wouldn't have invited you."

"I'll leave now," said Hannah. "That would suit me quite well!"

Olivia gave a little moan of frustration and fury. "You're usually so polite! You must be feeling really humiliated by Brian leaving you for an older woman."

"I am," said Hannah, and sobbed openly.

"Can I help?" Nigel Barraclough, tall, handsome, polished like a suspect apple by affluence and America, strolled up at Olivia's agitated signal.

"No, thank you," said Hannah, "I was just leaving."

"Please don't do that," he said persuasively. "I was looking forward to talking to you this evening." He offered a flawless smile and a Kleenex for Men. Hannah blew her nose thoroughly and rubbed her eyes. A Filipino butler was hovering with little pre-dinner snacks and the delicious smells reminded Hannah that she was hungry and there was no food at home; the anxious looks she received from the other guests pricked her social conscience, and she allowed herself to be given two drinks in quick succession and then installed at one end of an imitation Regency dining-table between Derek Cummin and Nigel Barraclough.

It was one of those evenings, Hannah reflected morosely, where the more she drank the worse everything seemed. Derek was telling her, in detail, about his last trip to Brazil and about the sociological, economic and political consequences of Japanese investment there. He had a long, pale face with thin lips like an appendix scar which seldom parted enough to reveal his pointed, uneven teeth. Brian had always claimed Derek fancied Hannah; Hannah had seen no evidence of it, but there was certainly a pale, fishy emotion glinting in the depths of his eyes, and he pressed her arm with more fervour than, on the face of it, Brazil would warrant.

"We have to consider the wider implications," said Derek with ventriloquist's skill. Hannah was imagining sex with Derek; she hadn't been listening, and said so. Derek took offence.

"You're not interested in Brazil?"

"I was thinking about something else."

"What?" said Derek, with contemptuous impatience, as if nothing Hannah could be thinking of would be of any significance compared to what he had to say.

"You really don't want to know," warned Hannah.

"Come, come my dear," said Derek. "I don't expect your dark thoughts will worry me."

"I was thinking that your prick is probably like an ice-lolly."

"You wouldn't last a year at the World Bank," he said venomously, with an unamused sea-lion bark. "You're impossible."

"I told you you wouldn't like it," said Hannah, turning to Nigel Barraclough and her food.

Each evidence of Olivia's wealth, fabulous in comparison with Hannah's present poverty, became more and more irksome. Each mouthful of caviare became a tile for the bathroom or a square foot of curtain material. And she felt unprotected and vulnerable, as if Brian's departure had left her socially belittled; as if she had thoughtlessly mislaid a major part of her personality or come out half-dressed.

She also felt lumpish and ugly. When the women left the table, eyes collected by a masterful and beady Olivia, and sought refuge in a bedroom at least as large as the whole ground floor of Hannah's new house, she could see herself reflected in the mirrors lining the walls. Beside the other women she looked home-made, her hair amateurish, her Afghan hem dipping. She knew that much of this was her own state of mind and made a conscious effort to be less passive, chatting to the other women.

Olivia had temporarily vanished into a lavatory and so they were talking about her. "It was feeding that baby," said one. "She went on feeding it till it was school age, for Christ's sake. It can't be good for your tits."

"She always had small boobs," said a beautiful Scandinavian in designer leather and a predatory air that warned she had probably skinned the animal herself. "Besides, I don't think new tits will help."

"I think they look very good," said Hannah.

"The point is, will Derek?" The Scandinavian gave a significant look. "His interests lie elsewhere."

"Oh," said Hannah. "Where?"

The other women exchanged glances. "You mean you really don't know?" Hannah shook her head and Olivia re-entered the room, already higher in Hannah's sympathy.

At eleven-thirty Hannah felt she could decently leave, though the other guests were entrenched. Nigel offered to drive her home but she refused and soon with a sense of intense relief was escaping into the Mayfair street. The air wasn't exactly fresh, it was too warm and petrol-laden for that, but at least it wasn't heavy with money.

She had to walk home; forgetting that she might not want to be given a lift, she hadn't brought enough money for a taxi. She probably didn't have enough cash for one anyway, even if she took the sticky odd coins from the depths of the sofa. So she wandered along Park Lane looking aimlessly about her and wondering why the dinner party had depressed her so much. She should have used it as an opportunity to find a proper job. Or perhaps she was too old, now, for recruitment to the kind of institution whose employees ate expensive meals and negotiated loans. In any case, the women made her feel unpolished and the men made her feel undesirable.

Lost in these reflections and slightly hazy from the wine, she didn't notice when a man driving a Volvo estate car slowed right down to cruise beside her. When she did realise he was talking to her, at first she thought she knew him and nodded and smiled politely before walking on.

"Come on, get in," he said urgently. "Do me a favour." He had a North London Jewish voice and a heavy, rather handsome face with drooping cheeks like a bloodhound. With astonishment Hannah realised he was trying to pick her up. Why not? she thought. Seized by an impulse, reckless and slightly drunk, she got into the car.

The man gazed at her in satisfaction. He was short, about fifty, paunchy and, from what she could see of his body from the open-necked shirt, with the remains of a considerably muscled body running to fat. That was all right with her. He was looking at her entirely uncritically, in fact with gloating anticipation, and Hannah was amused and flattered.

The car had a funny musty smell and there were rolls of carpet in the estate section. "My name's Simon," said the man. "You caught my eye straight away. I like that dress you're wearing. Bright, feminine, not obvious like the other girls." He talked awkwardly, laughing every now and then – his face twitched and Hannah realised she was now in a social situation almost as stressful as she had felt the dinner to be. Still, the sex might be good and would certainly be an experience. Apart from one Brigadier Soames, she had only ever had intercourse with Brian.

They drove to a deserted car park behind a warehouse – Simon's readiness in finding it gave the lie to his constantly reiterated "I don't often do this kind of thing, you know."

They parked, the engine clanging away into an eerie silence. "Let's get in the back," he said.

"Doesn't anybody use this car park?" defended Hannah, reluctant to move.

"We're just going to," he sniggered.

Hannah saw she had come too far to turn back. Besides, this ageing and presumably uncritical stranger would be a good test of her independence.

In the surprisingly comfortable back seat Simon settled himself and waited. Evidently he expected her to straddle him. She wrestled her tights and pants off, feeling less and less randy by the second, then plopped herself on to his unzipped lap. His skin felt warm and clammy; his penis was much shorter and narrower than Brian's with a curious bend in it and a poor sense of direction. Perhaps this is why he has to pick girls up in the street, thought Hannah. But he grasped her broad buttocks with welcoming enthusiasm and she began to think she might enjoy it.

Very soon he gave a wriggle and his penis went from sausage to chipolata. "Thank you," he said, apparently considering the episode over.

Hannah wasn't used to this kind of treatment and assumed that he would make some attempt to please her, so she sat on.

There was an uncomfortable silence. Hannah became aware of an itch in her left knee. Simon cleared his throat.

"If you reach over to the front seat you'll find a J-cloth in the box near the handbrake." Hannah found the box. He took it and started to mop vigorously. "We don't want any personal stains on the plushette upholstery, now do we?" Hannah, indifferent, said nothing but settled herself more comfortably on his lap.

Silence fell again. A clock struck in the distance.

"Do you have a family, dear?" he said.

Hannah described the children.

"That's nice," he said, scrabbling around in a pocket. "I have two sons. My eldest was just barmitzvahed, last week. It was a lovely occasion. I've got the photographs here."

Bemused, Hannah peered at them in the sickly light of the street lamp.

There was a tapping on the window. A policeman stood outside. Hannah jumped in shock but decided not to move. With yards of her hand-dyed dress billowing over them, she and Simon were a decorous, if comic, sight. She wound down the window.

"Good evening," said the policeman with heavy irony. "What do you think you're up to, then?"

"This gentleman was just showing me his son's barmitzvah photographs," said Hannah.

"Yes, officer," gushed Simon, obviously unnerved, thrusting photographs through the window. The policeman, middle-aged and slow moving, fumbled for glasses and studied the photographs by the light of his torch.

"Beautiful, beautiful," he said. "It's a very moving occasion, a barmitzvah, important in a boy's life. My third son . . . I've got the snaps in my wallet . . ."

So now Hannah, still astride Simon, was admiring two sets of barmitzvah photographs.

Next day Hannah woke with a throbbing headache and an acute attack of misery. She felt so wretched that for the first few hours she pretended to herself that what she needed was nourishment. She started with a full litre of orange juice for the hangover. Mid-morning she had breakfast: porridge with cream, white sliced bread toasted with butter and marmalade. After the sixth piece she didn't even bother to toast it, but covered successive slices of the soggy white doughy bread with butter and marmalade and stuffed them into her mouth whole, washed down with cups of coffee. She stopped only when the loaf was finished. Her stomach was sending up panic signals but she ignored them and hunted through the house for a missing bar of chocolate. At length she found it and ate that too.

By then, lying on the sofa, she could no longer avoid thinking. She knew that eating didn't help, but that hadn't helped her not to eat. The neurotic trap she was caught in seemed logical, even neat. She was depressed, so she ate; she ate, so she was depressed. And she was fat. And she wobbled when she walked along.

All women wobble when they walk along, she argued with herself.

Jane Fonda doesn't wobble.

How do you know?

She can't. Not after those exercise routines.
Well, face it. You're not Jane Fonda.
I think I'll have a tin of pilchards.
That'll make you feel sick.
I feel sick already. I've gone up two whole dress sizes in the last few years.
So what?
So what hope is there for Hannah?
You're just upset by that man last night and you're trying to avoid thinking about it.

To stop the conversation in her head, she ate the tin of pilchards. She opened it first, but only just.

She tried to think about Olivia. Had she alienated her permanently? Derek would surely tell his devoted, slavish, obsessive wife that Hannah had been very rude to him. If that was the case then Hannah need hardly ring up to thank her for the dinner party.

All that remained in the larder were three large tins of baked beans. She didn't like baked beans but she decided to eat some. Luckily, the doorbell rang and, still in nightdress and bare feet, she opened it a sliver, just enough to stick her head round and see who it was. A man stood there. He was about forty, medium height, muscular build, wearing jeans and a blue T-shirt. He had dark hair cropped very short and he carried a clip-board.

"Mrs Dodgson?"

"Hannah."

"Can I come in, Hannah?"

"Why?"

"To talk to you about your house."

"It's sold."

"Not this house. The house you're converting in Crimea Road. Bibi Ainsworth asked me to look at it for you."

"This isn't a good time," said Hannah. "I'm depressed, I've got a hangover, and I haven't many clothes on."

"I'll make you tea for the hangover and I'll wait while you change. There's not much I can do about the depression." He had a faint Welsh accent and an air of sturdy self-reliance. Hannah felt sure he was going to give her bad news about the house, and particularly did not want to hear it. But it was kind of Bibi to arrange his visit, even if it did come at the wrong time, even if the whole arrangement showed Bibi's distrust of Hannah's choice of builder.

"Do you mind waiting in the kitchen?" she said.

"Not at all."

When Hannah, dressed but no more fitted to face the world, returned to the kitchen, the Welshman had finished the washing-up and made tea. He had also tuned the radio to classical music. Under his care the room looked welcoming. Hannah wondered if she would be feeling better this morning if he had been the cruising scavenger to pick her up last night. But she was still trying not to think about Simon Gold so she concentrated on sipping her tea, which showed a marked reluctance to join the pilchards, the porridge, the toast, the bread, the marmalade, the bar of chocolate.

"I feel cold," she said, which was the nearest she could come to express her actual sensation, which was that she was gently but inexorably floating away.

"Here," said the man, and he draped one of her own sweaters round her shoulders. "I'm sorry this is a bad time but I wanted to see you before those builders of yours get back from holiday, and I'm off to France tomorrow to fix up a farmhouse for a mate of mine."

"Not another farmhouse in the Dordogne?" said Hannah cattily to show her indifference to him and all his concerns. "I thought people stopped buying those years ago." I sound just like Caroline, she thought, too ill to care.

He disregarded her, opened his clipboard and listed what he had found in the new house. Obviously her builders were botching their work, as Bibi had so often pointed out.

Hannah knew she should listen and ask questions. Much of what he said was incomprehensible. What was an RSJ? Why did she need at least two ring mains? Why had she had sex with a stranger in the back seat of a Volvo estate? Why couldn't she concentrate? What was this man's name? Bibi had talked about him for years – her miracle of a builder, reliable, honest, intelligent. David Bowen, that was it.

Possibly she had also had an affair with him. There was more to Bibi's sexual activity than she ever told Hannah, and she told Hannah a great deal. Bibi married in her late twenties.

Until then she had glittered through Sixties' and Seventies' London, sometimes the companion of a famous or notorious man, more often involved with some unknown she discovered in the course of her busy life. Caroline disapproved wholeheartedly of Bibi's tendency to think of the lower classes as real people, to turn up at parties with a waiter or a builder or the man who mended her car. Caroline prayed for the lower orders, reflected Hannah perking up at the thought, while Bibi showed Christian charity in a more tangible form.

"I'm not listening, you know," she said. "Don't waste your time. Leave me the list and I'll see to it."

"Why are you upset?"

"Didn't Bibi tell you? Because my husband left me and I still haven't got over it."

"How long ago did he leave?"

"Two months."

"That's not very long," he said. He was sitting with his back to the window and the light behind him emphasised the solidity of his body. He was very muscular, he sat very still. Hannah wished he would go away. His masculinity reminded her of what she had hoped for from last night's debacle.

"Couldn't you have put off moving until you were ready to cope?" he said. "That would have been better."

"That might have been better," snapped Hannah, "but it's not what happened. Lots of things in my life would have been better done another way, or not done at all, and I expect the same is true for you, but let's not go into it."

He said nothing; silence suited him. Hannah missed the noise of the children, of the dogs, of life anywhere in the house. She'd sent the children away to make packing and moving less of a strain for them; and when they came back from the Dodgsons they were going to America with Brian and Marjorie and then it would be a matter of days before their terms started. Probably most holidays would be like that. So for most of the year, Hannah alone would run a house and two pets of a non-existent family, like a house-sitter.

"They'll have to go to day school," she said out loud.

"Your children?" He spoke as if he knew about them. Briefing from Bibi, presumably.

"Otherwise I'll never see them," she explained. "If they're

at school all term and with Brian all holidays, I'll never see them."

"Are there schools near here they could go to?"

"I'll have to look into it." It was an invigorating idea, something to look forward to. The children at home! Seeing them every evening! She wriggled her toes with anticipated pleasure. She could make supper for them, find out about their day at school, shout at them just like a real mother. Such a simple thought. Why hadn't she had it before?

"I think I was in shock," she said.

"When do your builders start work again?"

"The week after next."

"I'll be back from France by then. If you'll let me, I'll supervise the work."

"You mean tell them what they're doing wrong and make them do it again?"

"Yes."

"But I can't ask you to do that, you're really expensive, aren't you? Besides, is it ethical? Wouldn't it be like calling in a second doctor without warning the first?"

"I don't expect you to pay. I wouldn't do it professionally. Think of me as a friend, helping out."

He must still be involved with Bibi, thought Hannah, unless she's paying him and he's not supposed to let me know. "That's too much to ask," she said. "Like inviting Baryshnikov to dinner and clearing a space for him to give a pirouette or two."

"You mustn't tell Bibi," he went on. "If she finds out I ever work free she'll pester me to cut my charges."

Maybe it's a genuine offer, then, thought Hannah. Why? Does he feel sorry for me? He looks too sensible to go round rescuing large ladies with hangovers from the consequences of their folly.

"That's settled. I'll just clear away our tea then I'll be off."

The telephone rang and she answered it. Nigel Barraclough's voice: "Hannah! how delightful to hear your voice!"

"But hardly surprising, since you dialled my number," said Hannah, who was then aghast at her own sprightliness; reminiscent of her much younger self, probably brought on by this voice from the past.

"Did you enjoy Olivia's party?"

"Not much. Did you?"

"It was good to see so many old friends. It's good to be back in Britain."

You've probably got more genuine friends in the snake house at the Zoo, thought Hannah. He sounded entirely American. She wished she knew what prompted him to pay attention to her. Was he married?

Bibi's builder dried the tea-cups and replaced them in the cupboard.

"Are you free for dinner tomorrow?" said Nigel.

"Tomorrow?" Hannah temporised. It would be forward to point out that she was free for dinner for the rest of her life; and did she want to spend a whole evening with him?

"We could talk over old times," said Nigel.

"We didn't have any old times. Not together," said Hannah.

"That's what I want to remedy."

Glib, thought Hannah.

"What time may I call to collect you?"

"Eight," said Hannah.

"Not earlier?"

"Eight."

She replaced the receiver. Bibi's builder was at the front door.

"Thank you," she called after him. "Thank you very much."

"Don't do anything rash," he said.

"What do you mean?" she called after him, but he had already closed the door.

Next day Bibi came back from holiday, a week early, alone.

Hannah was sunbathing on a small, dingy flat roof at the back of the house, wearing a faded old bikini. If she sunbathed naked the seventy-year-old man next door with a room overlooking her roof swore at her in Polish. She was lying on her back, eyes closed against the sun, counting the sounds of London. Traffic, a baby crying, reggae, a barking dog, Brahms, a family row, a police siren, a child practising the violin, a jet on the flight path for Heathrow. Far away, a military band, perhaps for the benefit of tourists left over from the royal wedding celebrations, played 'All the Nice Girls Love a Sailor'.

A night's sleep had more or less restored her equilibrium. She had eaten a human sized breakfast, one slice of toast – none of the insane gorging of the previous day – and still clung to her decision to take the children away from boarding-school; that acted as a beacon, a thought comforting as a hot water bottle on a cold night, welcome as the final curtain in a school play, necessary as a petrol station when the gauge has been on red for the last twenty miles. Compared to that the memory of Simon Gold seemed distant though still distasteful, like a slug in the far corner of the room. The violence of her reaction the previous day surprised her. True, her sexual experience was very limited: Brian, and Brigadier Soames; but her first encounter with the Brigadier had been as arbitrary and unloving as one could well imagine.

Drowsing under the fingering sun, feeling her body ease and melt into the aromatic tarmac finish of the flat roof, the scent of sun oil rich in her nostrils, she remembered Brigadier Soames and his Airedale, under whose well-trained stare she and the Brigadier had coupled on the sand. She remembered the ozone and seaweed air of the cave in Devon; the pounding of the sea and her own passion and the Brigadier's bronchitic spasms sounding in her ears.

For most summer holidays from school Hannah had gone to stay with her mother's sister's family in Devon. Ten . . . twelve . . . fourteen . . . the years ticked by and she got used to her cousins, Jill her own age and Jackie a year younger, and learnt to fit in to the hurly-burly of her aunt's household. Anne Atkinson was far less tidy than her elder sister, Jane Crester-Fyfe; she was also less obsessive and less ambitious. Her sandy hair was unkempt; the ill-disciplined Labrador left hairs on the chairs; amiable bald Arthur, her husband, pottered off every day to his country solicitor's practice. Into this casual household Hannah fitted happily enough. The narrow boxroom, Hannah's room, was the nearest thing to a sanctuary she ever had. She would lie in bed staring out through the skimpy curtains at the straggly branches of the oak tree outside her window or into the velvet darkness, and know that elsewhere in the house no one minded what she did. The dim mirror in the wardrobe reflected naked, developing Hannah with the charity of blur – as she matured she became self-conscious about her heavy breasts (why did the left one grow so much bigger than the right, for a whole three months?) and long, solid thighs.

Her cousins, mindless, even-tempered, grew out of ponies and into boys. Hannah was a late developer, immersed in books, in love with Heathcliff and Mr Rochester and Hamlet. All her sexual fantasies were a kind of literary rape carried out in the dark in case Hamlet liked small breasts or rosebud lips.

Self-conscious about her body, Hannah often went swimming alone. Swimming with the others entailed dashing from towel to sea to towel. So she pretended she liked getting up early in the morning and at six o'clock on fine days she ran down the path from the house and changed into her swim-suit in a cave.

The Brigadier took early walks, winter and summer. He prided himself on his regular habits. Hannah knew him only by sight; now and then he came to drinks before Sunday lunch, but Hannah kept out of sight as much as she could on those occasions. If she was forced to be present, she passed round the peanuts and cheese straws with uncalled-for zeal. She grew accustomed to greeting him on the beach: "Good morning, what a lovely day," was her formula (she only swam on lovely days). He would lift his summer hat, usually a Panama, occasionally a yachting cap, and bow slightly. Hannah would feel his eyes on her body as she hurried away from him. He never stared at her when she could have noticed and objected. She often turned quickly hoping to catch him but he always turned away in time.

She thought of him more and more and Heathcliff less and less. Whatever else could be said of the Prince of Denmark, he was certainly not alive and well and fancying Hannah; Brigadier Soames might be over sixty, red-faced and moustached, on the bony side of thin, but at least he was real – and at the same time as unthreatening as a fictional character. A transition, Hannah felt, a compromise. Her sexual curiosity, frustrated by her social awkwardness with her contemporaries, flourished with Soames as its unlikely object. He was so old he must be grateful for her, she reasoned, and this thought banished much of her self-consciousness.

One morning he prolonged their conversation. "At school still, are you?"

"Yes Brigadier," answered Hannah, eyes downcast, towel clutched to her chest.

"Enjoy it, do you? Have fun? Feasts in the dorm, and so on?"

"Now and then," said Hannah kindly.

"Strict school is it?"

"Quite strict," said Hannah. "It's run by nuns."

"Convent, eh?"

"Yes Brigadier."

"Wear a uniform, I s'pose?"

"Yes. Blue skirt, white blouse, black stockings, tie."

"Black stockings," said the Brigadier with a wealth of longing. "That'd suit a bonny girl like you. Couldn't help noticing you've got a fine figure."

"It is a nice uniform," said Hannah, not as innocent as she sounded. The combination of reading and Bibi had ensured a wide theoretical acquaintance with most aspects of sex. "Would you like to see it?"

"You'd wear it for me?"

"Of course. I'm proud of my school," said Hannah. He looked suspicious. I'm overdoing it, she thought. "I like dressing up, besides," she said wildly, "and I don't have many clothes."

"Atkinsons keep you short, do they?"

"Oh no, no, that's not it. I grow out of them so quickly."

The dog barked reproachfully. It wanted a game. Hannah moved away.

"Tomorrow, then?" said the Brigadier.

"OK," said Hannah.

Her feelings about sex were mixed. Her parents never spoke about it, either in the general or in the particular, and she had always imagined they had no sex life until one humid, open-windowed night in South America when sleepless Hannah heard her mother scream in disgust "sex, sex, filthy sex, that's all you ever want". Hannah was half shocked, half embarrassed, and she looked at her father through new eyes. She concluded from this episode that her mother thought that sex was dirty. Hannah had earlier discovered that her mother thought everything was dirty, so she gave no conscious weight to her opinion.

The nuns' picture appealed more. Keep yourself pure till marriage, when sex will be blessed by God. She liked that idea; it appealed to her romantic, idealistic mind. Brigadier Soames didn't fit into the nuns' patter. But Hannah was excited by the thought of what might happen between them; the day slid by unnoticed; she couldn't eat, she couldn't even read, and she woke before five next morning just as the darkness was touched by the grey of early dawn.

She closed the side door of the house cautiously and picked her way across the gravel, cold and shaking even in her winter uniform with an overcoat on top in case anyone caught sight of her and asked awkward questions about why she should wear school clothes in the holidays. Going down the steep path she several times missed her footing and once nearly fell to the beach far below. The shock pulled her up, and she clung to a tree half-way down. It was a winding, broken path. She looked back, up to the top of the hill, to the angular grey stone building that housed the sleeping Atkinsons.

Twenty years later, lying in the sun on her flat roof, Hannah could only remember fragments of the encounter in the cave. She could recall the pleasure of his touch on her breasts. His hands were old and dry as paper, the nails chalky. He kept talking as if she was a horse to be encouraged over a difficult fence, and she despised him for it, and for his uncontrollable excitement as he forced his way inside her. It was strange, uncomfortable. At once she felt unsexual and embarrassed, conscious of the damp sand under her buttocks and the Airedale's tufty-eyed scrutiny.

Afterwards she straightened her uniform and wondered if sex was always like that, and if so, why people made such a fuss about it. Hardly different from putting in a tampon, but messier.

"All right, are you? All right?" Soames blethered at her. She wanted to get away from him. All they had in common was her body. She felt foolish in her winter uniform with black stockings on the beach. She was sore, her lips bruised and roughened by the gobblings of his moustached mouth, her thighs aching and sticky.

She dragged herself, heavy-legged, up the path. The shuttered windows of the house looked disapproving and hostile. Fifteen, and no longer a virgin. How common was that? She didn't know. She'd ask Bibi.

That experience had put her off sex for the next few years. She couldn't look Soames in the face again and he had none of the charity or self-possession or even simple good manners to say something that would make her feel better. She was determined not to stop her early morning swims in case anyone noticed and asked why. He still took the dog for walks at the same time; still raised his hat to her as if nothing had happened. She felt as if what they had done was too horrible to be mentioned. She resolved never to have sex again until she trusted the man completely, trusted him to make it pleasurable for her and to be affectionate afterwards. She had trusted Brian.

So no wonder, she thought shifting her body on the towel in pursuit of the sun, that Simon Gold and his back seat activities had upset her. If she hadn't drunk so much at Olivia's she wouldn't have made such an idiotic mistake.

At this point in her reflections she opened her eyes to find Bibi perched on the low wall enclosing the roof, clutching a bottle of champagne. "Bibi!" she squealed, sitting up suddenly and shoving her breasts back into the bikini top. "Why aren't you in Corfu? I didn't expect you back till next week." Bibi looked holidayish, her T-shirt and shorts slightly crumpled as if she had travelled in them, her eyes hidden behind massive dark glasses, her arms and legs tanned.

"How did you get in?"

"I've still got the key you gave me last year when you went away on holiday. But listen, I've got marvellous news! I'm going to have a baby! Here, I brought glasses from the kitchen. Have some champagne."

Hannah was delighted. A baby at last! And no reason, now, to interrogate Nicholas about his mysterious, unfinished sentence to her. He couldn't possibly be sterile.

She hugged Bibi close, sympathetic tears of joy springing to her eyes. "Bibi, I'm so happy for you! So happy!" Bibi shrugged her off and poured champagne.

"Is something wrong?" said Hannah.

Bibi took her sunglasses off to reveal a lurid black eye just poised between purple and yellow. "Everything's wrong except the baby," she said miserably. "Nicholas – I don't know what's wrong with Nicholas. He hit me."

"Why?"

"I don't know. I thought he'd be delighted with the news.

I waited till I was absolutely sure. When I was a month overdue, I told him. Then he hit me."

"Did you come straight back to London?"

"I hung around for a day. I hoped he'd explain. He wouldn't even speak to me, it was very hard on the Haileys when their party suddenly went sour."

"Never mind about that," said Hannah, "they were lucky to have you in the first place. But are you *sure* you're pregnant?"

Bibi shuddered. "I wish you wouldn't use that word, Hannah, it always sends shivers up my spine. Granny was obsessed with not using common words. Pregnant, mirror, note-paper – ugh."

Hannah recognised this familiar Bibi feint and was undistracted by it. "Have you had a test?" she insisted.

"Not yet. But I'm sure. I've never been this late before. And I feel different. I do so hope it's a girl, I've always wanted a girl."

I hope it's a baby, thought Hannah, her mind racing. If she had been right originally and Nicholas was now sterile, then he might well be furious with Bibi if she announced she was pregnant. Furious, jealous, utterly confused. Hannah was sure that Bibi was faithful to Nicholas. Which meant . . . that Bibi was probably so wound up about having a baby that her periods had stopped.

"Promise me you'll go to a doctor and have a proper check-up."

"You finish the champagne," said Bibi evasively. "Alcohol is bad for babies."

Hannah covered herself with a tent-like dress she had snapped up for thirty pence at a Scouts' jumble sale and tried to listen to what Bibi was saying. Plans for the new baby, names, schools, whether to get a trained nanny or one of Caroline's willing girls from Ireland; then gossip from Corfu, funny, lively descriptions of people and events. But the sun was cold on Hannah's back and the champagne tasteless in her glass. Something was terribly wrong. Bibi was not pregnant but ill, she was sure, and a dreadful restlessness seized her. She wanted to rush Bibi to the doctor there and then. "Let's go inside," she said, but Bibi wanted to stay.

"I think it's nice sitting on your roof, Hannah, and we won't be able to toast ourselves here much longer. When are you moving out?"

"End of next week," said Hannah. She could hardly bring herself to talk to Bibi without expressing the worries in her mind. She couldn't look her in the face, in case she saw more warning signs of illness. I can't bear it, I can't, she thought. Bibi, please don't be ill. Don't let there be something wrong with you, especially not now when I rely on you to stay the same while everything else changes.

"Will you be godmother, Hannah?"

"Certainly not," said Hannah, relieved to have something genuine to say. "You know what I think of christenings, with a poor baby trussed up like a chicken in lace. Ask Caroline."

"Don't worry, I will. Do stop looking at me like that. What's going on in your mind? Aren't you pleased for me?"

"I am, I am," cried Hannah. "I just don't want you to raise your hopes and then find out it's a false alarm."

"Do stop carping at me. You're not usually so cautious. Tell me what you've been doing while I was away."

Hannah made an effort and recounted the details of Olivia's party. She omitted its aftermath. She didn't want a Bibi with enough information to be indiscreet at a later date.

"And you're going out to dinner with this Nigel Barraclough person? Do I know about him?"

"I doubt if I ever mentioned him to you. He was just an acquaintance at Oxford. He asked me out a few times but I was never able to go."

"Why?"

"Too busy," said Hannah, smiling half in disbelief in memory of the time when her evenings were engaged for weeks ahead. "Oxford was odd then. Not enough women, and most of those had steady boyfriends. So I never went out with Nigel. But we were at a party once and he got rather drunk and showed me pictures in medical books. Pictures of birth deformities. He said he wanted to heal the whole world."

"Do you still want to heal the world?" asked Hannah. It was after dinner; Nigel had been easy to talk to so far and he was good at dealing with taxi-drivers, head waiters and other potential tyrants. But there were three people sitting at the window table in one of the smarter London restaurants; Nigel, Hannah, and Nigel's memory of Hannah. She had made an effort to look attractive, masterminded by Bibi; she was wearing her own sundress and several of Bibi's antique scarves.

"Toss the scarves about with reckless abandon," Bibi had advised, "and you'll do. The neck and shoulders are all right, and at least your arms haven't gone."

"Gone where?"

"Sometimes at our age the upper arm sags and flaps in the breeze like bunting."

But though Hannah was modestly proud of her appearance that evening, it was clear Nigel didn't notice it. The Hannah of sixteen years ago was what Nigel saw. "Do you remember? Do you remember?" he kept saying, and most of it Hannah not only did not remember but did not believe had happened in the first place.

"You were the most charming girl I'd ever met," he said. "I kept hoping you'd notice me. You were brilliant, independent, beautiful."

Brilliant probably, independent possibly, beautiful never, thought Hannah choosing the most delicious of the sticky crystallised fruit.

"You always spoke your mind," said Nigel. "You knew what your values were. I admired that. I'll never forget the evening we spent together at Archie Patterson's party."

He took her packing-roughened hand in his manicured one and Hannah, more as a tribute to Bibi than on her own account, smiled mysteriously and tossed a scarf or two with her free hand. He leaned his head towards her. She gazed admiringly at his teeth, the pièce de résistance of his renovated transatlantic appearance. She found the emphasis on physical perfection disconcerting; first Olivia, now Nigel, had felt they were not good enough for public consumption in their original form. But once you start extensive repairs why should you ever stop? Eventually you would be like a much-restored old master, only the provenance original.

But she could see why he was a successful psychiatrist with a practice that consisted mainly of women. He was unthreatening, unsexual, reliable; something to fall back on. A marshmallow-coated water bed.

"I've never been married," he told her seriously. "Somehow, it's never been the right time. I've known some wonderful ladies, though. I was with Barbie-Ann for five years. She was my last live-in lady." He produced a very slim, very black leather wallet and extracted a photograph; Nigel in swimming trunks, a beautiful dark girl in practically nothing. "That's Barbie and me on holiday in the Caribbean."

"She's absolutely gorgeous," said Hannah, not even jealous. This girl was more perfect than Hannah could imagine wanting to be.

"She moved out – on an amicable basis, mind you – three months ago. So I'm still taking things easy. My healing-time, you might say."

"Why are you in England? On holiday?"

"The main reason is to see my parents. My father isn't well."

Not another one, thought Hannah, her mind flying to Bibi at the mention of illness. Bibi was still at Hannah's house, she had agreed to stay the night after much persuasion; Hannah didn't like the idea of her being upset without company.

With difficulty she dragged her attention back to Nigel who was now discoursing on his parents. "Not very stylish people, of course – they live in Dollis Hill – but the salt of the earth. So authentic, so real." Unreconstructed, was presumably what he meant. Hannah's sympathies lay in Dollis Hill, especially as she suspected that he would describe her to other people in the same terms. Nigel reminded her of Brian, trying to get as far as possible away from his background, his education, even himself, yet still attached to his family by ancient affection and guilt. Perhaps for him Hannah was a compromise; not as foreign as Barbie, not as dull as Dollis Hill. Perhaps also now Nigel had achieved so many of his ambitions – money, status in a fashionable branch of a dignified profession – he wanted someone who could appreciate all the nuances of the distance he had travelled.

"Olivia said you were working at a school. Is that right?"

"Yes, a small private school in Hampstead. I teach part-time."

"That's just a stop-gap, I suppose."

"I'm lucky to find that, with unemployment rising all the time. I'm totally unqualified, remember."

"But you were the top scholar of your year." Like most medical people, whose career structure is very much determined by their reputation as students, he had no understanding of the precarious and fleeting nature of artistic and literary careers.

"Believe me, Nigel, that's no use at all now."

"You'll think of something. You're very inventive." She would have been more reassured by this if his tone had been less professional. "I hope to see a lot more of you," he went on.

"How?" said Hannah. "You live in America and I live in England."

"I'll be back for Christmas. May I come and see you then?"

Hannah agreed and gave him her new address, neither believing nor disbelieving in his intentions. Christmas seemed so far away; after the move, after another term at school, possibly after the divorce.

When he took her home finally, after several more cups of coffee and further lavish compliments, he kept the taxi waiting while he said good night at the front door. Hannah went in to find the house apparently deserted. "Bibi? Where are you?" she called, and Bibi stepped out of the hall cupboard.

"Just being tactful," said Bibi. "In case you wanted to have passionate scenes on the drawing-room rug." She looked tearful, blotchy and drawn. "I can see you had a good time. Will we be seeing a lot of Nigel?"

"No, he's going back to America."

"Sure you don't mind me staying the night?"

"We've been through all that," said Hannah. "You've got four spare bedrooms to choose from."

"I rang Nicholas. He still won't talk to me."

"Give him time."

"But I don't understand."

5

It was the week before Christmas at 93 Crimea Road. Karen and a friend of hers were closeted in Karen's room, with an ugly sound of pop music coming from it. You couldn't distinguish the tune but the thump thump thump of the bass speaker reverberated through the house. Hannah was in the kitchen. It was a much smaller room than the previous Brian pine model, but pleasant, stretching the width of the house with wide windows overlooking the scrap of garden at the back. The curtains were open though it was four o'clock and nearly dark; the garden, piled high with snow, reflected the kitchen lights with an eerie glow. John was stumbling around in the mysterious heaps of snow building a drunken-looking snowman, from time to time waving to Hannah who was sitting at the table peeling potatoes.

Nicholas, armed with a cup of tea though he had evidently hoped for something stronger to top him up as the alcohol receded in his veins after the office Christmas lunch, sat at the table beside her. Hannah was making an effort to be kind to Nicholas. Since Bibi's cancer had been diagnosed he had been an ideal husband. Cancer of the womb, not a baby, the doctor had said, and after Bibi's first appalled and disbelieving reaction she had tacitly dropped the issue of Nicholas' reaction to her supposed pregnancy. It was as if the black eye episode had never happened. Nicholas was solicitous, attentive; so Hannah bit back any sharp remarks that sprung to her lips where he was concerned.

Just now, he was inspecting his teeth in a small mirror of Karen's he'd found. "I'm worried about my gums, you know," he said. "It could be only a matter of time before all my teeth fall out. Last week I was working on a toothpaste account. They'd done animations of germs attacking gums and uprooting teeth – I could feel my own clackers rippling in the breeze like a field of wheat."

"That sounds like copy for the ad."

"It is – not the clackers bit, of course, the wheat bit."

"When are you picking Bibi up from the hospital?"

"Not for another hour."

"Could you drop Mrs Harris off on your way?"

"Mrs Harris? The woman who used to live here? Is she still hanging about? Bibi said she was a terminal bore."

"She's lonely, and the house reminds her of old times," said Hannah. Mrs Harris was indeed a nuisance.

"Where is she, then?" said Nicholas.

"In the sitting-room, watching television."

"By herself? How does that help her not to be lonely?"

"She isn't by herself. David Bowen is working in there. Something to do with the fireplace."

"David Bowen the builder? Bibi's chap? Doing the work himself? That'll cost you."

"He's very efficient," said Hannah non-committally. David Bowen often dropped in to see her and made little adjustments or improvements to the house, putting up shelves, fixing curtain rails, re-hanging doors. After supervising the incompetent builders she had hired, he seemed to take an almost proprietorial interest in the house and in her life. He was easy to get on with: she found herself talking to him far more freely than she ever had to Brian. She never felt him to be critical of her, though they often disagreed.

"His wife ran off with an Australian, you know," said Nicholas. "Last year. Extraordinary thing. Wife just takes off with the children. Next thing he knows, a postcard from Perth. 'Having a lovely time. Glad you're not here.'"

"I didn't know it happened like that," said Hannah, reluctant to discuss David. He was a strong, independent person, much more considerate than Nicholas, whose personality seemed to Hannah as insecurely rooted as his teeth.

John tapped on the window. He was so bundled up against the cold that only his reddened nose and sparkly eyes could be seen in the swathes of scarf and balaclava. He was pointing at the completed snowman. Hannah duly applauded, as did Nicholas when his duty was made clear to him by a strategic kick on the ankle. The plaintive faces of Whisky and Soda were pressed against the window; evidently they had had enough fun in the snow. Hannah let dogs and child in and a gust of freezing air filled the kitchen with a reminder of the comfort of being indoors.

"Can I have tea? Are there any mince pies?"

"They're warming in the oven. Put away your coat and wellingtons and give the girls a shout."

"Karen won't want any pies. She's on a diet again."

"Let them know anyway."

"I don't want them sitting here. Karen's such a pain, and that friend of hers is no better. She's got a silly name."

"What is her name?" asked Nicholas.

"Charlotte St Leger. I ask you. She's a vile snob and all she ever talks about is money and boys."

Though Hannah thoroughly agreed with this sentiment, all she said was, "Hurry now. And don't be rude to Charlotte. She's a guest, remember."

"Worst luck," said John.

"I bet Karen's growing into a little knockout," said Nicholas. John made a face and disappeared into the hall.

"She's pretty enough," said Hannah, "but she's done terrible things to her hair. She's in love."

"Who with? Anyone I know?"

"Peregrine Sanderson. A youth of seventeen who keeps being nearly thrown out of Eton. He plays in a pop group and never washes his hands. His nails are absolutely ingrained with dirt."

"Sounds very like a first love," said Nicholas. "Mine was also called Peregrine. He acted in every school play and he wore green carnations, after Oscar Wilde."

"What happened to him?"

"Went into the Household Cavalry and married a general's daughter. Last heard of in the City. I saw him at a dinner the other night. He's gained chins and lost hair."

"Try telling Karen all that," said Hannah.

"What's this about me?" said Karen suspiciously, entering with Charlotte a shadow's shoulder behind her. They had apparently spent the day putting on lurid make-up and were identically dressed, in jeans tight on their little rumps, and fluffy angora sweaters. Karen was dark, Charlotte fair, their hair short and brushed up in spikes, their mouths pulled downwards at the corners in fashionable frowns. They looked like twenty year olds who had shrunk in the wash.

Hannah introduced Charlotte to Nicholas. She said "Hi!" without moving her lips, then perched herself on the best chair, the chair Hannah had been sitting in before she got up to make the tea.

"How's Bibi?" said Karen. She knew Bibi was ill, though not how ill, and she was sorry. Bibi was her godmother and had always been generous and attentive to her.

"The hospital's taking good care of her," said Hannah; Karen was intelligent enough to see that that was no answer, and sensitive enough to stop talking about it.

"Not mince pies," said Charlotte as Hannah took the racks of pies out of the oven. "How too sweet." She had a malevolent, patronising stare, and Hannah reminded herself that this creature was only thirteen and so probably had no idea how poisonous she was being.

"In what way, Charlotte?" she said. "How do you mean, sweet?"

"So traditional. My mother never makes mince pies, the cook does that. My mother's far too busy going to parties and shopping. My mother's beautiful."

"Is she?" said Hannah, much gentler now she could hear the child's distress. "Tell me about her. Is she fair, like you?"

"Would you like to see a photograph?" said Charlotte eagerly. "I've got one upstairs." She darted away and Nicholas raised his eyebrows at Hannah.

"Problems there?" he said with surprising sympathy. Hannah glanced at Karen; she was absorbed in a copy of *Vogue* that Bibi had left on the windowsill.

"I'm not sure," said Hannah. Even while doing sensible adult things like counting out the teacups and estimating how many mince pies her assorted guests could eat, she was sharply reminded, by Charlotte's prickly vulnerability, of the anguish of being a rejected child. She was reminded also of the vicious circle: because the child is unloved she is difficult to get on with, so she feels more unloved but hides it. I wonder if that's what I do, thought Hannah uneasily. Do I make it hard for people to love me? Could Brian have loved me if I'd let him, if

I'd shown him how important he was to me, instead of just refusing to clean the house?

Charlotte reappeared with photographs of her mother, who looked like a French film star, all blonde hair and spindly little legs.

"Isn't she smashing looking?" demanded Karen. "Did you know she used to be a model? And she's had parts in films?"

"She's lovely," said Hannah.

"We're spending Christmas at a hotel in Switzerland," said Charlotte.

"Wish we were going to a hotel. Daddy and Marjorie are going to be in a hotel, aren't they? In America somewhere?"

"San Francisco," said Hannah. She was peeved by Brian's tactless choice of America for a trip with Marjorie, since even her memory of the honeymoon would now be overlaid with the other woman.

"So where are you going for Christmas?" asked Nicholas.

That was a sore point. Hannah had agreed to go to her parents, taking the children. She didn't in the least want to and at first she had refused, but her mother had kept ringing up and John had liked the idea of being in the country for Christmas. She explained some of this to Nicholas, but Karen interrupted.

"Daddy was famous, wasn't he? A famous footballer? I've been telling Charlotte about it."

"He was very famous," said Nicholas, to help Hannah out.

"Then how come you've no money?" said Charlotte. "Karen says you've had to move into this house because you've got no money."

"I like the house," said Hannah.

"But look here, if your husband was a famous footballer, you just sell your story to the papers, it's easy, my mother always does it. 'Intimate secrets of the break-up.' It needn't be true, you can spice it up a bit, my mother always does, it sells better that way."

This solution had been suggested by Bibi, Nicholas (separately), the butcher, the incompetent builders' foreman, her bank manager, her solicitor, and Mrs Harris.

"I'm too shy to do something like that," said Hannah. "It's bad enough as it is, without telling the papers about it."

"I think it's a super-shitty idea," said John, "and just like a girl to suggest it."

"Ah, there you are," said Hannah. "Tell Mrs Harris and David that tea's ready if they'd like some, and wait to give her a hand if she can't get out of the chair alone."

Charlotte looked bewildered and hurt. Evidently her suggestion was meant as a goodwill offering. "*My mother always sells her story*," she muttered, and started biting at the skin down the sides of her nails.

It was after tea on Christmas Eve by the time Hannah parked the Renault near her parents' cottage. Traffic had been worse than she'd expected, she'd twice lost her way to the kennels, and the children had been slow over packing the car and had squabbled over who should bring what and who would sit in the front. Hannah's patience was shredded and she was badly missing Brian, who was useful on family occasions; he kept the children in order and enjoyed being sociable, even with Jane Crester-Fyfe who had always despised him and not bothered to hide it.

"Here at last!" said her mother in fluting reproach, ushering them in to the tiny drawing-room which at once seemed overcrowded. Since she had just arranged her things as she liked them in her own house, Hannah was unusually critical of her parents'. It seemed to her underlit, unwelcoming, stilted and uncomfortable. "We'd quite given you up!" Jane went on. "Wipe your feet carefully, children, Hannah, we don't want mud on the carpets, my goodness it's been a long time since I saw you all, you must tell me your news."

Immediately, none of her guests could think of anything to say.

"Well, Hannah, you've cut your hair, I see." Jane's own hair was in its usual rigid waves and she was tightly but suitably clad in a tweed skirt and a festive red twin-set. Hannah was in an inoffensive dark blue smock-like dress; though her mother scrutinised her closely she could think of nothing else to criticise so she turned to Karen.

"And what has Karen done to her hair?"

"Not a lot, Grandmother," said Karen cheerfully. She was quite undaunted by Jane. Hannah liked to imagine that this was because Karen was such a well-balanced, un-neurotic child, but she suspected that it was because she was as hard as nails.

"I'll start unloading the car," said John. This was exactly what Brian would have said at this point. With relief, Hannah let him get on with it, locked herself in the downstairs lavatory and read *Country Life*, ignoring her mother's perfectly audible cries: "Reginald! They're here, Reginald! Come and see them! Hannah, come and see your father."

The children went to bed at ten o'clock. Most of the evening to that point seemed to have been spent washing up; eating with the Crester-Fyfes was always more washing-up than food. When the children were in bed and the Scrabble game they had been playing cleared away, Reginald turned on the television, he claimed for the news; but it was clear from his grasp of the programmes that he was a television addict.

Jane Crester-Fyfe disapproved of Americans, Jews, Pakistanis, social workers, Arabs, news readers with common voices, the Irish, Europeans, Samaritans, blacks, trades unionists, homosexuals, single parent families, all politicians except Enoch Powell, actors, men who wore their hair too long, Japanese, and feminists. Since several of these people appeared on television, and Jane expressed her ideas forcibly, it made for lively viewing.

Jane's complaints dropped in volume a little when a nativity play came on. "At least it's suitable for Christmas Eve," she said, and watched the opening scenes quietly. Then came a protesting splutter. "The Virgin Mary! Look, Reginald! That girl is a *Jewess*!"

"Yes," said Reginald. "You're right, darling."

Hannah said nothing.

"It's disgraceful!" said Jane. "Look at her! Obviously Jewish!"

"Very suitable," said Hannah. "The whole family were Jewish. For more than sixty generations."

"Hannah!" said her mother crossly. "It's nothing to do with you. You're not even coming to midnight mass. Next thing, you'll be saying that Jesus was a Jew."

"Of course he was," said Hannah. She never knew, when her mother adopted ridiculous positions like this, if she was serious; and if serious, if she was sane.

"He was a Christian, Hannah," said Jane.

"But he was born a Jew."

"I'm not going to discuss it. And I don't think it appropriate for you to discuss it. A lapsed Catholic! A divorcee!"

"I'm not divorced yet," said Hannah mildly.

Her father stirred slightly. He was sunk in the depths of the most nearly comfortable chair. "Have they set a date for the hearing yet?"

"Towards the end of January."

"Do you want me to come up and keep you company?"

"I'll be all right," said Hannah. She didn't want to have to think about querulous Reginald as well as the pig-solicitor, Brian and her own feelings on her divorce-day, which was surely at least as momentous as a wedding-day.

Hannah tried to put Christmas morning off as long as possible. She pulled the sheets and blankets over her head and ignored repeated visits from Karen and John. The guest bed was too large without Brian. Her extended arms and legs touched cold sheets, and without conspiratorial company she felt mean when she deceived the children.

Eventually they tired of approaching her and settled to breakfast with Jane. Hannah could hear the muffled voices from the kitchen immediately below her. The much-laundered Liberty print curtains hardly kept out the snow light. Hannah wriggled round without letting any part of her body escape the covers; her breath was smoky on the air; the central heating hadn't been turned on yet. She peered out of the window. The whole well-kept home counties garden with croquet-lawn and flowerbeds was covered by yet another fresh coating of snow. Only a few bird-tracks marred the purity of its surface.

No dogs to enjoy it, thought Hannah. The spaniels hated kennels and would certainly be moping over their horse-meat. If they had been here they could have capered about and eaten turkey leftovers till their podgy bodies keeled over and they slept in front of the fire in canine ecstasy.

She began to dress under the bedclothes, thinking about

Bibi. She and Nicholas had gone to her mother who lived in a Georgian house in Rottingdean. They'd go to parties and drink gin and keep off the subject of illness, and children, and try not to look at Bibi too closely.

And she thought of Brian. Was it foggy in San Francisco? Would they drive along the coast, into the sun, and would Marjorie totter along the beach in her high heels?

At least the children seem to be enjoying it, thought Hannah as the household sat in reverent silence listening to the Queen's speech. They had pulled crackers at lunch and even Jane had worn a paper hat; it didn't suit her. Hannah looked longingly at the pile of books she had harvested for Christmas, knowing that it would be regarded as republicanism of the most blatant kind if she dared to read during the Queen's speech. Nevertheless, she picked up the top book – a social history of nineteenth-century England that Karen had bought in the Oxfam shop, guessing rightly that Hannah would find it interesting.

"Hannah!" said her mother warningly.

Hannah went on reading.

"I'll speak to you afterwards," Jane said.

When the speech was over Hannah left the room, but Jane followed her. "Where do you think you're going?"

"I don't want an argument," said Hannah, and closed the kitchen door behind them to shut out the silence that had fallen in the drawing-room. She imagined Reginald staring at his grandchildren as he had always stared at his daughter, unable to think of anything to say.

"It was gross disrespect to the Queen," said Jane.

"Let's not discuss it."

"I don't want to *discuss* it," said Jane. "I want to *show* you where your duty lies. It can't go on, Hannah. Divorcing, losing your faith, getting a job without telling me, and now this mad rejection of all that makes Christmas."

"What mad rejection?"

"Midnight mass. The Queen. You must go back to the old values, then your life will make sense again."

It was tempting to believe that Jane was speaking out of a genuine desire to help, but Hannah knew her too well.

"Do you want any help putting the good china away?" she said.

"Don't think that'll worm you back into my good graces."

"Be reasonable, Jane. I'm thirty-five years old and a guest in your house. If you can't be civil to me, I'm going home."

"If that's the way you feel, I won't stop you," said Jane, and a spring of pure joy welled up in Hannah's diaphragm immediately above the heavy accumulation of seasonal cheer.

"The man at the kennels wasn't pleased, was he, Mummy?" said John.

"I think he was drunk," said Karen. "Not surprising, on Christmas Day."

"The dogs were glad to see us," said Hannah. Whisky and Soda were wriggling all over John and the suitcases hastily crammed into the back seat. The car was crawling along; snow had started again and visibility was counted in yards, but the pleasure of not being at her parents' made up for the discomfort.

"Why did we leave so suddenly?" said Karen.

"I've told you. Grandmother and I had a disagreement."

"Do we have any food at home?" said John. "I liked Christmas lunch. Turkey and bread sauce and cranberry sauce and two kinds of stuffing and roast potatoes and boiled potatoes and sprouts and beans and gravy and the soup of course and Christmas pudding and brandy butter and mince pies..."

"Grandmother puts everything into separate dishes," said Karen. "Is that how you're supposed to do formal meals, Mummy?"

"Not as many separate dishes as Grandmother uses. Not unless you're giving a banquet."

"I even ate the green beans," said John, "and I don't like them usually."

"Was that manners?" asked Hannah, changing down into second gear.

"More like terror," said Karen. "John's scared of Grandmother."

"I'm *not*," said John. "I don't like it when she looks at me like a fish, that's all, as if there's nothing behind her eyes."

"I'm glad we're going home," said Karen. Hannah was pleased; perhaps Karen was settling in to the new house.

"Perry might call," went on Karen, in the elaborately casual voice she always used when she spoke of Peregrine. "I gave him Grandmother's number but I don't think he was listening. If he does ring he'll probably ring home."

Hannah peered through the windscreen; snow was piling up and the creaky wipers were only just clearing enough space to see. They seemed to be the only car on the motorway and Hannah was willing the car not to break down.

"He won't ring you anyway," said John. "He never does. You always ring him."

"Shut up," said Karen pinching his arm. He pulled away and buried himself in the corner of the back furthest away from her. "You don't know anything about it," she went on.

"I know who dials the phone and who answers," said John.

"You don't know that he doesn't ring me when you're not there."

"I know he's not interested in you. When he came round last week he spent the whole time talking to Mummy."

"But he came round, so there."

"Only to give you back the records you left by accident on purpose when you went round to see him."

"Lay off, John," said Hannah. "Try and read the motorway signs and tell me where we are."

"Terrific," said Karen sarcastically. "Outer Hebrides, here we come."

"Anyway I think he's a poof."

"What do you know about poofs?"

"More than you," said John. "They're always making passes at me."

"Look at the signs, John, and stop boasting," said Hannah.

"Boasting? Do you think I *want* poofs grabbing at me in the changing-rooms?"

"I have no idea," said Hannah.

"I thought you'd be shocked," said John indignantly.

"I'm shocked, I'm shocked. Now where the hell are we?"

"You forgot to turn the light off in the hall," said Karen scornfully.

"No I didn't," protested John. Hannah parked the car and let the spaniels out to run along the deserted street. "It might be burglars," said John self-importantly. "Give me the keys and I'll go in first."

Sure that it wasn't a burglar, she let him go, and started to take cases out of the car. Karen sat tight in the warmth.

"Give me a hand," said Hannah.

"In a minute."

"Now is when I need it."

By the time Karen came to help Hannah had finished. "Thank you," said Hannah ironically. "That was a real help."

"Don't sneer at me like that. I don't like it. No wonder Daddy left you."

Hannah was holding one of Karen's tote bags. "Carry your own stuff then," she said, and dropped the bag into a pile of muddy snow. Karen gasped with shock and affront.

"What did you do that for?" she demanded.

"Work it out," said Hannah.

"It's David," said John, "not a burglar. He's working in the kitchen."

Hannah called the dogs and hurried inside, ignoring Karen who was standing in offended silence. The house was warm and David, sitting at the kitchen table with screwdrivers and unidentifiable plastic components scattered round him, was a pleasant surprise for Hannah. He looked apologetic and put out; she realised how much she took his normal composure for granted.

He stood up and straightened the bits and pieces on the table. "I didn't expect you back till tomorrow. I thought an extractor fan in the kitchen would make your life a bit easier."

Hannah looked bewildered and he went on. "An extractor fan. To take the smell away when you're cooking, and keep the onions out of your eyes."

"I know what an extractor fan is," said Hannah. "But this is Christmas Day. You shouldn't be here."

David looked even more uncomfortable. "I'm sorry if it's inconvenient. I'll go now."

"I hope you'll do no such thing, unless you have to," said Hannah. "Please stay for supper. Only what I can find in the freezer, and I promise it won't be turkey." She was still ruffled from the fracas with her mother and from the brush with Karen, who was presumably sulking outside. David's company was very welcome, but threatening too. She didn't want to rely on anyone except herself and she was beginning to rely on him. His repeated kindnesses were not only touching in themselves, but they reminded her of all Brian had not done, had never bothered to do for her after their courtship. A woman was one thing, a wife another.

Of course the same might be true of David Bowen: eventually a conversion supervised plus a mantelpiece installed plus sixteen shelves plus four doors re-hung plus an extractor fan might equal a session or several with David on the double bed he had repaired. The thought was not repugnant. It was, however, embarrassing and she busied herself about the kitchen.

There was no need to enquire about David's Christmas. With him, social chit-chat was like pulling hippo teeth. He would tell her what he wanted her to know – otherwise she would have to ask a whole series of questions to which he would reply "yes" or "no" or sometimes just "um". This could have been annoying but she didn't find it so. She merely found it released her from the necessity of making conversation.

She was touched by David's thought for her – but how absurd to be touched by anything as unromantic as an extractor fan. She could imagine Brian's reaction. Just like a woman to go on and bloody on about a stupid little thing. But it was the accumulation and aggregate of little things, stupid or otherwise, that made a life; not just the meant, deliberate, star moments. But Brian believed in star moments. So did Karen. If Perry rings, life will be perfect.

Hannah remembered how, quite early in her marriage, their arguments had often centred round the same theme. "You just want to spend your life trotting out of the players' tunnel on to the pitch with the roar of a vast crowd battering your ears," she had complained.

"You've got no sense of magic," he shouted back. That was when she'd wanted to spend five hundred pounds paying gas and electricity bills and he wanted to go skiing in Gstaad. Certainly at this particular point in her life, Christmas Day of her thirty-sixth year, magic was elusive, whether in the form of trips to Gstaad or funds for utility bills. She would have to find work to do, work that paid real money to give her independence.

Enviously, she watched David's hands assembling the fan with precise and confident movements. It was too late now to take up a trade. But what marketable skill did she have?

Karen stuck her head round the door. "Oh, so he's here again," she said disagreeably. "Hasn't he a home to go to?"

"Yes, thank you," said David. "I happen to be helping *your* mother in *your* house. With things like book-shelves for *your* room."

Karen was taken aback by such a direct approach. Most of Hannah's friends would have politely ignored her. Brian would have shouted "Sod off, you cheeky little bleeder" and seldom had Hannah felt so spiritually in tune with him. But instead of shouting, she said coldly, "If you can't be civil, go to your room."

With a scornful "Oh, *really*!" Karen left, slamming the door, and Hannah sat down to recover from the wave of anger that consumed her. Karen could always provoke her to anger. Perhaps because she was the elder, perhaps because she was a girl, perhaps because she was Brian's favourite, the emotion between mother and daughter had always been awkward and intense. Hannah could hardly bear to be in the same room with the child without wanting to correct her in some way. She had read all the books on child care, she knew these feelings weren't appropriate or useful; while Brian was still with them he had eased the tension by his simple reactions. But now Hannah could forsee ceaseless struggle. After all, maybe she should leave Karen at boarding-school.

"Teenagers are often like that," said David. "I wouldn't worry too much."

"And the split-up hasn't been easy," said Hannah reaching for excuses.

"I think it's just her age, split-up or not," he said. "You can worry too much about children."

"You just said that," snapped Hannah, his equanimity irritating her.

"I said it twice because you didn't seem to have taken it in the first time."

Hannah's silence said "None of your business" and "Don't be so smug" and "Fat lot of good you've done with your own children – you don't even know where they are."

Then neither spoke. The central heating boiler whirred and coughed, a motor-cycle revved up in the street outside, and the dogs were sleeping audibly by Hannah's feet.

"Why did you leave your parents' early?" asked David.

"I couldn't stand my mother any longer. We had a quiet row. All rows with my mother are quiet. It would be fun to scream, now and again."

"Thirty-year-old women are often like that," said David, poker-faced. "It can be a difficult time. You'll grow out of it."

"I'm not thirty, I'm thirty-five."

"Even worse. That's a dangerous age. Young enough to be attractive and old enough to know what to do with it."

Hannah laughed. She was pleased by the compliment, but she found it wholly inappropriate. "I don't feel dangerous."

"But you are. Going round telling the truth to people."

"I haven't done that much lately. I've been concentrating more on telling the truth to myself."

"Much harder. Almost impossible."

"But you recommend it?" said Hannah.

"I don't know that I recommend it. I don't see what else you can do."

"You make everything seem simple."

"That's what my wife always said."

It annoyed Hannah when he said "my wife". It reminded her that she could no longer say "my husband". She was also irritated by the way in which he had refused to criticise his wife, even by implication, on the few occasions he had spoken of her. Hannah knew only that she was called Glynis, that she was in her twenties, lively, pretty (so he said – Hannah didn't think so from the photograph, she was all hair and teeth). She was also impulsive. She must have been, to leave for Australia taking her two children to live with a man she had known for only two weeks.

"Just because something is simple to understand doesn't mean it's easy to do," she pointed out.

"You can argue about theory till the cows come home. I bet you went to university."

"Oxford."

"That's a great place for theory. It didn't teach you much about building."

"And your building school didn't teach you much about English literature."

"Ah, but you can't live in books."

She was prepared to be annoyed once more, this time by his specious and facile arguments, but it was plain from his expression that he was teasing her and after a moment she decided to allow herself to be teased.

"That's good," said David. "You're smiling."

"Don't I usually?"

"Not much."

Hannah thought about it. She had always been a smiling person. Her mother had often complained "what are you smiling at?". So, come to think of it, had Brian. Finding life funny had often been one of the safest and most reliable refuges; if she was losing that, the prospect was dreary. "Keep reminding me to smile, then," she said.

"If I'm here, I will."

"Where might you be?" The thought of him going away caught her breath, as if she'd been hit in the throat. Over the past three months he'd been in the house at least four times a week. He knew all the practical things she didn't; he never seemed tense, he kept a steady perspective while her view of events juddered and lurched. Their relationship had never been closer than that of house owner and house repairer, and that too had been reassuring. She never needed to pretend with him. He had seen her at her worst and lowest point.

"I might be in Australia. A friend of mine thinks he's found Glynis."

Glynis, Glynis, nothing but Glynis.

"When he's sure, I'll probably go out there."

"To Australia? That's a long way."

"It's where my children are."

Devoted to her own children, Hannah should have understood and sympathised with his devotion, but she was still too insecure to be generous.

"How long would you stay?"

"It depends. If Glynis is settled there, I might just emigrate."

Hannah made a massive effort to show no emotion. "How old are your children?"

"Kate's nine. David's just turned seven. I last saw him when he was five. It's been nearly two years, Hannah."

Although his voice did not call for it, he deserved sympathy, Hannah knew. "I hope your friend has found them," she said, willing herself to mean it. "Is there any chance you and Glynis can get back together?"

"I don't think so. She made that clear in her letter when she left. I shouldn't have married her."

"Do you want to tell me why?"

"No need. It happened some time ago and no amount of talking will help." He was smiling at her as he spoke to show that his refusal was not a snub.

"Do you want some wine, then?"

"Please. Red if it's any good, otherwise white."

"You can have red; we're still finishing my presents from parents. I didn't know people gave presents to school-teachers, did you?"

"I don't think they do at comprehensives," he said with an exaggerated Welsh accent. "I wouldn't know about the other sort of school."

"But you know enough to like good red wine. You're a snob."

"Talking of which, a Nigel Barraclough rang. He wants you to ring him back."

"When did he call?"

"Just before you arrived."

"I'll ring him after supper," said Hannah gathering packets at random from the freezer, wishing she was organised enough to label food clearly and not have to rely on remembering every odd and dessicated left-over by the contours of the silver foil she used to wrap most scraps.

"And Bibi rang."

"Did she?" said Hannah, wishing her heart didn't sink when she thought of Bibi, and then wishing she didn't want so many things different in her life. What must it be like to be the kind of person who was more or less satisfied with themselves, with their job, their partner, their children? Were there such people?

"She sounded happy," said David.

"Have you seen her recently?"

"I did some work for her about a fortnight ago. She looked ill, if that's what you mean. Very thin."

"She always looks thin."

"And not only that. Her work is deteriorating. I suspected when I saw the latest effort in her flat."

"She's got the best doctors," said Hannah. "It doesn't seem possible that she should be ill – Bibi of all people. She always had so much life in her." The word "life" hung in the air and Hannah wished it unsaid. "People do recover now, don't they? In the last few years . . ." she couldn't go on.

"Don't worry about what can't be helped," said David gently. "Wait and see how it turns out."

Hannah shook her head, trying not to cry. She cried in front of David a good deal and she wanted to project a more independent, tough-cookie image, especially if he was going to Australia. She would have to be less soggy altogether.

"Did you ever use her birthday present?" he asked.

"I only remember one thing about my birthday," said Hannah. "It was the day I found out Brian had left."

David ignored this. "Bibi gave you a present. I know she did, we talked about it the week before and she asked my advice."

"But you didn't even know me then."

"She described you to me."

"Please don't tell me what she said," said Hannah, longing to know.

"Have you ever used your present? It was a subscription to a health club, and Bibi paid five hundred pounds for it."

"As much as that! And I don't even know what I've done with the membership card! How dreadful of me. Why did she spend so much? She usually gives me ordinary presents." Hannah's mind ran through the places the card might be. She'd certainly have to use the rest of the membership Bibi had paid for; presumably Bibi would have nudged her into it if it hadn't been for the debacle of Brian's departure. "As soon as the holiday is over, I'll go along," she said. "What a fool I'll look in leotard and tights." Five hundred pounds! By Hannah's standards, Bibi was very well off; she earned good money herself and her grandmother had left her three houses in Brixton which she had promptly done up and sold for ridiculous prices, just before the property boom collapsed. She had then invested the money cannily. Nicholas also earned money but only enough to keep himself in clothes, drink and trips abroad. So Bibi had cash to spare; but to spend so much on Hannah!

John joined them in the kitchen, a towel wrapped round his head turban-fashion. "What's for supper?"

"So far it looks like pork chop, breadcrumbs and pizza," said Hannah unwrapping the foil packets. "Chicken fricassee. Raspberries. Haricots verts."

"Sounds terrific," said John apparently without irony. "I've never had that. When do we eat? I'm starving."

"Did you wash your hair?"

"No. My turban is part of a game, and I'm not going to tell you about it, so don't ask."

"OK, I won't."

Karen came down to supper when it was ready and ate in sulky silence. From time to time she looked at David with hostility but he ignored her and talked to Hannah and John. Finally she broke in to a remark John was making. "I wish Daddy was here," she said loudly.

"Do you?" said Hannah.

"Then *he* wouldn't be," and she pointed her spoon at David.

David seemed unmoved by this so Hannah ignored it. "Daddy's coming back from America soon," she said, all her guilt revived as Karen had intended it should be.

"Then at least we can see him in Marjorie's flat which is a lot nicer than here," continued Karen.

"Shut up," said John.

"I'm going to ring Perry," said Karen, and left her raspberries and ice-cream half finished. John immediately appropriated it.

Hannah's first instinct was to worry about Karen, to go after her and try to talk her out of her temper, but David was watching her and she could see he thought she was fussing. And he was probably right. Let the girl have her outbursts of temper. She'd grow out of it.

"I'm going to watch television," John announced. "Anyone coming?"

"Perhaps," said Hannah. "When I've cleared away." She wanted to stay and talk to David but John had been alone too much recently.

Karen reappeared. "Perry says he'll take me to the club tonight."

"Which club?"

"Some club in Wardour Street. We've been before, last week when Charlotte was here."

"I remember. Perry's mother went with you. Is she going tonight?"

Karen blew her lips out in a derisive sound. "You must be joking! No one over twenty goes to the club. It's too noisy and crowded, and the music's too advanced."

"But I spoke to her on the telephone. She definitely said she was going with you."

"That was just to keep you quiet."

"It's too late tonight for you to go anywhere on your own."

"I won't be on my own. I'll be with Perry."

"No," said Hannah. "He's too old for you. I don't think it's a good idea for a thirteen-year-old to associate with older men." She was trying to keep her authority gentle, and she spoke lightly. Karen thought she was being laughed at and stamped her foot.

"You *can't* keep us apart like this! I *love* Perry!"

"Come on, Karen, if you throw yourself at his head any more he'll get concussion," said Hannah. It took Karen some seconds to work out what this meant.

"I'm going, whatever you say." Slam, bang, crash, and Karen had gone to her room.

"Are all girls that silly?" said John.

"Wait till you're in love," said David. "Everyone's that silly when they feel strongly about someone."

"Have you ever been like that?" asked John. "You're not at all . . ." His hand waved in the air seeking a conclusion to the sentence and the thought.

"I've been just like that," said David. "Worse, probably."

Karen was lying on her bed sobbing when Hannah came in. Clothes were scattered round the normally immaculate room. "Can't you decide what to wear?" Hannah picked up the nearest garment, a knitted skirt in pink and blue stripes. "What do most girls wear at this club?"

"Depends," said Karen knuckling away the tears and looking

like an eight-year-old. "Doesn't matter, does it, since I'm not going."

"That may not be true," said Hannah. "How important is it to you?"

"*Very very* important. The most important thing in my life so far. Perry asked just me, by myself. There's only me and him going. It's his mate's band – The Field Game, have you heard of them?" Hannah shook her head. "They're a head-banging Eton band. They're great. We won't be all that late, Mummy, really. The club closes at eleven-thirty."

Hannah had been imagining a night club, but now she saw she was on the wrong track. "Tell me about the club. What happens there?"

"It's just a big room. The band plays and we jump up and down, mostly, and shout. There isn't room to dance. We can buy drinks at the bar but you know I don't like the taste of alcohol." She clutched Hannah's hand. "Please let me go, please."

"You can go on one condition."

"What's that?"

"I pick you up from the club. At eleven."

So at eleven Hannah walked the dogs up and down Wardour Street while John went in search of Karen. He emerged from the dustbinned doorway muttering, "It's a nightmare in there. I can't possibly find her. I can't even get in."

Soho was extraordinary on Christmas Day; empty except for scavenging cats and patrolling policemen, the chill in the air not disguising the smell of rotting vegetables, and only the head-banging band's rhythm leaking through the bare concrete walls of the club breaking the eerie silence. At a loss, Hannah leant against the car, tired from the various experiences of the day, wishing she hadn't insisted on fetching Karen, wishing she'd accepted David's offer to come with her.

Still, she thought, bracing herself for a plunge into the world of youth, it'll be a step on the road to standing on my own feet.

"Yercantcumminere," said an emaciated pink-haired boy who was standing just inside the door, almost visibly leaning against the battering tidal wave of sound from the band and the shouts of the crammed audience. "Yercantcumminere" he repeated. "Yergorrabeamemer."

"I don't want to come in. I want to fetch my daughter."

He shrugged and indicated the audience, about four hundred of which were teenage girls. The dark ones all looked more or less like Karen. The band was at the other end of the room and the audience was facing them, standing in tightly packed rows like a bizarrely dressed congregation.

"When I went to concerts we had more room," said Hannah. The band changed tempo and the audience started jumping up and down, still in rows. The smell of bodies was overwhelming and she seemed to have brought the only fresh air in with her.

"Idunwannaereabahtit," said the youth.

"What don't you want to hear about?" Hannah scanned the room looking for Perry. He often wore leather flying caps or deer-stalkers.

"About the old days," said the doorkeeper with mocking, exaggerated diction. His naked arms were covered with rope-like veins which seemed to have an identity of their own.

"Do you know Peregrine Sanderson?"

" 'Course I do. Owns half the club, doesn't he?"

"Can you tell me where he is? Karen's with him and I want to take her home now."

"What's it worth to you?"

"I haven't any spare money and if I had I wouldn't waste it paying you to do something which I can do myself," said Hannah flatly. The veins flexed and writhed in his arms and his face went pinker than his hair. He reminded Hannah of her pig-solicitor. "If you listen to this row every night, won't you go deaf?" she asked.

"Can't hear you."

She pushed her way through the crush of bodies. The band had changed tempo again and the jumping had stopped to be succeeded by a unison moaning. As an entertainment, Hannah considered it about on a par with Christmas lunch with the Crester-Fyfes. She felt very old among all the utterly serious, smooth, painted faces. "Karen! Time to go!"

Karen argued, was shown Hannah's watch, argued about the watch, and followed Hannah to the exit. Perry hardly noticed her go. He was dressed in tight jeans (not a good idea with legs like hairpins) and a leather flying jacket, fur-lined, over a naked and sweating chest. He was moaning with the others, though not as enthusiastically as some.

Outside, even the rotting vegetables smelt sweet by contrast and Hannah took deep breaths while John complained. "Mummy, you were *ages*! What were you doing? Karen, why were you late? I've been waiting in the cold."

They all huddled into the car and set off home through the half-lighted streets. "I had a smashing time," said Karen. "Really smashing. Didn't you think the band were great?" She seemed almost relieved not to have been left with Perry. Hannah had to concentrate on driving. It was very cold and the freezing slush was treacherous. The car slid and gripped unpredictably. "Perry owns part of the club," Karen went on. "I met the whole band. It was the most amazing Christmas evening I've ever spent."

Next morning Hannah returned her telephone calls – Bibi first.

"Happy Christmas! Happy Christmas!" carolled Bibi. "It's bloody cold in Rottingdean. What's London like?"

"Cold, quiet, lovely."

"Your ma sounded furious when I rang, from which I gather all was not calm and bright at your family festivities."

"You are entirely right. How do you feel, Bibi?" she sounded brittle and forced and Hannah couldn't ignore it.

"Oh, Hannah, you've no idea," said Bibi. "I feel so sick all the time and my bones ache from the treatment, and my face is set into a smile trying not to show what's wrong with me. I don't want to burden my mother with it – she worries so much about us anyway. And poor Nicholas, any mention of pain or sickness frightens him to bits, and he's in a panic about his teeth falling out. You don't mind me saying this to you . . ."

Hannah shut her eyes. She didn't want to think about Bibi's suffering either, her whole body shrank away from imagining it. She was lying snugly cocooned in her post-Brian duvet in the depths of her marriage bed. Her children was safely asleep in other rooms, the dogs were curled up on the window seat watching the yellowish London snow drift on the windowsill, and if she didn't let her mind rove too freely she could imagine

131

she was not unhappy. Bibi was an intruder with her reminders of mortality.

Then she put herself in Bibi's place. What must it be like not only to be seriously ill with all the attendant discomfort, pain and fear, but also to find the illness separating you from the people you most wanted to be close to? It must be the loneliest condition of all.

All the useless rationalisations went through her mind again. There must be something we can do. Perhaps another method of treatment? There are amazing cures. She could comfort herself with these ideas and she still hadn't answered Bibi.

"Of course you mind," said Bibi. "Sorry."

"I mind about you being ill. Aren't the drugs helping?"

"A little. It's not just the pain. Do you think I'll ever get better, Hannah? Tell me the truth."

"I don't know anything about it. How can I answer that? What do the doctors say?"

"They say that you never know, with cancer. Which means I probably won't."

"I expect they mean they don't know."

"Not very cheerful, is it?" said Bibi. "If I am going to die of this, I wish it would hurry up and kill me." This was so much what Hannah was also hoping that she couldn't comment. Bibi went on: "Let's change the subject. Tell me something I don't know. Give me the benefit of your stock of useless information."

"The capital of Upper Volta is Ouagadougou."

"That's dull. An *interesting* useless fact."

"I fancy David Bowen."

"Remind me to talk to you about that some time," said Bibi, "but you've reminded me why I rang – to tell you Brian has been asking round trying to find evidence."

"Evidence of what?"

"Affairs, mostly."

"Surely he remembers who he screwed and when?"

"Not his affairs. Your affairs."

"I haven't had any," said Hannah blankly. Simon Gold didn't count – nobody could find out about that. "What does he want evidence for?"

"Aren't you arguing about the children's schools? Maybe he wants to prove you an unfit mother so he can get custody."

"Fat chance," said Hannah. She was angry and hurt, but also relieved; once she was fighting with Brian over specific issues it was easier to harden her feelings against him.

"I thought you ought to know," said Bibi in a passably good imitation of Caroline's "doing my duty" voice. "I'm only telling you for your own good."

"Have you seen him?"

"Nicholas had a drink with them last week."

Hannah bit her tongue trying not to ask questions. Bibi paused, expecting some.

"Thanks for telling me," said Hannah. "I'll pass it on to my solicitor. Then he can misunderstand, write his garbled version on a piece of paper, put it in my file and then lose the file."

"Is that what he does? Hannah, are you keeping an eye on him? Divorce can go dreadfully wrong. Remember that poor friend of Caroline's who left the Divorce Courts stuck with her husband for the next five years?"

"I'm being very careful. I've bought several do-it-yourself divorce books and I'm checking all he does."

After Bibi, she rang Nigel. He always answered the telephone soothingly, as if he expected the caller to be a patient on the verge of suicide. "Doctor Barraclough speaking. Who is that?"

"Doctor Hannah."

"Who?" Nigel was confused.

"Hannah, Nigel. You asked me to return your call."

"But you said 'Doctor'."

"I am a doctor – of philosophy. It's not only you gut-carvers who get doctorates."

There was a pause. Nigel was running the conversation through his head in an attempt to understand it. He had a superstitious reverence for Hannah's intelligence and was scrupulous not to miss an implication.

"Did you think it was pompous of me to announce myself as Doctor Barraclough?" he guessed finally.

Don't always try to get it right, thought Hannah impatiently. "How is your family?" she asked, remembering one of his parents had been ill, not interested.

"I'll tell you that when we meet. It's difficult to talk at the moment. Are you free for dinner in the next few days? I've been looking forward to seeing you ever since the summer." This warm sentiment evoked no response, and he ploughed on. "What about the day after tomorrow?"

"I'll have to arrange a baby-sitter," she said. Karen, scrambling into bed beside her, started to protest, "We don't need..." but Hannah muffled her with a pillow.

"The day after tomorrow, then," she agreed, and rang off.

"Who was that?" Karen asked, snuggling up to Hannah's shoulder. "You're lovely and warm." Hannah explained about Nigel. "Does he have lots of money? Does he want to marry you? Is he good-looking? Do you like him?"

"Yes. I don't think so. Probably. Quite."

"Perry kissed me yesterday," confided Karen. "I didn't think he would. When Charlotte was here she told me he told her he wanted to kiss me but I thought she might be making it up. But I knew he'd told Susannah..."

"Who's Susannah?"

"She's my new best friend. Charlotte, Susannah and Emma. Oh, and Sophie when she's in a good mood. Anyhow, at Tristram's party he told Susannah he really liked me."

"Oh good."

"I can't wait to tell Charlotte. I wish I knew her telephone number..."

6

For days before the court hearing of Dodgson v. Dodgson, Hannah thought about little else. What she would wear. What she would say to Brian. The points she had to make sure her solicitor understood. The practicalities swamped but did not submerge her emotional reactions. Once she dreamed that Brian came back to her and asked her to forget the divorce. In the dream she accepted him at once and felt entirely happy about it. The dream felt real, far more real than many conscious experiences, but when she woke up and asked herself if she wanted the dream to be true, she felt honestly uncertain. Life without Brian was often lonely but when things went wrong there was no one to blame but herself. She wasn't constantly having to make excuses to herself for what someone else had done; she didn't have to pretend. The only reason she could now imagine for whole-heartedly wanting Brian back was for the children's sake, and she knew that without the strain of Brian she was getting on better with them.

The court hearing was on a school day, so she went to see Miss Thirkettle the week before, explained the position and asked for permission to be absent. The headmistress grunted. She was looking even more eccentric than usual; her hair stuck out in tufts like the wig an amateur actor would choose for Mr Pickwick and one of her seamed stockings went round and round her leg, barber's-pole fashion. She was slumped behind her desk.

"Seen Mrs Fanshawe lately?" she demanded.

"Not for a week or two. Hardly, since the beginning of term. She's got flu, I heard."

"Avarice," said Miss Thirkettle. "A chronic condition. Sheer beastly greed." Usually her doom-laden pronouncements were delivered with relish, but today she sounded drained and spiritless. "In confidence. Can you respect a confidence? The school's running at a loss this term. That Iraqi girl left for Roedean, poor stupid Clarissa's father shot himself in the holidays as you know and they can't keep up the fees so we're carrying her as a passenger, and they had to do work in the holidays on the dining-room ceiling and there's no money left in the building fund."

I'll be out of a job again, thought Hannah. "So what is Mrs Fanshawe doing?"

"She owns shares in the school. Not a majority holding, thank the Lord, but enough to have a say. And the school site is valuable. If we sold it we should get at least a million. Amanda Fanshawe wants us to sell before the school overdraft gets too high and eats up her assets."

"Why isn't she coming to school?"

"She's looking for a buyer. You can't look for a buyer and teach sewing at the same time, so she tells me. I hate that girl," said Miss Thirkettle. "You'd never think she was Emily's niece. You know that Emily Mercer founded the school with me?"

Hannah could hardly not have known. The portrait of that bulky and dough-featured lady hung in a prominent place in the entrance hall, labelled OUR FOUNDRESS – Miss Mercer (MAOxon) 1910–1978.

"You've seen her portrait," Miss Thirkettle went on. "She had the kindest heart and the finest mind I've ever known. I was lucky to work with her. She had the vision that built this school; she was the driving force. I was always the practical one who plugged on behind taking care of the details." She stopped talking and looked at Hannah sharply. "I'm rambling. What was the point?"

"Mrs Fanshawe. You were saying you hated her."

"So I do. In confidence. You're a sensible woman, got your wits about you. Anything I say goes no further than this room. Hey?"

"Yes," said Hannah.

"I can't go on for ever. The school's finances are dicky enough anyway. If we had to pay a full headmistress's salary, we'd run at a loss. I only take pocket money. What's to be done?"

Hannah hesitated. She could think of few suggestions. "I assume you've thought of selling off the tennis courts for building?"

"No planning permission."

"Cutting overheads?"

"Cut to the bone already. You know what the pay is like."

"Making alterations so we can take more girls?"

"Too expensive."

"Then close the school," said Hannah. "It's demoralising to stagger towards failure."

"Remind me not to ask you for advice again," said Miss Thirkettle. "What about the staff? What about the girls?"

Overhead, the bell shrilled. It was the warning for afternoon lessons. "I should go," said Hannah. She could hear the high-pitched chatter of her English class. "I wish I could think of a solution to the problem," she said, feeling protective towards tousled and battered Miss Thirkettle.

The headmistress snorted. "Don't be stupid, girl," she snapped. "You have given me a solution. Probably the only solution. I don't like it, that's all, but I can't run an entire school as a charity concern. It's not financially possible. What'll you do if we close? Get another teaching job?"

"What'll you do?" countered Hannah.

"Ah. I'll be well off. Go to Greece. Buy a villa overlooking the sea. Read all the books I've missed." She pointed to the piles of unopened packages of books stacked against the wall under the big window. "All those. Think of the pleasure; books, the sea, the sun on your back."

Alarming shrieks were emanating from Hannah's class and she edged towards the door.

"Remember," Miss Thirkettle cautioned Hannah as she opened it. "In strictest confidence."

"What was in confidence?" Daphne, the school secretary, lurking outside the door, held on to Hannah's arm in an impromptu rugby tackle. "Was it anything I should know?"

"Nothing, really," said Hannah to one of the eyes. "Truly, nothing," she repeated for the benefit of the other eye, wishing she knew if one was glass or if the woman was afflicted with poor muscular co-ordination.

"If it's important, I should know," insisted Daphne, bringing Hannah to a stop with her superior weight. Her face loomed close to Hannah's; moist lips and minty breath, grim and self-interested determination in every lineament.

"I must teach," said Hannah.

It was wet. Not just drizzle but sheeting, bouncing-up-from-the-pavements-and-drenching-the-inside-of-your-skirts wet. Umbrellas-won't-stop-your-hair-falling-out-of-curl-and-into-a-tangled-mess-in-thirty-seconds wet. Hannah was hoping to appear smooth, unruffled, attractive, so that the court officials would be amazed that anyone would want to divorce her. She was six pounds lighter than she had been at Christmas; three sessions a week at the health club were beginning to pay off, though she was still by far the fattest person in her exercise class and she always stopped exhausted long before the others, waiting for minutes at a time until lithe Carly the dance supervisor stopped extolling the virtues of pain and capering about like a monkey in a wildlife documentary. But the pounds were dropping off, her muscles were stretching and her stomach was more flat than pot. It gave her confidence.

She dismounted from the taxi and darted across the shimmering pavement to Pendlebury's office, entirely dressed in new clothes – Bibi's Christmas present, impossible to refuse. "Mrs Dodgson," said Pendlebury when Hannah was announced by the world-weary receptionist. His enunciation was blurred by a doughnut. "You're looking exceptionally well." He sounded badly disappointed.

"What's wrong with that?"

"Doesn't help our case. You look well turned out and cheerful and, if you'll forgive me for saying so, attractive."

"This is so sudden," said Hannah. Pendlebury smiled through crumbs, placatingly.

"Never mind," he said finally, having sucked his teeth clear of goo. "It'll all be quite straightforward. Adultery, joint custody, your care and control."

"Has Brian agreed to the day schools?"

"There's a slight difficulty. He wants to keep them at their present schools. And he wants your son to go on to the public school you'd arranged for him."

"Then he still won't agree. What'll happen if the dispute comes before the court?"

"Hard to tell. The judge could decide the issue himself; he could appoint a welfare officer to establish the children's wishes. Mrs Dodgson, I must say this. Harrow has an excellent reputation."

Hannah would have been puzzled were it not for her extensive experience of Pendlebury's lack of grasp of the facts of her case. As it was, she merely prompted "Eton".

"That, of course, is also an excellent establishment, but hardly germane to our discussion."

"It's quite germane. It's the school John was supposed to go to."

"Ah," said Pendlebury, refreshing himself with a gulp of creamy coffee.

"What was your point?"

"The judge may feel that a well-established institution like Eton . . ."

"Or Harrow," suggested Hannah helpfully, to be rewarded by a glare.

". . . has manifest advantages. Your daughter's school, too, has . . ."

"Manifest advantages."

"Quite."

On the cluttered mantelpiece beside his desk was the announcement of a forthcoming performance of *HMS Pinafore* by the Caterham Young Conservatives. "Are you one of the main parts?" enquired Hannah, tapping the poster. He flinched as if she had made an improper gesture.

"Merely a humble member of the chorus."

"Tenor?"

He blushed unbecomingly. "How did you guess?" Hannah smiled encouragingly for as long as she could bear to, then brought him back to the subject at hand. "What you think is that the judge may well agree with Brian."

"Very possible. Especially if the other side makes play with the fact that you are a lonely woman who wants the children at home. Judges don't like possessive mothers."

"Ah," said Hannah. "So I'm to convince the court that the children should be at home with me without seeming to need them at home with me."

Pendlebury examined this statement from every angle before committing himself. "In a word – yes," he said finally.

The Gothic halls of the divorce courts were in deep shadow. Hannah walked just behind strutting Pendlebury: he led her down two corridors to the wrong court and they had to retrace their steps, the marble floors echoing and hard. Clunk, clunk, clunk, went Pendlebury's scuffed and muddy shoes. Tap tippity tap went Hannah's heels. The rain beat against the skylights of the odd, rambling, Victorian building.

In a way, Hannah had looked forward to this. The one place she should be at home would be the divorce courts; there she would be what the courts were designed to deal with. She half expected some of the cosy camaraderie of the ante-natal clinic where she could swap experiences with other nearly divorcees. But the assorted human beings waiting outside court 57 (imagine, thought Hannah, all the divorces in progress even now in courts 1 to 56) were not interested in sharing experiences with her. They were huddled together in family groups, mostly consisting of several generations of women right down to the toddlers, their mouths and feelings plugged with sweets. From the groups of solicitors, barristers and clerks came occasional laughter and purposeful talk. Clearly these courts were not run for the benefit of divorcing people, but for the lawyers. At any rate the lawyers were the only ones enjoying themselves. All the litigants and friends seemed to have a grievance. We would not be here at all, their tone and bearing conveyed, if the world had gone right with us, if we had what we deserved.

Hannah's euphoric sense of confidence and ease subsided. She read the catalogue of typed names on the door of the court. Dodgson v. Dodgson was in the middle of the list. "Won't be heard for at least an hour," said Pendlebury bustling back from a conference with the clerk. "Would you like to go and have a cup of coffee?"

"I'd rather wait. I brought a book," said Hannah brandishing a paperback, eager to avoid an hour's conversation with him.

"What are you reading?" he asked, with a "putting my client

at her ease" expression on his face. Showing off for the other lawyers, thought Hannah. *"Anna Karenina,"* she said.

"Very appropriate, if I may say so. Think how different her story would have been under a more civilised system of divorce law."

Hannah smiled and agreed, but her heart wasn't in it. For once not even literary discussion tempted her. It had been a bad mistake not to bring someone with her for moral support. David Bowen had offered; Bibi had offered; Nicholas had been offered by Bibi. And Reginald Crester-Fyfe had rung up the previous day and meandered on about a girl needing her father at a time like this. But she had thought it important to be independent, look after herself. It had been her decision to marry Brian, to have the children. Now she should take care of the consequences.

She sat down on a wooden bench and stared unseeingly at Tolstoy's prose. "It's Hannah, isn't it?" said a man's voice. He was shabby, mid-thirties, with not enough charm to carry off his intimate manner.

"Do I know you?" said Hannah. The type was familiar; he was some kind of journalist, probably a free-lance. She looked for Pendlebury.

"Who are you looking for? Brian's not here yet."

Pendlebury wasn't there. Probably gone for his precious coffee and doughnut. Hannah walked away from the journalist and read the list of cases again. "Just a few words, Hannah," he coaxed, following her. "Tell me what you feel about Brian's new woman."

"No comment," said Hannah. This was the first journalist to approach her for years. Ironic that Brian's fading celebrity should even plague her here. She sat down again, opened her book, made no replies to the shabby man's questions. She breathed the air reluctantly; it was stale, damp, tobacco-laden. All round her human beings in wet clothes were steaming. She was afraid of smelling them if she opened her nostrils too wide. And the journalist; his breath smelt, his clothes smelt, and his puffy pasty face was thrust inches from hers. Pendlebury was still nowhere to be seen. Yes he was. He stood with a tall dark man in a pin-striped suit. Hannah caught his eye and he came towards her.

"Please go away," she said to the journalist. "I want to talk to my solicitor." And suddenly, surprisingly, he did.

"Just having a word with the other side," said Pendlebury. "Good firm, Truscott & Truscott." He patted her shoulder encouragingly. "Won't be long now."

It was then that Hannah realised. Brian wasn't coming. There was no necessity for him to appear, she knew that from her do-it-yourself divorce books. She was the petitioner and the divorce was undefended. If she had thought about it she would have known. Of course he wouldn't come. He didn't want to see her normally; he wouldn't want to confront her here. The meeting she had wasted so much time imagining would not take place.

Panic. Any moment now her case might start. Brian wasn't there to convince about the children's schools. The judge might take Brian's side. Doughnut-brain Pendlebury was grinning foolishly at her. "I want to meet Brian's solicitor," she said.

"Time enough for that afterwards," smirked Pendlebury.

"Now!" snapped Hannah. She would not ally herself with the whining, passive victims all round her. This place with its prosperous male lawyers and derelict female clients, its miasma of damp and delay rising presumably from the actual marshes it was built on if not from the emotional morass it was designed to define but not resolve – she would not accept its values and its restrictions. "I want to speak to him now," she repeated, and when Pendlebury still hesitated she walked over to the tall man. Close to, he was attractive. He had a lean lined face and intelligent eyes. Forty-five? Fifty? "Mr Truscott?"

"I'm the young Mr Truscott," he agreed. "The other two are retired."

"I'm Hannah. How do you do? Listen carefully, please. Can you talk to Brian on the telephone?"

His face closed into a professional lawyer's expression. "Why do you ask?"

"You'll need his agreement, I expect."

"What will I need his agreement for?"

"To withdraw his proposals for the children's education. If he doesn't, I'm not going to ask for a divorce."

He surveyed her calmly. "Don't get upset, Mrs – "

"I'm not upset," said Hannah, "and please talk to Brian quickly, otherwise they'll call us into court and I'll withdraw, and your client won't get his divorce for five years. *I'm* the one doing *him* the favour, and I want the arrangements for the children to reflect that."

Where books were concerned Hannah was at home. She comforted herself with this, watching him walk – scurry, rather – to a telephone. She had read the divorce books again and again, and the facts were clear. But she hadn't wanted to blackmail, she'd wanted Brian to agree of his own free will. Perhaps she still wanted too many people to agree. She should take her own way. All that intellectual training wasted, dragging on men's arms, wanting their agreement, when all she had to do was establish the facts, interpret the situation, decide and carry out her decision. But she was inhibited by wanting to please lawyers with attractive faces.

The judge presented no such difficulty. The courtroom was like a coffin – airless, wood-panelled, largely silent – and he was its rightful occupant. He was old, thin, bent, and he spoke on spurts of breath as feeble as sighs. He seemed to have outworn all emotion but malice. Hannah stood in the witness-box and waited for him to speak again. He shuffled through the documents on the bench in front of him, the skin on his hands papery against Hannah's carefully prepared account of her marriage, translated by Pendlebury into legal grounds for a divorce.

"So your husband er . . . your husband Brian . . . committed adultery."

"Yes, m'lud," said Hannah. Everyone in the courtroom, except herself, was male. Even the pigeons tapping on the window were probably male, and legally qualified.

"I'm not clear as to the arrangements for the children." Somehow this statement, on the face of it an acknowledgment of his own failure to understand, was a threat. Both solicitors stirred on their coffin-benches.

"The children are to live with me and attend day schools," said Hannah. The judge darted her a piercing, venomous look.

"So you proposed. But your husband had other plans, did he not? Which he has withdrawn."

"Yes," said Hannah. She knew he was prowling round, looking for an opportunity to pounce. All she had to do was keep quiet and wait him out. Her impulse was to chatter, explain, excuse, ingratiate. She bit her tongue to keep it still.

"Now let me understand your situation," he said. "You work, do you not?"

"Yes," said Hannah.

"As a ... as a ... teacher."

"Yes."

"Do you think your work will make it difficult for you to make a home for your children?"

"No, m'lud."

"What was that? I didn't hear you," he said querulously. "You'll have to speak up. I know this is an emotional time for you but this is a court of law."

"I said 'No, m'lud', m'lud."

"Ahhh," he sighed. "You do not think it will affect your home-making endeavours at all? In any way?"

Crafty old reptile, thought Hannah, briefly amused despite her tension. Then she looked at Pendlebury's anxious face and Truscott's alert one and saw that they shared her perception that the judge was threatening her plans for the children. Intellectually she could see that the law had to establish the best possible arrangement for the children of divorced parents. She could also see that many children would be better off at boarding-schools, and that a parent under stress might not be the best person to decide. These would all serve as justifications for this man's whim. He wasn't trying to understand the marriage, Hannah, Brian or the children. He was trying to score points in an intellectual game. He was challenging Hannah. I am much cleverer than you, his eyes said. A pity to waste your old age with such concerns, thought Hannah in riposte, but she kept her expression bland. "I beg your pardon, m'lud," said Hannah borrowing his tactic. "I didn't hear the question."

He repeated it.

"Yes," said Hannah, "if I work, that must affect the amount of time I have to spend on home-making. It need not damage the quality of care and attention given to the children."

"Ah," said the judge. "In your opinion."
"Yes, m'lud."

"You handled him very well," said Truscott. They were walking through the echoing corridors towards the outside world. Pendlebury, who had started to walk with them, had paused to greet an acquaintance. "He's an awkward old chap, but he doesn't mean any harm. Judges often get like that."

"I think he did mean harm," said Hannah. "I think he meant to change the arrangements for the children just to show how clever he is."

"Ah well," said Truscott with the easy tolerance of non-involvement. "You got what you wanted."

"Only just."

"Is Pendlebury taking you to lunch?"

"No," said Hannah, reluctant even to imagine the tedium of such an event. "Why do you ask?"

"Solicitors often do."

"Ah."

"And it would give me great pleasure if you would lunch with me."

"I doubt it," said Hannah.

"Doubt what?"

"That it would give you great pleasure. It's hardly the moment to make polite conversation, do you think? Unless you're offering yourself as a temporary consolation prize. I've just lost a husband so I can borrow a solicitor."

Truscott laughed, a deliberate sound which made Hannah think some woman must have told him that he had an attractive laugh. She was a little flattered by the invitation, but not so flattered that she could spin the feeling out for an entire lunch, neither did she want to be entertaining for him.

"I'm sorry we can't lunch. Perhaps another time?" he said tenaciously.

Hannah murmured without agreeing. They were at the heavy wooden doors, and she paused. Beyond the doors was rain, she could hear it, and London traffic. She was going home to an empty house, or possibly to Bibi, if she was finished with her hospital session. The thought was appealing. She wanted to draw peace round her like crepe bandage round a dodgy knee.

She pushed the door open, forestalling courteous Truscott, and saw the shabby journalist. He was standing with an even shabbier man whose nicotined fingers grasped an expensive camera. Click click, went the shutter, click click click. Hannah ignored it. No point in protesting; she composed her face not to look gleeful, not to look upset. Odd to have photographs from the divorce and none from the wedding – nobody had remembered, in the scramble and squabble preceding the wedding, to arrange it.

"I'll get you a taxi," said Truscott.

"No. I'll take a bus." Hannah wanted to save money. Now the financial details were settled she knew exactly how poor she was. And the school might close. Her stomach twisted and gurgled with hunger and anxiety.

She rode the two buses home oblivious to things around her. In just over six weeks the divorce would be final, then Brian could remarry. Mrs Brian Dodgson would no longer be Hannah, it would be Marjorie. How many months, years before Hannah could hear Mrs Dodgson without turning her head to answer, and why were the details more painful than the fact? Random memories of Brian, some good, some bad, rattled round her head like a gerbil's wheel.

"Terrible rain, I said terrible rain. The rain's terrible." First Hannah smelt the man who had just sat beside her. His appearance matched his smell and exceeded it. Blackened teeth hung at random in his open mouth; he was over seventy and each year had been misspent, or so his lined, stained and puffy face suggested. He was a bore. He fixed Hannah with a determined stare and talked. About the weather, about London Transport, about young people today. He was opposed to all of them. Hannah found his sourness obscurely invigorating. She felt no obligation to listen or to agree. Instead, she felt the impersonality of the city. This man could be smelly and boring, Hannah could be divorced, London didn't care.

The house was warm when she opened the front door. From the kitchen, Radio Two chatted confidentially. Bibi had taken to listening to it day and night. She greeted Hannah with a hug;

Hannah forced herself not to pull away at the first touch of bone under cloth. "I've made lunch," said Bibi proudly. "Salad all ready, omelette coming up. Do you want mushrooms?" She was amazingly perky. Usually after her treatment she was too ill to do anything except lie down and occasionally vomit. "I wouldn't let them do anything to me today," she explained. "I couldn't bear it. I wanted to hear your news." She was dressed in layers of Italian clothes, new, in shades of black and tan. She was elated. Hannah sat down and accepted a glass of wine and Bibi's friendly bossing. "So how was it? Tell!"

"I got the divorce. Brian didn't come."

"Didn't *come*?" Bibi wheeled round from her position at the cooker. "What a cowardly snake! Perhaps he thought you'd dismantle him like the car. But after all your plans... I've two messages for you. Nigel Barraclough telephoned."

"From America?"

"From London. He's staying on for the weekend. I got the impression he'd come over just to be with you." Bibi was watching her expectantly, fish-slice poised in mid-thrust.

"I wish Nigel hadn't come," said Hannah. "He's very hard work."

"He's very well off."

"Tell me the other message."

"David Bowen left you that." She nodded in the direction of a big, squashy, brown-paper parcel. "And he said he'd come and see you about eight tonight. To talk about the loft insulation, he *said*."

Even though Bibi was watching her closely and Hannah didn't want to betray herself, she couldn't resist a delighted smile. "Just as I suspected," said Bibi. "You're in love with David."

That accusation Hannah could whole-heartedly refute. She knew what being in love was; she'd been in love with Brian. Her feeling for David was very different, much more like a seasoned friendship spiced with desire – on her side at least. What David felt, who knew? She unwrapped the parcel; it contained a plastic padded object, some kind of cushion. Bibi immediately identified it. "To use in the bath, of course. When you spend all those hours reading. Keeps your neck comfortable."

David often commented on the length of time Hannah spent in the bath. She found it a refuge and a pleasure; warm water swilling round her, a good book, obligations shed with her clothes. And now a padded cushion to lean against, albeit a padded cushion covered with a repulsive flower pattern.

"I like the design," said Bibi.

"You can't. It's disgusting."

"You've got no taste."

"I've got my own taste."

"David must care for you. I had a snoop round the house and I recognised his handiwork everywhere. What's he charging?"

Hannah didn't answer. She remembered that David hadn't wanted her to tell Bibi he was working free, but couldn't remember why, or if the reason still applied. Bibi so ill seemed set apart from previous arrangements and understandings; no longer effective enough to keep things from. "He's not charging at all," she said.

Bibi grimaced. It was meant to be amusing and lively but it crumpled into pathos. "You're a lucky girl, Hannah. Easy to love."

"So are you. Bibi, what's this nonsense? Nicholas loves you, I love you, you've an indecent amount of friends who love you."

Bibi slid the omelettes on to heated plates. "Not at the moment. Nicholas is obsessed with his teeth. I didn't know you could have so many aids to oral hygiene. Floss and sticks and little tooth-brushes and larger tooth-brushes and plaque disclosing tablets – oh, I know he's partly using it as something to worry about that isn't me, but I feel left out. He spends hours in the bathroom staring into his mouth. He's even got a set of those dentist's mirrors and he's all deft and professional with them. Looks at every angle of every tooth."

"He's concerned about you," said Hannah.

"And most of my friends don't like talking to me any more. They're often out when I know they're in, and they don't ring back."

"Illness frightens people."

"Cancer frightens people. But I don't feel loved. Do you remember the hippies?"

"Of course."

"Peace, man. Love. Remember the summer of '67?"

"Not well."

"You were twenty-one. Just before you met Brian. I was with Oscar Mandel."

Hannah remembered Oscar vaguely. Short, Jewish, sexually athletic, a non-stop talker who now poured his flood of words over various television game shows. He was particularly good at insulting inoffensive members of the public.

"Then we broke up because he said hippies were self-indulgent, unrealistic, immature. I liked the idea. I wore beads and gave flowers to policemen, and went barefoot till I stepped in dogshit for the third time."

"That reminds me. I must take Whisky and Soda for a walk."

"It was my last year at art school. Then I grew out of it, gave the beads and sandals to Oxfam – talk about coals to Newcastle – and set out to be a dynamic young designer, hip to tech, no fool."

"You were never a fool."

"But now I think I was right first time. There were virtues in the hippies. I find the idea of peace and love and flowers appealing. Do you think cancer has mellowed me?"

"Softened your brain, more like," said Hannah bracingly. "I don't notice the Sixties' look in your clothes."

"I've been thinking about it. Now it doesn't matter what people say about my taste, I could wear absolutely anything I like. I've closed down the business, you know."

"Why?" Hannah was shocked. She'd been relying on work to keep Bibi occupied.

"All sorts of reasons. I feel too ill to concentrate, and the last job I went for, they turned down my designs."

"That happens all the time."

"No it doesn't. Other designs sometimes appeal to clients more, or they want a different feel to a place and I do more sketches for them. These were turned down because they weren't any good, and they weren't any good because I was jealous."

"What were you jealous of?"

"The clients. I didn't want to think of anyone living in the house after I was dead, with my decorations round them.

So I had to close down. You can hardly be a sizzling ambience specialist if you begrudge your clients' every breath."

Despite the gloomy tenor of Bibi's conversation, she sounded a great deal more like her old self. It was as if she had reached a decision. "I'm not going to have any more treatment," she said, reading Hannah's mind.

"No more radiotherapy? Is that what they said?" Good or bad, thought Hannah running through all she had read about cancer, a disorganised jumble of upbeat articles in the *Reader's Digest* full of breakthroughs and positive thinking, and *Guardian* women's page features about courageous women who refused to let male chauvinist surgeons cut off their breasts.

"No more radiotherapy. No more chemotherapy. Just pain-killing drugs."

"That's good."

"It's what I want. They went berserk when I told them. I read my notes, you see."

Hannah was beginning to see the outlines of a tragedy emerge from Bibi's vivacious account. "Tell me what happened, Bibi. Slowly."

"I read my notes when the doctor left me alone in his office. The cancer's everywhere. Bones, liver – the results of the scans were all there. It's well beyond operating."

"You don't know that the radiotherapy won't help."

"Not when it's that far gone. I've lots of chums from the waiting-room of the oncology clinic. Isn't that a horrid word, oncology?"

"Only because you know what it means." Hannah was humbled. Her own day, divorce and all, seemed enviable by comparison with Bibi's.

"You learn a lot in the waiting-room. Some people have been going to the clinic for years, and they know more about it than the young doctors." She paused. "Is it a good omelette?"

Hannah had no idea, and said so. "It's food. Do you expect me to taste anything when we're talking about this?"

"So don't eat it," snapped Bibi. "You'll get fat."

"Tell me what the doctors said."

"They said what they have to say. 'Consider your husband...

don't give up now . . .'. Platitudes, rubbish. They don't have to go through the sickness. I feel like death and have to go on living."

"Should I encourage you to go on with the treatment? Are you being sensible, Bibi?" Hannah's large clear eyes were fixed on Bibi's face, her whole being focused on her friend.

Bibi stared back, entirely decided. "I've made up my mind," she said.

"OK," said Hannah, returning to the food. "Are you going to tell Nicholas?"

"I'll have to. The doctors will probably call him in and talk to him, anyway. They think he's the sensible one, just because he's male and wears a pin-striped suit and doesn't cry all the time. If they tried living with him and his teeth, they'd soon know different."

"He'll be upset."

"At first. He'll give me my own way in the end and convince himself he thought of it."

They ate in silence for a while, then Hannah began to describe her divorce. As she talked every detail came back and she could visualise Truscott's lean face and Pendlebury's sweaty red neck bulging over his collar, the judge's dispassionate look and the journalist's avid stare. "People look at you a lot when you get divorced," she observed. "In case you make a scene."

"They don't look at your face at all in an oncology clinic," said Bibi, "probably for the same reason."

"It was an odd morning," said Hannah. In retrospect her experience made even less sense. "Private feelings on public show, rather like walking down Bond Street naked. And then there was a drunken bore next to me on the bus. He complained about modern life. I think he was National Front. He seemed to ascribe most of Britain's problems to blacks and Pakistanis."

"What did you do?"

"I gave him my copy of *Anna Karenina*."

Bibi put down the fork she had been prodding her omelette with. "Why?"

"To surprise him. To exasperate and disconcert him. As an anarchic gesture."

Bibi considered this. "Did it have to be *Anna Karenina*? Would any other book have done as well?"

"Only if it was foreign. 'Bloody foreigners,' he said, 'think they can come over here and write books. Take jobs from our boys.'"

"Is that what he said?" Bibi was captivated by the idea, diverted from gloomier thoughts. "All those unemployed Tolstoys cluttering up the Labour Exchange."

"Job Centre."

"He should get his mates together and picket the Festival Hall when they play Beethoven."

"Or the National Gallery. All the Impressionists taking up British wall space," said Hannah, rousing herself to unaccustomed enthusiasm, hoping to keep Bibi's interest alive; but Bibi saw through the attempt and resented it. "So I'm safely divorced," said Hannah, offering another distraction, "unless something goes wrong in the next six weeks. That's when I apply for a decree absolute. Brian wants it concluded as soon as possible."

"So he can marry Marjorie?"

"Probably. It wouldn't suit him at all if he was left womanless, homeless and jobless. She's employing him in one of her businesses, you know."

"So Nicholas tells me."

"It won't be fun living dependent on her whim. What if she goes off him?"

"He's a lot younger than she is and a lot more attractive."

"But in the weaker position. He's got a duff knee, remember."

"It's hardly his knee she's interested in. What *are* you talking about?"

"I mean now he can't play football he's not equipped for anything," said Hannah crossly, made foolish by her irritation. Bibi hooted with derisive laughter.

"Marjorie's not complaining."

"As far as we know," said Hannah, briefly luxuriating in the prospect of a discarded Brian begging in vain to be taken back chez Hannah.

"Brian's got a strong sense of self-preservation. He'll keep his knees well in under the table, duff or not."

"What table?" said Hannah, deliberately obtuse, determined to pick a squabble.

When a man comes all the way from America for three days just to see you, it is hard to escape dinner with him. But nothing would have persuaded Hannah to dine with Nigel the night of her divorce hearing. She had too much to think about; questions to settle, decisions to make; when to tell the children about their change of school, how to present the divorce to them. And there was the problem of work. What was she to do about a job? If the school closed down she'd have to move quickly, but even if it didn't the world was much too harsh a place to confront on one's own with the kind of income the school provided.

Moreover, she was not going to regard marriage as the answer ever again. Dependence was a weakness of hers, she would be tempted to sink herself into a man's life without the capacity for unselfishness, unreflectiveness or a combination of both which would enable her to be an old-fashioned wife.

She also had the children. No matter that the marriage had ended, Brian was still their father and they could hardly be taken round like dogs in search of a good home and thrust into a family where some man who knew nothing about them would try to consider them as his. If she did find a man she wanted, much better to negotiate from a position of solvency and independence. But how to get there?

She lay in the bath. It was six o'clock, the portable radio close to her ear pumped out Beethoven, pine foam clung to her exposed shoulders and bubbled between her toes. More hot water trickled in to combat the heat loss in steam and the draught from the ill-fitting window. That was the next thing David planned to do, tighten the old sash window in its frame and replace some of the rotten wood. Already the bathroom was a display-case of David's improvements: a towel-rail, several stubby pegs on the back of the door to hang dressing-gowns on, a mirror over the basin (say looking-glass, her mother's voice admonished her, only common people say mirror). Mirror mirror mirror, thought Hannah, and swished water over her shoulders. David had also, common person though he was, sealed the edge of the bath with expanding plastic, cut and laid the scraps of carpet Brian hadn't wanted from their bedroom in the old house, and replaced a washer in the hot tap so that it didn't dribble valuable fuel away.

Beethoven's sonorous dignity made Hannah feel girlish. A rare surge of happiness gripped her. Nothing was perfect, but everything was possible. The children would be better off with a mother who lived in the real world, not the reading and eating zombie Hannah had so recently been. Rich Brian would be less querulous, if no more adult. Tomorrow's tiresome dinner with Nigel wouldn't last long; Hannah could make clear to him what was increasingly clear to her, that she couldn't seriously contemplate putting up with him for more than a few hours at a time. He was too intense about the wrong things, and she couldn't live up to his fantasies about her.

Once Nigel was out of the way . . . David had given her a plastic cushion for the bath. She wriggled her shoulders against it, and looked at her body, its shape gradually re-emerging under the layers of fat. Bibi's birthday present had been a success, would be more of one if Hannah kept going to the exercise classes; in her present mood she felt able to attend one a day and two on Saturdays. Her only problem was making money. That was a practical problem which would respond to thought and hard work. Self-help Hannah squared her shoulders and felt decisive.

The telephone rang and rang. The caller wouldn't give up. Perhaps it was about one of the children; Hannah heaved herself dripping out of the bath, grabbed three towels and padded downstairs barefoot. As she went through the tiny hall cold air chilled her. A premonition, she thought, moving from foot to foot as she heard her mother's voice.

"Hannah, is that you?"

"Yes. I've just got out of the bath, let me ring you back."

"A bath? Are you going out this evening?"

"No."

"Are you ill?"

"No."

"Then this is a *very odd* time to have a bath," said Jane Crester-Fyfe.

"Why are you ringing? I'm cold," said Hannah.

Her mother took a battle breath. Hannah could imagine her quivering nostrils and the tight whiteness round her mouth.

"Hannah, this just can't go on. Your divorce hearing was today and you didn't even tell us."

"Didn't even tell you what?"

"Your father offered to be with you." Her voice was eloquent with injury. "Why do you treat us like this? Why did you behave so badly at Christmas? We're not just nobody, do you realise that? Your father was highly thought of in the Foreign Office, and he's a very good-looking man."

This hardly called for a polite reply. Hannah rewrapped the towels and patted at her damp bits. One of the dogs licked her toes and the other snored on a sag-bag. "Aren't you going to ask me how the divorce went?" She didn't hope for sympathy or tenderness from her mother, but she was struck by the absence of common courtesy. Since Hannah's decision to stand up for herself, the relationship had settled down to hectoring on her mother's part and retreat on Hannah's.

"I'm not going to ask," said her mother haughtily. "If you wanted us to know, presumably you would have telephoned."

"It's over," said Hannah. "No hitches." She didn't want her father worrying.

"I won't ask for any details," said her mother avidly, and waited.

"How is Grandmother?" said Hannah. When last heard of, two months ago, the old woman was on the point of death.

"No change."

Two generations of unloving daughters, thought Hannah, and Karen may well make it three. Especially when I tell her she has to leave Charlotte St Leger. As a small conciliatory gesture, she offered information. "Did you know that Bibi is ill?"

"Beatrice Ainsworth?" said her mother with loathing. "What's the matter with her?" To Jane, illness was a privilege to be earned. Only people she admired were allowed to be ill. Others were malingering, or had brought the disease on themselves by anti-social or immoral behaviour.

"She's got cancer," said Hannah.

"Of the womb, I expect."

"Among other things."

"Promiscuity. That's what that comes from. I never liked the girl, though" (perfunctorily) "I'm sorry. But she was never the kind of friend I hoped you'd make."

"I'm cold. Is there anything else?" Hannah regretted mentioning Bibi's illness as a titbit for her mother's cormorant circle of gin and tonic gossips.

"How much money did you get from Brian?" said Jane. Then, providentially, the doorbell rang, so loud that Jane could hear it. "If that's the doorbell I hope you won't answer it in your dressing-gown," bossed distant Jane.

"I'm answering it in a towel," said Hannah. "Goodbye."

It was David Bowen, an hour early. For a moment Hannah stood and blinked at him, still reflecting on her mother's unpleasantness, clutching her towels against the cold air. He was foursquare as ever in jeans, a green husky and a lumberjack shirt, but he was unusually spruce: the shirt was clean and pressed, the jeans new, the husky not his battered workday one. He was also freshly shaved. He was carrying a bottle of wine. "You'll attract a crowd," he said, pushing her back into the hall. "Get back in the bath, and I'll open the wine. Unless you've other plans."

Other plans, thought Hannah joyfully running back to the bath, washing, changing into her best stay at home and flirt garment – not a jot or a tittle or a very suspicion of another plan. She was still not slim enough to wear fitted clothes but she felt supple and sinuous under her smock. Her bath-time happiness, checked by Jane's antarctic influence, was seeping back. Each garment she put on was chosen with a view to taking it off again. Satiny French knickers that concealed the curve of her flesh below the navel, push-together semi-transparent bra, clouds of scent most of which landed on the carpet and the bed (might come in handy later). She looked at herself in the mirror, satisfied enough with what she saw, hoping that sex was like bicycle-riding, not easily forgotten. Although, come to that, she'd made a distinct mess of her last bicycle ride – on Karen's bike during a dull sports day. She'd wobbled along a path which was deserted – fortunately for Karen's amour propre – and ended up in a pile of leaves and a flurry of woollen tights. So much for not forgetting how to ride a bicycle.

"I'm glad to see you," she said joining him in the kitchen, just as something to say to cover her entrance (Would he notice she'd dressed up for him? Didn't they always? Who knew? Bibi probably knew). "I didn't expect you till later."

"I told Bibi between seven and eight," he said busying himself with the wine bottle. (How can it take ten minutes to open a bottle of wine? Is he as nervous as I am? Why?)

"She told me eight." (Am I making too much of this?)

"That's not like her."

"I suppose not," said Hannah, uneasily conscious of her nipples not exactly hardening but giving notice that they might. For all practical purposes she hadn't had nipples for the last few months, since Simon Gold had groped at them in a febrile, disheartened way.

David poured the wine and Hannah sipped it. White wine, her favourite not his, German wine which tasted as if hordes of spring flowers had cast themselves lemming-like into the bottle.

"Nice," said Hannah, sipping on with great attention. Shortly the glass would be empty and then what would she do? David's clean clothes, shaved jaw and alert manner, as well as the considering look in his eye, all signalled sexual intention.

She had forgotten courtship. Brian's self-confidence and sureness of touch both metaphorically and literally had removed from Hannah all responsibility for their courtship: she hadn't needed the skills since. But now as David showed every indication of shifting the gears and the ground of their relationship – as, on one level, she wanted him to – she was panic-stricken. What if sex were disappointing, for either of them? Most likely, she'd lose David altogether, even as a handyman and companion. Or, worse still, what if it went well and she loved him, and then he left for Australia? Still sipping the air at the bottom of an empty glass, she huddled inside herself, tiny despite her mature shape and size, hiding.

"Would you like to go out for something to eat?"

"Mmm. That would be fun," said Hannah in a social voice. Fear was throwing her back on earlier defences and social masks.

"How was this morning?" David asked in his normal manner, interested without being curious, but Hannah's tension was past normal reassurance.

If he presented her with a signed statement that he would certainly enjoy every minute of sex with her, would find her body desirable in every particular, and would never leave her, it would have fallen short of the comfort she needed.

"I don't know," said Hannah, affectedly casual. "It was all right, I suppose. Brian's solicitor was rather attractive. He asked me to lunch." Even as the words escaped her free-wheeling mouth without intervention from her brain, she regretted them. "But I didn't go," she added.

"I was asking about the arrangements for the children," said David.

"Oh, that went all right," said Hannah, aiming for an everyday tone and failing miserably, sounding like a brittle and bright young thing remaindered from a BBC Twenties serial.

"Good," said David. He was beginning to sound puzzled, as well he might. He had never seen Hannah like this. Slightly keyed up himself, he was slow to imagine the depths of her insecurity or the reasons for it. "Is something wrong, Hannah?"

"Oh, nothing. Nothing at all," said Hannah, attempting a laugh. "The divorce wasn't nearly as bad as I expected."

Sensing that there was no communication between them, David lapsed into silence and poured more wine.

"Thank you for the wine," said Hannah.

"Not at all," said David, catching her formality.

Better perhaps not to go out to dinner, thought Hannah. Better to send him away and hope that she wouldn't be so frozen another time. Every moment passing carried him further away from her; he was clearing his throat, shifting his feet, withdrawing. And every moment passing, Hannah longed for him more acutely. Not wanting to meet his eyes, she stared at his hands and tried to remember if his wife was really pretty and if her name was actually Glynis. Early in Hannah's childhood she had learnt not to want anything too much, because to want was not to get. So instead of touching David's hand she thought about his wife and felt older and plainer.

"Hannah, what's going on in your head?" said David. "Is it Nigel? Bibi told me he'd called."

"Nigel doesn't matter," said Hannah. "He's taking me to dinner tomorrow night: I couldn't refuse. He'd come all the way from New York."

"I think you could have refused," said David.

Instead of being flattered by his jealousy Hannah was irritated by his male insistence on over-simplifying. She made an effort not to escape into the irritation. She would be less vulnerable irritated than she would be trying and failing to make contact with David: but there was no promise, no future in irritation.

"I want to get on with you," she offered tentatively.

"Is it so difficult?" he flashed back, aggressive for the first time. "You never found it difficult before. You were happy enough to have me around working on the house. Do you want to keep me assigned to general maintenance for ever?"

"Let's not . . ." Hannah began.

"Is it that you don't want to be seen at a restaurant with me? Because I'm dressed like this? Because I'm only David Bowen the builder?"

"I don't care what you do or what you wear," said Hannah. "I'm just bad at relationships."

"You haven't tried with me yet. And I haven't asked for a lifelong commitment, only dinner."

"Well then," said Hannah, clear at last in her own mind that she wanted to be alone, "I don't want dinner out. Not tonight."

"It's all in the breathing," said Angela Richardson, squeezing lemon into her tea. "Get breathing right and all else follows." It was break at St Ethelberta's: Hannah was penned into a corner by Guide-uniformed, panting Angela. "The first moment after birth, you should *Breathe in! Great big breaths!*" She illustrated her thesis with lavish lung-inflation. "But the stupid doctors slap babies to make them breathe and of course the poor little things are terrified so they take fearful shallow breaths." She gave a vivid impression of a frightened baby hyperventilating.

Hannah watched her worn and sallow face, cheeks puffing in and out like a dissipated cherub after a hundred yard dash. Angela's eyes had a baby's uncritical, ungiving, uninterested regard.

Mrs Fanshawe was also discouraging. "Idealism is all very well. I'm as idealistic as the next person but one has to admit, money is important, and if dear Clarissa's mother can't afford the fees then we're not doing her a kindness, letting the child stay on here. The sooner she gets used to her new station in life, the better. She'd be just as happy in a comprehensive."

"*Breathe in,*" said Angela smiling seraphically, "*Breathe out. Great big breaths.*" Around her the conversation eddied, ignoring her. Hannah thought about David. When the wine was finished, he had gone home, not hostile but not warm either, disappointed. Hannah had tumbled muzzily into bed and dreamt, against her will, of David and his wife happily reunited. This morning it had taken a massive effort of will to go to school. She wanted to see David, she could think of nothing else. She closed her eyes and imagined the feel of his lips and the pressure of his body on hers and in hers.

"That's right!" said Angela approvingly. "*In*, out, *in*, out, breathe!"

"One wonders what her father thought he was doing, killing himself, leaving his family to face the music? If life was as easy as that, we'd all do it. An excellent way to avoid school fees!"

Amanda Fanshawe reminded Hannah of her mother; a repository of narrow-mindedness, prejudice and spite, restrained only by the need to be well-thought-of by society. How fortunate that it was England in the Eighties and not the Third Reich to whose mores they wished to conform. Then her thoughts were drawn irresistibly back to David. He had a very muscled neck. Slowly his body was replacing Brian's in her imagination, so that her fantasy of male thighs were longer, thinner, more shaped than Brian's knotty block of kicking muscle. She could imagine David's thighs straddling her. In preparation she stretched her own legs and pulled her stomach in and caught her reflection in the dingy glass of the window.

Around her the staff-room lived its life. Lorene filled in forms for the San Francisco marathon, Angela found the one road to peace for the hundredth time in her unsatisfactory life – what would she have been like if her intelligence and energy were lodged in a sensible personality? Or had she started normal and been fragmented by a parent?

"The cleaners haven't been in again," said Sarah Austin, her county enunciation clear above the conversation. "Could you look into it, Mrs Fanshawe?"

"It's hardly my business," said Mrs Fanshawe.

"It's not like you to make such fine distinctions," said Hannah sweetly, and by the time Mrs Fanshawe understood the insult, Sarah was in full spate.

"Contract cleaners are an absolute disgrace. Jeff has the same problem at his office in the City. Half the time they just don't turn up."

Hannah thought of Zabriskie Cleaners and Mr Patel who certainly had turned up, when she was in the bath, and then she remembered David's arrival the previous night. If only she could respond to him like a normal human being . . . Her sensual reverie was interrupted by a nagging feeling she had overlooked something, a connection, an idea, a possibility. Mr Patel? Illegal immigrants?

"The bell's gone, Mrs Hannah," said Amanda Fanshawe reprovingly. Hannah was recalled from her mental search. The staff-room was empty. A faint trace of Sarah Austin's Miss Dior scent and the closer smell of lavender from Mrs Fanshawe hovered gentle over the more potent school brew. "What are you looking so happy about?" demanded Amanda Fanshawe sharply. "Miss Thirkettle told me she'd discussed the school's private business with you. Very remiss and indiscreet of her, I'm afraid, but then she's getting old." She waited for some indication of Hannah's reaction; when none was forthcoming she went on. "Have you noticed that the Headmistress is vaguer than usual? Deafer? More forgetful?"

"I hadn't noticed," said Hannah.

"Perhaps it's time for a younger woman to take over the reins," said Mrs Fanshawe, delicately glowing with alertness and verve.

"I don't think I'd be suited to the job," said Hannah, deliberately misunderstanding. Mrs Fanshawe gave her a venomous look.

"When you first joined us I had high hopes of you. But latterly I'm afraid you seem almost cynical and you linger in the staff-room when you should be teaching."

"I'd better go to my lesson, then," said Hannah.

"Cynicism and carelessness; modern faults, I'm afraid."

"Do you find them in your own charming children?"

"Certainly not."

"I expect they can embroider beautifully," pursued Hannah, enjoying herself too much to stop.

"Camilla is an excellent needlewoman. Thomas doesn't sew, of course, don't be ridiculous."

"What a pity. Apart from the equal opportunity aspect, I do think it's important for a man to be able to sew. It comes in so handy."

"How could it possibly come in handy?"

"If there's a third world war and it's fought with conventional weapons and still contains old-fashioned elements like prisoner-of-war camps, then Thomas can pass the time by sewing."

"You are talking complete nonsense," said Amanda Fanshawe, her pale hair fluffing as she quivered with exasperation.

The English class was subdued when Hannah reached them. She tried to push aside the disquiet roused in her by Amanda Fanshawe's transparent attempts to muster support for a takeover bid. It was ten minutes into the lesson before she realised that the girls were being exceptionally quiet, and doing a comprehension passage too, work they normally loathed, without protest. She glanced round the class. Kimia busily writing – she always finished first – Felicity Wakefield breathing heavily as her tongue traced the feeble scratchings of her pen. Cheese lay apparently asleep on her desk making no attempt to write. Hannah was about to tell her off when Kimia looked up and shook her head firmly. When the bell went Cheese sat up. Her eyes were puffy as if she had been crying not only recently but for all the previous night, and her ever-present smile was gone. The other girls didn't look at Hannah looking at her and they streamed out of the classroom as soon as the bell went. Cheese waited.

"Anything I can help with?" said Hannah. Cheese started crying again, exhausted tears.

"I don't want to go to sewing, Mrs Hannah. I feel ill, really I do."

Kimia stopped by them, her dark eyes meeting Hannah's and locking. "Have a talk to her," she said.

"Cheese, come with me," said Hannah. "Kimia, explain to Mrs Fanshawe that I'm taking care of her."

They went downstairs. Classes had begun and the only sign of life in the school was the murmur of teachers' voices and the scraping of chairs on wooden floors, behind the thick well-fitting doors. Hannah took the girl into a coaching room, a tiny stuffy little room tucked away at the back of the hall and over the kitchen, with hooks for the coats of long-ago visitors and a powerful smell of cooking fish.

"So what is it, Cheese? Why have you suddenly taken against sewing?"

"Will you tell Mrs Fanshawe what I say?"

"No."

"I don't want to see her. That's why I don't want to go to sewing. I'm lousy at it, anyhow. What normal person wants to embroider bloody cushion covers?" She had stopped crying and perched herself on the rusty old radiator. "That's probably why she took against me in the first place. You have to keep your sewing neat and pretend to enjoy it if you want to get on with her."

"Get to the point. I'm wasting a free lesson on you."

"You won't believe it."

"Try me."

"You know my mother got married again last term and I said her new husband didn't like me much? He's turned out all right now and he trusts me much more and he thinks I'm OK and I think he's OK."

"OK," said Hannah.

"But he's really old-fashioned and strict. It's odd, he nags me more than my mother does. He wants me to do well in my O levels and he thinks education is very important. For jobs and that."

"Sensible chap."

"And I'm not as dim as the teachers think," said Cheese defensively.

"You're not dim."

"That's what I thought. I worked really hard towards the end of last term and Kimia helped me in the holidays. I bunked off the first two sewing lessons this term because it's a waste of time. I've got stacks and stacks of Science work to catch up on, so I took the sewing time to copy up notes. Miss Richardson's been coaching me as well. She knows masses of Science. The Science teacher at my last school didn't know any, she taught Geography as well and I don't think she knew much of that, except where to find the Red Lion in the lunch hour."

"The point, Cheese."

"Mrs Fanshawe sent for me yesterday and said I'd be expelled."

"Expelled? For missing two sewing lessons?"

"Not just that. She showed me some pills and said she'd found them in my locker."

"And had she?"

"Only if she put them there."

"What kind of pills?"

"They looked like Valium."

"And they weren't yours? Tell me the truth, Cheese." The girl looked the picture of guilt, blushing and shuffling.

"I promise. But nobody'll believe me. Not against her. She'll get me expelled and then my new dad'll think I'm not trying. And if I'm expelled from here there's nowhere left to go."

"Tutorial college or technical college. Lots of places," said Hannah briskly, but she could see that for Cheese the real issue was to preserve the fragile relationship with her new father. "What exactly are you saying? That Mrs Fanshawe put the pills in your locker herself?"

"They're probably hers and she's just saying she found them in my locker."

"Come and tell your story to Miss Thirkettle," said Hannah.

"What a bitch," said Bibi later that afternoon. Hannah had been to exercise class and was now lying in the bath again, this time hoping to soak away the pain: Bibi was perched on the bathroom stool lighting a cigarette.

"But you don't smoke, Bibi."

"I do now. Hardly important what it does to my lungs, is it? No, seriously Hannah, the woman is dangerous. Why does she want the girl expelled?"

"I'm not sure," said Hannah, inspecting one leg to see if the strain her muscles had been subjected to was at all visible on the surface. "Miss Thirkettle saw that Cheese was telling the truth, so it's over."

"This particular part may be over but the rest of the iceberg is still rolling slowly in the deep waiting for the *Titanic* to strike it. A great deal of money is involved in the sale of the school, didn't you say?"

"Amanda Fanshawe's share would be in the hundreds of thousands."

"If I were your headmistress I'd lock my door at night."

"Are you joking?"

"Not entirely."

"Mmm," said Hannah. Her mind was still dominated by David. When would he come to see her again? She couldn't ring him, she didn't even know where he lived. She could ask Bibi but that would lead to questions and her feelings were too raw to stand exposure. Bibi was in a gossipy mood, she would pick over and analyse the relationship between Hannah and David and although the procedure would not be ill-intentioned, Hannah knew she would find it uncomfortable. At the same time it seemed unkind to deprive Bibi of anything that distracted her from her illness. "I'm scared of sex," she said. "It's been too long."

"Are you thinking of Nigel tonight?"

Better let her think so. "Um," said Hannah.

"I didn't think you fancied him."

Not in the least, thought Hannah, but he would do to practise on. She so much didn't want to take the risk of putting David off. If she was clumsy, embarrassed, awkward with him in bed – supposing she even got that far – what if he went away and never came back? She could imagine the postcard from Sydney. "Perfectly happy with Glynis and children. Glad you're not here." She didn't want to have sex with Nigel but she didn't find the idea repulsive.

"What's worrying you?" said Bibi, avid for a problem to solve.

"Well," said Hannah, more as a therapeutic interest for Bibi than seriously, "my breasts."

"Let's have a look then."

Hannah heaved her torso out of the bubbles and they both looked at her breasts. "Gorgeous," said Bibi. "What's the problem?"

"But look." Hannah turned sideways and they drooped down her chest.

"Don't lie on your side."

"It's worse if I turn over." Hannah went on her hands and knees, breasts hanging straight down in front of her.

"You look like the picture of the wolf who suckled Romulus and Remus in our old Latin grammar book."

Hannah settled back in the bath. "You see what I mean."

"If a man fancies you he won't mind. Most men care more how you feel than how you look. If you feel nice and they believe you desire them, that's OK."

"What if – Nigel – " (Hannah remembered just in time) "likes to look?"

"Try sellotape," teased Bibi. "Like the models do. A strip under the arms. Works wonders."

"Not on my size breasts. Besides, it'll feel odd."

"Take it off when you get down to it."

"Terrific suggestion, Bibi. First I dance around the room starkers except for a roll of scotch tape, tits lofted to the breeze, then I plunge the scene into darkness and dismantle myself."

"What happens if you lie flat on your back?"

"The breasts each sag to one side. Like unfresh fried eggs."

"Mine disappear when I lie on my back," said Bibi.

"And I've got stretch marks on my stomach," said Hannah. "Perhaps I should operate entirely in the dark."

"You could remove the light bulbs. Or the fuse."

Hannah remembered the last blown fuse and her lust for Nicholas. Now she was fully occupied lusting for David she couldn't imagine another man attracting her.

"You're stupid, of course," said Bibi, tapping ash off her cigarette. Both dogs were curled up at her feet and one of them sneezed as the ash landed on its nose. "Sex has no more to do with what a woman looks like than it has to do with the size of a man's prick. You must have realised that by now."

"In that case why do you stare at men's crotches so?"

"Merely in the interests of taxonomy. I like classifying them." Her face was animated: momentarily, the watery sun filled her spiky hair and charged it with light, softening away the lines of pain. She looked entirely well. Maybe you'll live for years yet, thought Hannah, let's be terrible old women together.

Bibi stood on the lavatory to see her bottom in the mirror. Its shape was clearly visible under her stretch jeans. "I've been thinking about the next few months. What on earth shall I wear? I'm bound to get even skinnier. My bones will protrude and people will cut themselves if they bump into me. The drugs'll make me sleepier and sleepier. I don't want the trouble of choosing proper clothes that fit and hurt me where they touch my body."

"So?"

"So I'm going to revert to the late Sixties. Hippie dresses, bare feet. Long loose garments and unkempt hair."

"Sounds like the way I dress now."

"You do it by accident. Mine would be studied, detailed and complete like a costume play."

"If you say so."

"It's a definite style. If I'm to be robbed of old age, at least I can claim an old person's privilege in advance."

"You can claim away. Nicholas won't like it." Hannah was captivated by the idea which was very Bibi. She had always gone her own way, made up her own mind. That was the quality that most irritated Caroline. Hannah imagined what Caroline would say of a present-day Bibi festooned in peace gear. "Bibi's gone too far again," Hannah imagined Caroline's mouth pursing round the words.

She remembered the summer term of their O levels; all three in the best dormitory, a delicately proportioned room on the first floor of the original Georgian building, overlooking the sunken garden, the rose garden, the cloisters. At night with the windows open for any breeze to stir the June heat the smell of roses was cloying, disturbing. Hannah and Bibi slept naked, covered only by a sheet to protect Caroline's susceptibilities. One night there was a noise outside the window and a shower of gravel scattered into the room, landing on Caroline's clothes which were laid out, folded in the regulation manner (pants underneath), on a chair. Dragging their chastity sheets behind them Hannah and Bibi made for the window. Caroline slept on.

It was the gardener; not respectable old Mr Flynn, but his new assistant, a well-built young man whose body in cotton shirt and worn grey flannel trousers was the focus of many lecherous fantasies.

"Come for a walk," he whispered. Hannah knew it was Bibi he was after; they must have had a previous meeting. Bibi dressed in a flash; she put on black gym knickers and a long, floppy sweater, then scrambled down the fire-escape and was gone.

She didn't come back for an hour. Hannah was beginning to panic. She prayed to Maria Goretti, patron saint of the dormitory, for Bibi to come back safely. Then she remembered that Maria Goretti had died from forty stab wounds rather than submit to her cousin's improper advances – at only fourteen, too – and decided the saint might not be entirely sympathetic to Bibi's case. Then Caroline woke up and they waited together, in silence once Caroline had run out of recriminations.

At last Bibi reappeared, tousle-haired and swollen-lipped.

"Oh, Bibi," cried Caroline, "have you *gone too far?*"

"No," said Bibi. "I went just far enough, it was lovely." She glowed with a sensual delight and Hannah had envied her; Hannah was still embarrassment-ridden by her own lustful endeavours with the Brigadier. Just as Bibi had radiated pleasure then, remembering the gardener, so now she radiated excitement and daring. Such a simple enterprise, the Sixties dressing, but it had obviously lit a spark of self-will and determination in her.

Six o'clock that evening, and Hannah badly wanted Bibi to go home. She wanted time alone to decide what she should say to Nigel; whether her plan to go to bed with him was practical, if somewhat cold-blooded, or merely a distraction. But with some impish devilment Bibi, who knew quite well that Hannah was not being frank with her about her feelings for David or her motives with regard to Nigel, threw herself into Hannah's preparations for the evening, all enthusiasm to help. She monitored Hannah's dressing and made her put on the same French knickers and bra she had intended David Bowen to see the previous night. "But they're still damp, Bibi, I only washed them this morning."

"We must suffer to be beautiful."

With Nigel and the bitter weather in mind, Hannah's own preference was for thermal underwear, but Bibi's beady eye wouldn't have overlooked such a giveaway.

There was a blessed respite while Bibi nipped out to a late-opening chemist – Hannah believed, for some pain-killing drug. But then she reappeared brandishing a tube of KY jelly. "For you," she said, thrusting it into Hannah's limp hand.

"I thought this was for gynaecological examinations and buggering," said Hannah.

"It's also dead useful if you're nervous."

"Oh," said Hannah, knowing Bibi was teasing her, stubbornly determined not to talk to her about David. "Do go away, Bibi. Give me some peace."

"I'm going. All in good time. I'm just being helpful. Knowing how anxious you are to make a good impression on Nigel."

Hannah avoided the challenge. She tucked the KY jelly away in the bathroom cupboard, by torchlight since Bibi had removed the fuse from the bedroom circuit in literal execution of her whimsical suggestion. She took off the sensible dress she had chosen and put on a silk shirt and a full skirt that Bibi had given her for Christmas. She looked blowzy but ripe. Nigel's eyes gleamed with appraisal and appreciation when he saw her but he spent several minutes making small talk with Bibi, who left winking most horribly behind Nigel's back.

When they were alone he took her hand in a manicured, therapeutic grasp and once more his eyes gazed into hers, unnaturally blue, angled downwards from his commanding height. She compared him with David. Too tall, his limbs overgrown and spindly like an unpruned rose bush or a marrow that should have stopped at courgettehood. Could she possibly go to bed with this man?

She was still asking herself that question after dinner. Good enough dinner, again, and Nigel's way with waiters hadn't deserted him. Perhaps he should stick to waiters. Hannah drank steadily, wine white and red, some sticky liqueur. Nigel seemed very far away. She called him David twice and had to force herself to listen to his words. He was evidently boiling up to a seduction. His fingers were no longer merely reassuring; they strayed about her shoulders and arms in a proprietorial way; and he was telling her how much he earned. It sounded an utterly ridiculous amount for a big bland Englishman to earn simply for listening to people's troubles. He was kind, however, even if it was professional, fifty dollars an hour kindness. When he took her home she asked him in and they sat in the kitchen consuming coffee and brandy. The brandy was Nicholas's

Christmas present to Hannah, intended probably as a supply for Nicholas himself on his visits. Its warmth clouded Hannah's thought processes still further; she was resigned to letting Nigel take the initiative.

She remembered the dogs. Recently they had taken to sleeping on their sag-bags in her bedroom. They would whine and bark if she went to bed and tried to shut them out. She dashed out of the kitchen, bumping into walls, bullied them awake, outside and into the car. When she rejoined Nigel in the kitchen he advanced towards her with the determined air of a real man who eats broken bottles as hors d'oeuvres. Light-headed Hannah allowed him to embrace her. He murmured into her hair, soft breaths of appreciation, and his hands stroked her body in a firm, thorough massage action. It was pleasant in a wholesome way. He was so large that Hannah could lean against him without any fear that they would both topple over. She didn't resist when he made to lead her upstairs, apart from saying, "It's no good turning on the lights. The upstairs fuse has gone."

"I'll fix it afterwards," he promised, leading her confidently into Karen's room.

"This way." Her own room was friendly and the thought of lying down, appealing. She still wasn't sure whether she preferred to lie down with Nigel or without him; she longed for David with all her heart. Why had she lost her nerve last night?

Nigel established them both on the bed. There was enough light from the moon to reflect patterns of the branches of the sycamore tree on to the ceiling. Nigel started to unbutton her blouse. He was deft and quick: not long before the push-together bra was revealed. Hannah felt contented but unsexual as his fingers unhooked her bra and her breasts travelled sideways. This seemed merely amusing.

His face was heavy above hers. "We could make sweet music together," he said.

"What?" said Hannah.

"We could make sweet music together." It didn't bear repetition.

Cold air passing over her nipples peaked them. His touch began to tickle, though she was still too dreamy to laugh. His hands started work on her legs. Suddenly Bibi's KY jelly seemed a good idea. She'd go into the bathroom, brush her teeth, lubricate herself, sober up a fraction, think.

"Back in a minute."

"I'll be ready," promised Nigel, starting to undress.

In the bathroom, unfamiliar in the dark, Hannah rummaged through the cupboard until she found the smooth, untouched tube. The joke's on you, Bibi, I'm using your wretched stuff, she thought, squeezing a lavish supply on to her fingers and anointing herself. Then she brushed her teeth thoroughly and long, trying to eliminate all traces of garlic and lobster and cheesecake, wondering that the garlic taste overpowered even toothpaste. Then she leant against the wall and tried to think. Did she have to go through with this? Her confidence was back. She was sure she could manage sex now. With David and perhaps a little alcohol, all would be well. But the thought of Nigel inside her, KY jelly or not, made her flesh crawl. Her body didn't want him and she couldn't argue with such a fundamental objection.

Her thighs felt very sticky and dry. Surely the KY stuff was a jelly, like Vaseline? She smelt her fingers. Strong peppermint. Like toothpaste. Light dawned. She grabbed the KY tube and took it to the window. The moon glinted eerily on a toothpaste tube. She had slavered her genitals in ounces of toothpaste. She ran her tongue experimentally round her teeth. She had a very well lubricated mouth.

"Hannah! Hannah!" called Nigel with an urgency that did not sound passionate. He was standing in the middle of the bedroom, clad only in a shirt, his penis dangling in the moonlight. It was long and thin and extremely limp, like a Victorian tasselled bell-pull. "Do you have a torch, Hannah? I lost my contact lens."

"I didn't know you were short-sighted."

"I'm not. They're for cosmetic purposes only. To make my eyes more blue."

You're *certainly* not going to screw me, thought Hannah. What a wet! Imagine going to all that trouble! And a man who wore blue contact lenses would definitely notice and mind about stretch marks and drooping breasts. She crossed her arms over her naked chest. "There's a torch on the bedside table."

He immediately dropped to his hands and knees and began feeling the carpet, inch by inch. "You've got some animals in the roof, as well," he said. "Probably mice or bats. There's been some odd noises. Hell, Hannah, don't you ever vacuum the rug? I've found three of your hairpins and a toy plastic soldier already." He sounded American.

"Oh, good," said Hannah, "I'm running out of hairpins." She felt relieved by his change of mood. Sex was forgotten. He sounded irritated. Her brain, hampered by the alcohol, took longer to solve the problem of the mice in the attic.

"Come and help," said Nigel. "This is my last pair, I've been unlucky this trip, I lost the others first day back."

"How?" Hannah imagined a similar scene: another girl half-naked, Nigel promising sensual delights and a steady income, ending with both of them patting the carpet.

"Does it matter?" There was a loud thud from the attic. "Sounds more like rats," said Nigel, as if that would be appropriate in Hannah's house. She had lost him for ever, she could tell by his tone. Never mind. They could always break up on an amicable basis like he and Barbie-Ann.

"David's in the roof," said Hannah. "It's not rats."

Nigel leapt to his feet, penis swinging. "What? Who?"

"David Bowen. He's . . . he mends things around the house. A handyman, I suppose. He's insulating the roof."

"At this time of night? It's past eleven!"

"He has his own work in the daytime. He . . ." Hannah's voice trailed away as she remembered. David knew quite well that Nigel was taking her out to dinner. He might also have guessed that she would bring him home. So David was here on purpose . . .

The trap door opened and David's legs, then David himself, appeared on the landing. He was silhouetted against the beam of light from the attic.

"How come that light works?" demanded Nigel irascibly, groping for his underpants.

"I replaced the fuse," said David, pressing a switch. The overhead light in the bedroom flooded on illuminating Nigel halfway into his royal blue underpants and Hannah naked to the waist. "Sorry," said David. "Did I interrupt?" His voice was Welsher than usual but otherwise expressionless.

"Get out of here," said Nigel. He was angry but suppressing it: the attitude of composed tolerance was too ingrained to be thrust completely aside.

Hannah looked at him. He seemed ridiculous: in that situation anyone would: but he evoked no sympathy. She was more struck by David's litheness as he swung from the trap door. "You wouldn't like to climb up and swing down again?" she asked. "It was very impressive."

"Here." He picked her shirt from the bed and draped it round her shoulders. She put it on, half-turning from David, not caring if Nigel saw. He was too preoccupied with his own clothes to notice.

"I think I'll make some tea," said Hannah. David followed her down the stairs.

"Are you angry, Hannah?"

"Angry? Why?" She filled the kettle mechanically, only glad that he was there, hoping that finding her with Nigel hadn't put him off completely.

"Because I barged in on you at the wrong moment. Because I'm here at all."

"I'm grateful to have the roof insulated."

"That's not what we're talking about, and you know it. I thought you were supposed to be honest. Don't evade me and put up smoke-screens."

"To tell the complete and total truth," said Hannah, buttoning her shirt across bare breasts and incidentally admiring the effect, "I nearly went to bed with Nigel to see if I'd forgotten how. I didn't want to be a disappointment to you. Because I cared about you and not him, I thought he'd do to practise on."

"That's the silliest thing I've ever heard."

"But then I decided not to."

"Why?"

"Didn't want to."

"Have you been drinking?"

"Yes. Masses."

David sat down and pulled her on to his lap. "I'm sorry, Hannah."

"What for?"

"That I came round yesterday so obviously on the make. It

was stupid. Tactless. On the day of your divorce. No wonder you were confused. I wanted you so much I . . . I couldn't wait. I was afraid you'd find someone else."

Tell me more, this is the stuff, thought Hannah gleefully and wiggled her bottom in an inviting manner. He slid his hands under her skirt and stroked her legs.

"Watch out for the toothpaste," said Hannah. "I mixed it up with the KY jelly. In the dark."

"KY jelly?"

"You know. For the older woman."

"You're not that old."

"True. Just as well. Toothpaste isn't that helpful."

"Ah-hum," coughed Nigel, standing intransigently in the doorway. Hannah, captivated by David's warm and welcome lovemaking, driven by courtesy, half-struggled to rise.

"Would you like a cup of tea, Nigel? Or some more brandy?"

"Thank you, no. I have to drive."

"Thank you for a delightful dinner." To David, whispering: "Let me up."

"No," said David. She struggled and he held her firmly. It was a sensual, demanding grip.

With a final effort to be civil, she said at random, "Did you find your contact lens?"

"No. Goodbye, Hannah. I hope – " he broke off, looked at David with resentment, and left, slamming the front door behind him.

"Good," said David.

"I'll have to make the tea," protested Hannah. "The kettle will be boiling."

"Not immediately. You didn't plug it in."

7

"So the thing is, Hannah," said Caroline's voice, "do you want a man?"

"No thank you," said Hannah, shifting the receiver to the other ear and pulling a sheet up over her breasts to protect them from David's straying hand, "I just had one."

"What *do* you mean? I'm talking about Bibi's party at the ball. She said you had some difficulty about finding a man. I know a terribly nice widower who'd simply love to meet you..."

David was making getting-up gestures and Hannah knew she would have to let him go. He'd taken two afternoon hours away from an important contract as it was, and they were sated. In the three months since her dinner with Nigel, she and David had made love so often and so thoroughly that Hannah couldn't believe that each time she could come to it with the same enthusiasm. But almost each time, she did.

Making love with David was totally different from Brian. To start with, there had been no room for initiative with Brian. He decided what they would do, and it always involved him in the starring and active role. Hannah merely had to stand, sit or lie in various positions wearing various garments. David, on the other hand, just liked sex. What he did to her or she did to him was not for advantage or to show off but simply for pleasure.

"What's that noise?" demanded Caroline.

"David getting out of bed," said Hannah. Caroline gave a shocked giggle.

"Oh, Hannah! Really!"

David bent over and kissed her neck.

"Are you honestly with a man? Shall I ring back?"

"No. And thanks for offering a partner for Bibi's do, but I think I've persuaded David to come with me."

"David? Your builder person?" Caroline whispered to make it less offensive. "Will he enjoy it?"

"Ah. That's what he doubts. He doesn't like formal clothes and parties. But Bibi's very anxious for him to go. Why are you surprised? I've told you about David and me."

"I understood you were having a *fling*. Not the same thing at all as appearing in *public*. I'll put my widower back in cold storage, then. But he may come in useful yet. You never know. When you get tired of . . ."

Hannah said nothing. Caroline continued, "Bibi seemed much better yesterday." She persisted in the belief that Bibi would recover. She was bombarding all the saints she knew and several obscure ones she didn't with personal requests, and nuns all over England had been recruited for a prayer drive.

"She's not in so much pain. I hope she's strong enough for the ball, she's so looking forward to it. I think she's got some dreadful plot hatching. Has she told you who else is in her party? She won't even talk about it to me."

David had washed, dressed, was on the landing. Hannah windmilled her arm at him and he said, "I'll be round at eight."

"Goodbye," she called.

"Has David gone?"

"Yes."

There was a pause while Caroline gathered up courage. "Hannah, what's it like? You know . . . doing it with someone you're not married to. Don't you feel frightfully guilty?"

"Not in the least. But then I don't have a husband. Why?"

"I don't know," said Caroline wistfully. "Lately, things have been . . . I don't know."

"Any word from Gerald?" Caroline's husband was now somewhere between England and the Falkland Islands, sailing with his regiment.

"No."

"Are you worried about him?"

"Well, partly. But he is a soldier and you're prepared. They may not even have to fight if the Argies back down. I was more worried when he was in Northern Ireland." Pause again. "Hannah, could we lunch tomorrow? When does your term start?"

"Not till next week. But, Caro, I'm sorry – " and Hannah was, Caroline's request had sounded like an appeal – "tomorrow I've arranged a business lunch."

"Business lunch? Who on earth with?"

"A man called Patel. He runs a contract cleaning firm."

"You don't need contract cleaners for your house, surely? I could easily find you a nice Maltese girl – "

"I don't want to employ him, I want him to employ me."

"As a cleaner?"

"Organising his cleaners. Getting contracts for them, supervising the work. On a percentage basis. Eventually I want to be a partner."

"When did this come up?" Caroline's unwieldy thought processes were making heavy weather of such an un-Hannah-like enterprise.

"I've been planning it for months. Ever since I realised that there was room for an efficient firm of contract cleaners with a large and expanding supply of cheap labour."

"Where does this supply come from?"

"Immigrants. Some of them illegal, I suspect, but I wouldn't have to know about that."

"But what do you know about cleaning?"

"Nothing. But I know a great deal about finding out about things from a position of total ignorance. That's what they taught me at Oxford."

"I've often wondered what you did there." Caroline was offended: turned down for a Pakistani; not consulted in Hannah's business venture. She rang off.

Hannah washed and dressed. Much to do. She vacuumed the downstairs rooms, started preparing supper. She'd leave a casserole in the oven and take the dogs for a walk before her exercise class. She only had to feed David and herself. The children were staying with Brian and new Mrs Brian until they went back to school. In such a short few months her life with David had settled down into a routine. Both were slow to commit themselves completely. Though David slept most nights in Hannah's bed (John: "I thought women your age were past yucky sex stuff"), and ate most meals at Hannah's house, he always asked if Hannah minded and paid his share of the food.

On one level she was very happy with the arrangement. He was a marvellous lover, an excellent companion, though always reserved. But on another level she wanted to know more about his attitude to her and the future of their relationship. She knew she was being feminine not feminist and she kept trying to restrain herself, but she wanted some feeling of permanence. He never suggested any, never talked about the future. "You're nice to be with" or "Let's go to bed" were the heights of his verbal commitment. The hours of work he had put into the house and his gentleness and patience with her were commitment of another kind. But accustomed to Brian's lavish promises, aware also that David was always guarded in his speech, Hannah felt the cold breath of disappointment to come always lurking behind the happiness of the present. Deliberately she fished, but David avoided her hooks with ease. Even a clever and skilled fisherman can be seen coming.

"What'll you be doing for a holiday this summer?"

"Not sure. I don't always go away in the summer, it's a good time to get on with my work. Houses empty, no interruptions."

And another day: "Any news about Glynis and the children?"

"No."

And another day: "Are you happy with me?"

"I'm here, aren't I?" (Gently.)

Mostly she managed to ignore her anxiety: a cloud, no bigger than a man's hand. Once she used exactly that expression to herself. Then the thought of a man's hand took her back to the living presence of David sitting at the kitchen table making notes and calculations while she peeled potatoes. Odd that she had begrudged cooking for Brian. It was probably because he talked about eating all the time, mispronouncing the foreign names of dishes, preferring pretentious French sauces and food that took hours to cook. David, on the other hand, was grateful for food at all. Possibly Glynis had been too pretty and sexy to lower herself to such mundane matters. Often David cooked for Hannah, not well but efficiently, and he did the washing-up afterwards.

Hannah's opinion of the fugitive Glynis sank even lower. Why had she left him? It wasn't as if he was dull. He was too reserved and independent ever to be that and he enjoyed all manner of things: sex, concerts, jokes, foreign films, walks, television. His greatest drawback was a tendency to be right all the time, but Hannah was teasing him out of it. And he was a very successful builder; he specialised in the restoration of pre-Victorian houses, he was well paid and was his own master.

"You're lucky with David," Bibi said one day not long after the start of Hannah's affair. "He's the kindest man I know."

"But he doesn't love me," said Hannah.

"How do you know?"

"He's never said so."

"Give it time."

"Bloody useful, that is," said Hannah. "I expected a more original suggestion from my worldly-wise friend."

"Do you love him?"

"I don't know." She thought about it. "Love isn't a useful word. Too vague." But in her heart she knew she would love him if he would love her back, however vague the word. She wanted to be part of his life.

He never volunteered information about his family or friends; by digging assiduously Hannah found out his parents were alive and in London, and that the flat that he lived in (which she was never asked to visit) was two scarcely furnished rooms in Highgate he had bought after his family had left. Hannah, whose native medium was words, who talked to those she loved like the Orinoco in spate, had retailed all her life to him and received hard pebbles of fact in return. One night in bed she settled herself in the crook of his arm, hand on his chest (he was much hairier than Brian and his body smell was less sweet), and asked, "Why won't you talk to me about yourself?"

"Nothing to say. Kids do that in bus shelters and bedrooms."

"What?" Often his inexpressive language defeated her at first and she had to cross-examine him. "What age kids?"

"Teenagers. Lovers. My parents don't understand me. I want to be a pop star. That."

"You mean it's adolescent to talk about yourself?"

"Yes."

"Does it irritate you when I do?"

"Sometimes."

She pulled away, affronted, and turned her back on him. "Did Glynis talk about herself?"

"Not often. She didn't talk much."

"Perhaps that was what went wrong with your marriage," snapped Hannah, regretting it as she spoke.

"I doubt it," said David. "I don't think talking matters."

"So you just said."

"But I like it when you talk. You say funny things."

"You said I irritate you."

"Only sometimes, and only when you talk about yourself. You're interesting to listen to, otherwise." He kissed her and Hannah gratefully immersed herself in the simplicity of passion. That was usually how her uncertainties ended, not resolved but buried in flesh.

So consequently she kept more things to herself and one of the things she kept to herself was her plan to work for Patel. As she went over it to herself it seemed sound.

Hannah had chosen the restaurant carefully. Not Indian (in case Patel took offence; in case she chose one so inferior that no Indian would eat in it; in case it was specific to a region from which he did not come), but French. Close to Zabriskie Cleaners; they might need to go straight there after lunch. An expense account place, that would show respect to a business guest. She had booked a week earlier and specified a table by the window.

She arrived and was led to a table near the kitchen by an English head waiter who combined insolence with servility.

"I want a table by the window, please," said Hannah.

"I'm afraid none are free. Madam."

"I particularly mentioned a table by the window when I booked."

"Why don't you just sit down here. This is a nice table. Madam."

"I reserved a table by the window and I want one."

"Wait and see what your gentleman friend says. Madam."

"This is a business lunch and I am the host. There are several window tables free."

"Those are all booked."

"One of them, by me," said Hannah, as she chose a table and established herself at it.

Patel arrived several minutes later; he was led up to the table and looked at her uncertainly. She was neatly turned out and she looked happy, totally unlike the undefined and defenceless creature whose house he had cleaned the year before. In her turn she looked at him with eyes less obscured by self-pity. He was smaller than she remembered, and more prosperous. Gold cufflinks, pale pink silk shirt, suit of expensive material and cheap cut, and eyes of a startling pale green. He also had very precise small hands which nervously stroked the starched tablecloth; Hannah could easily have swallowed his hands up in hers.

He was vegetarian. It would have been better at an Indian restaurant. He insisted all was well, he would order vegetables, she was not to worry. The head waiter looked at them with contempt, his pasty and heavy-jawed face making no attempt even to appear civil. Hannah was not his type – too managing, too big, too old; the little black man asked how the vegetables were cooked, and what business was it of his? Hannah and Patel were not united under his hostility. She felt the foolishness of her mistaken choice of restaurant, and the ignorant arrogance of her countryman. Patel insisted all was well when it clearly wasn't. Lying civilities compounded themselves in suffocating heaps.

"This is a very smart restaurant. Very nice," said Patel for the fifth time.

"I hoped it would be pleasant for us. I have a business proposition to discuss with you."

"So you said." At once Patel was less affable, more predatory. He watched her closely as she outlined her plan, food forgotten, crumbling a roll into little pellets with his delicate hands.

"All this is based on the assumption that business is going badly," concluded Hannah.

"Not so well. Same problem. Few clients call us, and I am too busy with my other concerns to tout for custom."

"But you could provide plenty of workers, if the need arose."

"If the need arose. So you wish to work for me?"

"No, I'll be self-employed. You'll pay me a percentage commission like an agent."

"What percentage did you have in mind?"

"Fifteen per cent."

"Five."

"Ten."

"Ten is possible," said Patel.

"I must be able to use your office for telephone calls, and you give me stationery and pay printers' bills for leaflets. I'll have to know the hourly rates of your workers, and what to charge for overheads. Then I'll fix prices."

"I use the office also for my video rental business. We must agree on the details later."

"And if I'm successful, after a year we'll discuss a partnership."

"*If* you're successful. Forgive me, Hannah, but what do you know about cleaning?"

"We'll see," said Hannah briskly. Her self-confidence was impressive. If only she could organise her emotional life so easily. She thought of David. She wondered if he thought of her as much as she thought of him. Perhaps this emotional preoccupation was exclusively female.

"Some sweet?" asked the head waiter. He insisted on continuing to serve them, possibly considering that a lesser waiter couldn't torment them so thoroughly. Hannah, indifferent to more food, could see that Patel's expression quickened at the prospect.

"Could we see a menu?"

"We have nice apple pie, chocolate mousse, various sorbets..."

"A menu, please."

"The sorbets are excellent. A speciality of the chef."

"Is there a menu shortage?"

The man showed his teeth in a servile snarl. "Most of our regular patrons find a menu unnecessary to make a choice of sweet."

"Perhaps experience has taught them what to avoid," said Hannah.

"Miss Thirkettle was busy today but I'll catch her on Thursday," said Hannah scraping leftovers from the fridge into the dogs' bowls and tidying the kitchen table. She had five minutes to spare before getting ready for Bibi's dinner and the ball. "I don't see why the school shouldn't use my cleaners. They'd be a lot better than the present crew. And two more firms agreed to try us today. That's six contracts I've got in a week."

"You'll be a tycoon any minute," said David. The sentiment was right but the tone was wrong. She paused in her whirlwind of activity. His expression was glum in the extreme as he opened a Moss Bros box and examined the garments inside. "Last time I wore this gear was at a wedding."

"Not a white tie. Morning coat for weddings."

"The last time I wore poncey gear from a dark green box smelling of moth balls and hire money was at a wedding," persisted David.

"Your own?"

"I wore a suit at my own."

This tricky subject avoided, Hannah was prepared to be conciliating. "Are you regretting that Bibi persuaded you to come?"

"Yes. But..."

Hannah swept in hastily, not noticing that he had something else to say. "We won't stay to the end; Bibi'll give us a good dinner, and you can be as unpleasant as you like to Derek Cummin."

"Who's he?"

"I knew his wife at Oxford and Bibi decorated a London flat for them a few years ago. He works in the World Bank. You can be as rude as you like to them – Olivia's paranoid and she expects it, and Derek will be rude back."

"I thought Bibi wasn't telling you who she'd asked."

"She wasn't. That's because she knows I dislike Derek. She couldn't resist telling me this morning."

"How did she sound?"

"Cheerful enough. Somewhat spaced out from the drugs."

"Hannah," said David, "there's something I want to say...", but she was heading up the stairs.

"Tell me later. I must have a bath, I'm late."

"Thank God you've come," said Nicholas opening the door and releasing party sounds. "Are you going to San Francisco," sang a voice from the past, "you will meet some gentle people there," and a man laughed loudly ner-haw ner-haw, over a basis of chatter.

"Sixties' music to go with Bibi's clothes, what fun," said Hannah. Nicholas clasped Hannah's hands, pointedly excluding David.

"You're late. Bibi was afraid you wouldn't come." His face, fleshy and dissolute, bulged Oscar Wilde-like over his stiff collar. He looked puzzled and childish. "The doctor says Bibi won't last long but that's just between us. She seems better to me. Tell me what you think later. Everyone else has arrived and Olivia Cummin and Rosabelle Trench are squealing at each other because they've discovered mutual friends in New York."

"Shall I put my coat in Bibi's room?"

"Do. You know the way. Join us when you're ready."

David followed her along the corridor to the big bedroom and looked around, shaking his head. "I told her this wallpaper was a mistake at the time." Hannah put her coat on the bed, glanced at herself in the mirror to check she was neat; David put his hands on her bare shoulders and kissed her neck. In the mirror they were linked, happy. Hannah hoped without expectation that he would enjoy the evening. She felt happy, herself. She knew she looked good in the dress Caroline had lent her. It couldn't possibly have suited Caroline: it was off the shoulder and on her flat-chested barrel frame it would have been off the waist. It was also deep red, exactly the colour that made Caroline look anaemic and characterless, but suited Hannah's strong colouring and features.

"I feel a berk," said David. He looked ill at ease, but no more so than most men look in hired suits, and his burly muscularity remained.

"You look like Kirk Douglas," Hannah attempted encouragement. "Out-doorsy and masculine."

"Rubbish," said David. He was determined to be unco-operative.

"Like Burt Reynolds, then." Hannah was determined to be cheerful.

"Hannah, I . . ."

Bibi rushed in, a Sixties' ghost in white caftan, pale lipstick, and the pungent scent of joss-sticks. "Peace and love!" she greeted them.

"Right on," said Hannah.

"This is going to be the best ball ever," said Bibi. "The bursary fund will benefit and we'll enjoy ourselves."

"You've never worried about the bursary fund before, even when you were on the committee," Hannah pointed out.

"What bursary fund?" asked David.

"The old girls' association of the Convent of Mary Immaculate, where we both went to school," said Hannah. "They organise this ball every year and the profits go to the school's bursary fund."

"Caroline's on the committee, of course," said Bibi. "She goes every year. It can be fun seeing other old girls and thinking how much better we've aged than they have."

"On the other hand," said Hannah, "old girls keep getting younger and younger, like policemen, so it can be disheartening."

Bibi linked arms with both of them and headed for the drawing-room.

"Who is it going 'ner-haw'?" Hannah inquired.

"I'd say 'nyah-her' myself. It's Adrian Trench, one of the partners at Nicholas's firm. You know his wife Rosabelle. Poor girl, her son Charley just failed Common Entrance to Eton so try not to talk about schools or children."

"And don't you mention ice-lollies or you'll upset Derek Cummin."

"Why on earth?"

"Last time we met I told him he had an ice-lolly for a prick. Purely a hypothesis, no experimental verification."

"You mean he didn't slip you a length?" said David. It could have been intended humorously or disagreeably.

"More a shrimp, I'd have thought. Oh blah, wait till you see the first course," said Bibi.

"I don't understand," said Hannah.

"You will. Here's Hannah and David," said Bibi to the room at large.

When they sat down to dinner Derek was on Hannah's right so she turned first of all to the man on her left. He was in his mid-forties, slightly foreign and half-familiar.

"Oscar Mandel," he introduced himself. The spare man for

Caroline, the television personality, Bibi's boyfriend of years ago, one of the most notorious lechers in London.

"I'm Hannah, how do you do," said Hannah. Caroline, on Oscar's other side, was deep in conversation with Nicholas. She was bulky in expensive blue. "Of course I've seen you on television."

"Ah," said Oscar, and waited for an appreciative comment. His face was well-featured but puffy about the eyes and pouty about the mouth. His gaze was bold and challenging; his whole manner frankly sexual. Hannah looked at David who was looking at her. She smiled and he returned the smile, but reluctantly. He seemed preoccupied and Hannah began to wonder what he had been trying to tell her earlier.

"Don't you think so?" Hannah realised, with a start, that Oscar had asked her a question. "Don't you find Lady Caroline a most attractive, womanly woman?"

"Well, er – yes," said Hannah. "She has five children. That's quite womanly."

"I meant more her manner, her – being. There is a feminine quality about her missing from so many modern girls."

"She was brought up to pretend to be idiotic when there are men around, if that's what you mean." Loyalty to Caroline precluded pointing out that she was also fairly dim by nature.

"She's so fresh, so unspoiled. My work takes me into an artificial world, among pretentious, insincere people." Horses for courses, thought Hannah. "But every now and then, I meet an enchanting creature with a pure air of the real world of trees and sky and slow-moving, billowing clouds about her."

"This is how you see Caroline?"

"But yes."

"Her husband's in the pure air of the South Atlantic," said Hannah. "He's sailing with the Task Force."

The maid, an Irishwoman who always helped out at Bibi's parties, presented a dish. Hannah took a vol-au-vent which on investigation proved to be shrimp in a cream sauce. Bibi was looking at her, laughing. Now she understood Bibi's reference to the first course. Unsuspecting Derek, between her and Bibi, was directing a monologue across Bibi at Adrian. Hannah imagined his penis curled up like a little shrimp. ". . . Not that these people understand the first thing about financing. I'm not in it for my health . . ." Adrian, a thin man with a pronounced Adam's apple, was nodding encouragingly and releasing an occasional "ner-haw".

Bibi's face was whiter than her caftan. Hannah wondered why she was prepared to spend her valuable time, her running-out minutes, with these not special friends.

"Hello, Hannah," said Derek, turning to her abruptly. "Bibi tells me your divorce is through now."

"Correct." He was settling in to be unpleasant, which was all right by her.

"Brian's landed on his feet, I hear?"

"She's very charming. And well off."

"But older?"

"Older than I am. Older than Brian is. Not older than Margaret Thatcher or Nancy Reagan, or Ingrid Bergman . . ."

"Don't start rabbiting on. You're a terrible bore, Hannah."

"Am I?" said Hannah, considering the proposition. "I wouldn't say a *terrible* bore, just an everyday one, like most people are from time to time."

"Your boyfriend is, on the other hand, a *genuinely* terrible bore," said Derek, baring his assorted yellow teeth in an almost smile. "I was stuck with him before dinner. Where did you drag him in from, Hannah?"

"Poor you, wasn't David impressed enough by your financial wizardry? Olivia's right, you are sensitive."

"Enough bickering, my children," said Bibi lightly. Hannah tried to catch David's eye, she wanted the reassurance of a smile from him, but he was talking to Rosabelle Trench. She felt suddenly insecure. What if David was tired of her and was trying to tell her so?

She made an effort to enjoy herself, turned to Oscar Mandel. "There is nothing more erotic, more challenging to a mere male than a pure woman," Oscar whispered urgently into Caroline's ear. She was blushing, bridling like a skittish plough-horse on a frosty morning. Hannah didn't have the heart to spoil her fun and turned back to Derek.

"I've just started to work for a cleaning firm," she began.

"Just *love* your wallpaper, Bibi," said Olivia. She was looking at herself in the mirror, rearranging the frills on her black

Japanese-designed dress. She was pleased with herself. "Best decision I ever made, having my boobs augmented."

Bibi was lying utterly still on the bed, conserving her energy. Rosabelle Trench was Olivia's audience. Caroline took Hannah aside. Her eyes were gleaming with excitement and wine and her white neck was blotchy. "Isn't he gorgeous? Isn't he incredible?"

"Oscar?"

"Isn't he the most attractive man you've ever met or heard of?"

"No."

"You're just eccentric, Hannah. He is, he is, he is! And he fancies me!"

"He's got a reputation for fancying lots of women."

"But I'm different, he told me so."

"Yes, yes," said Hannah impatiently. She wanted to speak to David, she wondered how he was faring alone with the job-lot of men. She thought Caroline was too old to be taken in by Oscar Mandel, or not old enough.

"Listen, Hannah, listen, there's something I want to tell you. Please listen. I haven't told anyone else."

Caroline stood on tiptoe to reach Hannah's ear and whispered, "It's about Gerald. He's I-M-P-E-R-T-E-N-T."

Caroline never could spell, thought Hannah, hovering between "important" and "impotent" and deciding on the latter.

"How long for?" asked Hannah.

"Years, on and off," said Caroline. "He doesn't like to discuss it and lately it's been difficult for me." She blushed. "You know how it is, when the children are small or you're carrying a baby, then all you want is sleep. But for the last three years I've missed it."

"But – he must have managed at least five times."

"Oh, much more than that," said Caroline loyally. "About once a month in the early days. Not so much recently. Not at all in the last year. Promise promise *promise* you'll tell no one, specially Bibi. On your honour as an old girl of Mary Immaculate, promise and swear."

"I won't tell," said Hannah. "Why shouldn't Bibi know?"

"I don't want you talking about it behind my back. Come on, Hannah, what do you suggest?"

"How impotent is Gerald? Does he try?"

"Yes," said Caroline wriggling uncomfortably, keeping a weather eye on Bibi to see if she was listening. Olivia and Rosabelle were exchanging addresses at the tops of their voices and scribbling them down in small leather books. "Yes he tries, but no go. It upsets him, not succeeding. I feel responsible when it won't get hard, as if it's all my fault."

"I don't expect he worries about your clitoris."

Shocked giggle, puzzled expression. Hannah was more surprised by Caroline's interest in sex than by Gerald's incapacity. "What do you think?" demanded Caroline again.

"We can't talk about it now."

"But I want to, I must. It's been a secret for years."

Hannah was snappish and tense when they arrived at the ball. More than anything, she wanted an opportunity to speak to David alone, but it seemed as if he was deliberately avoiding her. She stood on the steps of the hotel with Oscar and Caroline and watched David drive the car away to park it, not even certain that he would park it and return, with a clear mental picture of him driving on and away and leaving her abandoned in a ridiculous dress.

The ball was well attended. It was held in the usual hotel, not quite of the first rank but overlooking Hyde Park; big enough to have a ballroom, established enough to make the occasion passably dignified without being impossibly expensive. When Hannah first entered the ballroom with its smell of flowers and floorpolish and cigars she felt relieved. At any rate in these surroundings, amid so many familiar faces including even a few priests and nuns, Caroline would be held to the strict line of her duty by the pressure of circumstances. In the car on the way from Bibi's, Oscar's hand had been pressed to Caroline's breast. Goodness knew where they were now.

She joined Nicholas and Bibi at their well-placed table not too near the usual band. "Oscar's a quick worker," she said. Nicholas made a face. He hadn't ever come to terms with Bibi's ex-boyfriends.

"I didn't think he'd do so well with Caroline," admitted Bibi. "She's kicking up her heels a bit. You're not enjoying yourself, Hannah."

"Not much," said Hannah.

"Anything I can do?" said Nicholas. "Would you like to dance?"

"Go on," said Bibi.

Hannah went to dance, her heart mutinous, her lips smiling. Nicholas took her in a decisive but incompetent grip and they embarked on a compromise shuffle. "Strangers in the night," he hummed, "ta ta ta ta ta, lovers at first sight, tarum ti ta ta."

"How are your teeth, Nicholas?" asked Hannah, all her concentration focused on the absent David.

"Not too good. I've been transferred to the gum and denture specialist. Only a matter of time before they fall out."

"Ten years ago thirty-seven per cent of the British population had false teeth."

"You look most attractive in that dress." The hand resting on her hip tightened. Hannah pulled herself slightly away from him, nodded to a familiar face (the beefy prefect she had been in love with, what on earth was her name? And why had she chosen lime green chiffon?).

"Mind if I cut in?" said David, and Hannah grasped him with a positive wail of relief.

"I thought you'd gone. Oh, David, I thought you'd gone."

"Without saying goodbye? Don't be silly. Are you a keen dancer?"

"Is this small talk?"

"Because I'd rather sit out. I dislike dancing and I want to talk to you." They retreated behind a pillar. "It's about Glynis and the children. They've moved back to Britain, I found out today. They'll be living in Aberystwyth, near Glynis's family."

Hannah felt apprehension, foreboding, and irritation with wretched Glynis who couldn't even stick to one continent. But she knew David wanted to see his children; she imagined what it would have been like to lose Karen and John. "I'm glad," she said. "That means you'll be able to see them. That's marvellous news."

He looked uncomfortable.

"What haven't you told me?"

"I'm going to Wales tomorrow."

"How long for?"

"I don't know." He took her hand. "I honestly don't know, Hannah. I want to find out if there's work for me, and look for a flat."

"A flat? Why?" She was stupid with shock. "You've got a flat in Highgate."

"Hannah, try and understand. I haven't seen the children for years. If I don't live near them they'll grow up not knowing me."

Let them. Bloody let them, screamed Hannah silently, swallowing the words. "But what about me?" My children are in day schools here, I work in a school here, I'm just starting a business here. What about me?

"That's it. That's why I didn't know how to tell you. But we don't belong together anyhow. Look at this kind of party, it's second nature to you, and I hate it. We come from different worlds."

"That's a cheap excuse. I go to parties like this once in a blue moon, and I only came to this one because Bibi's dying and she asked me to."

"You're at ease with men like that." His gesture indicated their table.

"Only donkeys are at ease with men who go 'ner-haw'."

"What do you expect me to do?"

"Marry me," said Hannah, goaded beyond endurance.

"I can't marry you. I've got my life and my children and you've got your life and your children."

"And you don't want to."

"And I don't want to. We'd lose tax relief on our mortgages, for a start."

"Come to that," said Hannah, her blood thoroughly up, "I don't want to marry you either. I'd just prefer not to be married to you in Highgate rather than Aberystwyth. Can't Glynis live in London like anyone else?"

"You're not talking sense."

"I'm *talking* sense, you aren't *listening* sense. You know perfectly well what I mean. Oh, David, I'll miss you so much." Large tears ran down her nose and plopped on the upper curve of her breasts. He thrust a handkerchief in her direction. "And don't tell me how pretty I look when I'm angry," she spluttered.

"That was the last thing on my mind," said David.

Oscar and Caroline approached them, hand in hand. Caroline had a dazed, fulfilled expression that Hannah found particularly irritating. No danger of Oscar Mandel going to Aberystwyth, or anywhere west of Shepherd's Bush.

"Are you having gorgeous fun?" asked Caroline. "Is this a Cole Porter song they're playing? It reminds me of that lovely film with Grace Kelly, do you remember Hannah, where she kisses Frank Sinatra by the swimming pool? Don't you think Oscar looks a little like Frank Sinatra?"

"About as much as you look like Louis Armstrong," snapped Hannah.

"You're beautiful when you're angry," said Oscar Mandel. "Have we said something to upset you?"

"And a logo is very important," said Adrian Trench, pushing Hannah in a subtle reverse spin that suited ill with the Beach Boys medley the band were playing. "Take Exxon, now. They spent hundreds of thousands of pounds to find a logo that meant nothing in any known language."

"They could just have taken a line from the *Guardian*," said Hannah.

"Ner-haw ner-haw, no but really. That's where Nicholas comes in. He's a logo man, he's an eye for a selling design. Terrible about Bibi. He's taking it well, what do you think?"

"Surprisingly well." David was sitting at the table with Caroline who was drinking glass after glass of German white wine.

"I'm glad the wine's been a success," said Adrian, following her gaze. "A new account. Not exactly vintage stuff, but decent enough, and cheap."

"Caroline's obviously enjoying it."

"Not like her to be so unbuttoned, ner-haw, still, can't be an easy time with hubby doing press-ups on a deck somewhere in the South Atlantic. Did you see the film on the News last night? Fit as anything, our chaps."

Hannah remembered the propaganda film; bright-eyed young soldiers thudding up and down in feats of physical endeavour, a reassuring BBC voice-over, a map of the Falklands with a Union Jack in the corner in case the viewer forgot what we were fighting for.

"Teach 'em a lesson," said Adrian. "Can't mess with us. What d'you think of Maggie Thatcher? Good man, eh?"

"I think she's very Victorian," said Hannah. "Right and wrong confused with us and them, and a gun boat or ten if the foreigners don't see it our way."

Adrian held her at arm's length. "You mean you don't agree with her policy?"

"I think it's going to be expensive," said Hannah. She didn't want to be contentious; Adrian meant to be civil, or at least she gave him the benefit of her liking for Rosabelle. "I hope Gerald comes back safe and sound."

"So do I." He spun her round again.

Back at the table Caroline was in the middle of a story about one of her children. "They damn near sacked him. The headmistress rang up last week, wanted to speak to Gerald, couldn't of course, spoke to me instead. Damn near sacked him, sorry shouldn't swear."

"What had he done? Who is it, anyway?"

"Young Gerald, the eldest. They'd caught him sniffing glue. Peculiar thing to do, Hannah. Sniffing glue."

"It's fashionable at the moment."

"He always liked stationery. Sharp pencils and rolls of Sellotape, funny interests children develop."

"So what happened?"

"Headmaster gave him six of the best and a talking-to. Oh good, here's Oscar. Move over, David, that's Oscar's place."

"Thanks awfully, Bibi, it was a smashing evening," said Hannah. They were waiting for the bewigged elderly cloakroom attendant to find their coats.

"Don't give me that," said Bibi, "you're bloody miserable."

"That's David, not your party. Oh, Bibi, he's going to Aberystwyth."

"Back to Glynis?"

"To be near his children."

"Give me a ring tomorrow and we'll talk about it," as Caroline approached. "Do you want a lift, Caro?"

"No, thank you. Oscar's taking me," said Caroline carefully, and closed her piggy ancestral eye in a lewd wink.

*

David and Hannah drove home in silence. She was too tired and dispirited to talk. There was nothing to say. Early morning London looked familiar, dishevelled. Aberystwyth was probably tidy in the early morning, with only milkmen about their legitimate business, and no drunks or junkies in doorways. She couldn't live in Aberystwyth. She hadn't been asked to live in Aberystwyth. She felt like a ninepin in a bowling alley, hardly up before it is knocked sprawling once more.

When they reached her house David said, "Do you want me to come in?"

"Why not?" said Hannah. "It's late enough, you must be tired."

She let the dogs out, coercing them into the chilly dawn garden; she made two cups of tea, took them upstairs, undressed, lay beside David sipping the tea. Hip to hip, silent, things weren't quite so bad.

Two days later Hannah was explaining about the cleaners to Miss Thirkettle. "I wouldn't mind," said the headmistress. "I wouldn't mind at all. The cleaners we have now are useless, as you say. But I have to warn you . . ." she hesitated. "In the strictest confidence."

"I said nothing the last time you asked me to keep a confidence. About Mrs Fanshawe trying to sell the school."

"I know you said nothing. That was a grave disappointment to me, I expected you to leak the news to the whole staff-room."

"Did you want me to?"

"Yes. Prepare the teachers for the blow, when it comes. It was an error of judgment on my part. Very few women keep secrets, and I didn't suppose you were one of them."

Crafty old bat, thought Hannah. "About the cleaners?" she prompted.

"This is in complete confidence, as I said. The announcement to school and parents will be made next week; St Ethelberta's will close at the end of the summer term."

Miss Thirkettle didn't look unhappy; she looked smug.

"Explain what you're pleased about," said Hannah.

"I've sold it to St Margaret's round the corner. They'll take in any of our girls who want to stay, and there may be work for some of the teachers. Almost certainly for you, if the cleaners scheme hasn't got off the ground yet."

"That is good news."

"And there'll be redundancy payments, of course."

"That'll hardly involve me."

"A small consideration, yes. I wanted to be fair to everyone. My lawyers have arranged it so that redundancy payments are substantial. More substantial than they need be."

Hannah was beginning to follow. "Will there be much left over for Mrs Fanshawe?"

Miss Thirkettle gave a great bellow of laughter and stamped her brogues. "Not much! Not much at all! The lawyers fixed it up all right and tight."

"What about you?"

"I'm nicely, thank you."

"But what you're saying is that the cleaners may not be needed after the end of this term."

"That's it."

"I'll go and see them at St Margaret's. They might need my cleaners over there."

Even to herself Hannah sounded despondent. She knew that, whatever her feelings about David, she should press ahead determinedly with the cleaners scheme. That is what budding tycoons were supposed to do. But it wasn't easy, especially faced with the prospect of St Ethelberta's closing. It seemed to Hannah that no sooner had she settled down and got used to something, than it closed or moved. The school represented a kind of security, a haven of English dottiness – Betjeman suburban and Larkin drab, but individual; and for many, happy. For Miss Thirkettle, however she rejoiced in thwarting Mrs Fanshawe, it must be an enormous wrench.

"Won't you miss the school?"

"Human nature to resist change," said Miss Thirkettle. "Doesn't do to indulge it. Been here since 1938. Good innings. Nearly seven hundred girls, give or take a few."

The break bell rang. It was a bright spring day, warm, blue sky with powder-puff clouds and sunlight gilding the dusty evergreen bushes. It was the first day of the year that Miss Thirkettle had allowed the junior girls out for their break. Hannah could hear them thunder down the stairs and out the side door; they scattered on to the grass in front of the headmistress's window. Two senior girls supervised them. Felicity Wakefield and Kimia Panahizadi, fair head and dark head, efficiently carrying out their duties as prefects, dispensing break buns and orange juice in the simple ritual, established for years.

"St Paul's have agreed to take Kimia," said Miss Thirkettle. "Brilliant girl, born manager. Lucky she's not an African. End up as a dictator with heads of her enemies in the refrigerator."

"What's happening to Felicity?"

"Nursery nursing. Two-year course. Give her the opportunity to look after people, and if they're very young people they won't be irritated by her."

"That's a good plan."

"I will miss them. Of course I will," said Miss Thirkettle, her bristly grey eyebrows knotted in an attempt to appear casual. "The school's given me an interest, prevented me from turning into Amanda Fanshawe, lying and cheating and throwing good money after receding looks."

The girls' shouts, like punctuation to their conversation, like an elegy for the school, echoed in the April air.

8

"Mummy," said Karen. She sounded exasperated. Hannah, washing her hair at the kitchen sink because John was in the bath upstairs, shook water from her ears.

"What?"

"I've been trying to talk to you for ages. It's amazing. In the paper. A photograph and everything."

The children were home for summer half-term; it was only the second day; already Hannah was in a state of controlled exasperation. "I couldn't hear you. My head was under water."

"In the paper here." Karen was excited. "There's a photograph as well, look."

Hannah wrapped a towel round her head. "Is it Charlotte St Leger's mother? Or that Etonian head-banging group?"

"No. It's Caroline, your friend Caroline, you know. It says she's going out with Oscar Mandel. They're in a night-club, see?"

Through shampoo-stinging eyes, Hannah saw, unsurprised. Recently Caroline had been brazen, flaunting her affair with Oscar, putting herself beyond discretion and recovery. In the photograph she looked vulnerable, appealing in her stolid innocence beside Oscar's polished profile suitably arranged for the camera. On the page opposite was a picture story of the brave men now garrisoning the conquered Falklands. Only a week after the Argentine surrender and most newspapers had dropped the Falklands. This rabid Tory publication would presumably be publishing photographs of grinning soldiers with visibly high morale for months. By which time Gerald would have returned to marital disaster. It would be a brutal shock, unless Caroline had already sent him a "dear Gerald" letter. The whole episode disturbed Hannah. She could see no possible good in it; but there was no arguing with Caroline.

She moved in a haze of infatuation, impervious to reason, deaf to sense, coated skin deep in Oscar's oily sexuality.

"I thought Caroline was respectable," said Karen. "I thought..."

"Do keep the newspaper out of the marmalade," said Hannah.

"Is she really carrying on with Oscar Mandel? Oh yuck, he's so *obvious*, all those winks and leers and hugging the women on his telly programme."

Hannah wasn't listening. She was planning her day. Two hours at the office should be enough for the backlog of paperwork; scouting for new contracts could wait till the children were back at school; lucky St Ethelberta's half-term coincided with theirs. Back here, make lunch, go out in the afternoon – boating on the Serpentine, John could show off his rowing and Karen her legs. Supper, children's choice, probably spaghetti bolognese, then watching television and sorting through price lists of heavy duty cleaning equipment. Not an exciting day, but placid, satisfying, like so much of her life at present and in prospect.

Even the children were happy. Karen had finally, grudgingly, admitted that the school she would move to in September had its advantages. "And of course Peregrine will be in London so we can see a lot of each other..." And John was looking forward to being at home and watching television in the evenings. Hannah would have been content – if only the absence of David didn't cobweb everything she did.

Karen was still talking. "You've lost weight, Mummy, I can see through your nightdress. Is David going to be here today?"

"No. He's in Wales, at the moment, decorating his new flat. Remember I told you he was getting a flat near his children?"

"Oh yeah," said Karen, indifferent. "I wanted him to fix my wardrobe. When'll he be back?"

"Soon. He's still working in London. There isn't enough of his special building work in Wales." Talking about him was a pleasure, even to an apathetic audience. Hannah was uneasily aware that she had mishandled her dealings with him over the move to Wales. He had offered compromises: he would still be working in London, he could see her then.

"But your main home will be in Aberystwyth. You'll sell the London flat?"

"No, I'll need a base here."

"You have a base here. With me."

He smiled and shook his head. "Won't do. You'll get fed up with me."

"How do you know?"

"Let's not risk it."

He wouldn't commit himself, he wouldn't make promises, he didn't say what he felt for her. The more she pressed him, the more silent he became. She gave an ultimatum. Unless he made his position clear, she preferred not to see him.

"I thought my position was clear."

"What position?"

"Weekends I live in Aberystwyth and see my children. Most weekdays I work in London, and see you."

"With what in mind?"

"Nothing. You know I don't think, or so you always say." He was irritated but she ploughed on.

"Then I'd rather not see you."

"If that's what you want."

"Don't you mind?" she said, fishing for consolation.

"I'll miss you in bed," he said. Perhaps he meant a compliment. Perhaps he meant it jocularly. Hannah was in no mood for runic interpretations.

"Is that all?"

"I like your company."

"Is that all?"

"You make me laugh."

He was himself, unyielding, so frustrating to Hannah that she longed to be indifferent to him. His refusal to bend to her wishes angered her. When she cared so much for him, how could he care so little for her, give her so little reassurance?

"You can come to Aberystwyth," he offered. "On weekends. You can . . ."

"I don't want to go to bloody Aberystwyth," flamed Hannah. Even as she spoke it sounded childish to her, but determined self-pity prevented her from accepting his offered half-loaf.

So for the last week he hadn't come to see her. He was probably happy with his children. She told herself she was pleased for him. Her passion for him had acquired a considerable substratum of affection and she wanted him to be happy. But when he talked about the children, showed her photographs, recounted every detail of their new older appearance and ways, his obvious pleasure in their company was a bitter contrast to his inability to express affection for her.

"No, David won't be coming," she repeated wistfully.

"You just said that," said Karen scornfully. "Phone. I'll get it." Pause. "For you."

"Ask who it is."

"Some hospital."

Bibi, thought Hannah taking the receiver, watching Karen's slender mini-skirted back view springing up the stairs in a spontaneous display of youth and health.

"Mrs Dodgson?" said the crisp female voice. "I'm calling from the private ward of St Mary's Hospital, Paddington. Mrs Ainsworth has just been admitted."

"Is she . . . how is she?"

"Resting comfortably," said the voice. "Unfortunately Mr Ainsworth can't be reached."

"He's in Germany for a couple of days," said Hannah.

"So I understand. Mrs Ainsworth collapsed in the street and was brought in by an ambulance. She would like you to bring in some nightdresses and washing things for her. She said you had a key and you'd know what to bring."

"How long will she be staying?"

The voice hesitated and Hannah imagined Bibi dying as they spoke. "I'll just bring a few things quickly," she hurried on to prevent the woman from replying.

Bibi's flat was silent and tidy, her duvet shaken into orderly submission, not even a coffee cup in the sink. No sign of the nurse who should have been there since nine o'clock. Perhaps Bibi had been feeling better enough to get up and go out on her own. Hannah clung to that idea, replaying it like a video-cassette. Bibi feeling unexpectedly well, going out into the summer morning, then fainting – nothing more serious – weak from being in bed, fainting, and now in a comfortable private room, strength being restored by food and care. This fantasy sustained her into the walk-in cupboard.

She sorted through the nightdress shelf, Bibi's dresses hanging each side of her, ghosts of triumphs past. Another video-cassette played on her mental screen, this time herself sorting Bibi's clothes after her death. Thank heavens Nicholas would probably do it alone. But that wouldn't be for months yet, even a year, Hannah lied to herself.

Three nightdresses, that would do, delicate cotton, decent enough for hospital. A pale green silk kimono, Bibi's favourite summer garment. Silk matching slippers. Leaving the cupboard, she stubbed her toe on a parcel, bent down to move it out of the way, saw the Mothercare wrapping paper. She couldn't resist looking inside. It was a jumble: nappies, bibs, nappy pins, zinc ointment, terry rompsuits, a riot of baby whimsy covered in little animals and flowers. Bibi must have bought them last August, during the short time she was convinced she was pregnant. Why hadn't she got rid of them? She wasn't a hoarder like Hannah. Bibi's housekeeping was organised, winter clothes cleaned and stored in bags when summer came, one bottle of shampoo finished before another was started, spare loo rolls under the basin, shopping unpacked and put away as soon as it was brought home. She hadn't talked about babies since discovering her cancer, not a word. Who knew what she had hoped?

It was a warm day but overcast and Paddington was grim and dusty. Hannah parked on a double yellow line and scribbled a note: "Traffic warden. Visiting patient in hospital. Please don't tow away."

The flower stall offered only attenuated town flowers, spindly and disheartened. Hannah bought some anyway. The hospital was familiar; Caroline had produced all her children there and Hannah threaded her way through the corridors and up the stairs to the private wing. The notice said, "All visitors please report to Sister's office"; Hannah did so. Sister was the owner of the voice on the telephone, a small youngish woman with a brisk manner that softened slightly when Hannah announced her business. "Can I see Mrs Ainsworth?"

"She's been heavily sedated, she may not recognise you."

"I'd like to see her anyway."

"Room 86. Over there."

It was a small room dominated by the bed and a television set. Bibi's body in a hospital gown hardly interrupted the tightly pulled sheets. Her head was sideways on the pillow. She was gazing at the window. The curtains, a lurid acid yellow, were lifting in the breeze. They seemed to have a life of their own. They certainly had more life than Bibi.

"Hello," said Hannah.

Bibi didn't answer but she rolled her head on the pillow with a lazy motion. Her face looked as sunken and pinched as usual, but her eyes were glazed and kept wobbling out of focus.

"It's me."

"Hannah," she said.

"I've brought you some flowers."

"Thank you," said Bibi, then focused on them. "They're *awful*," she said. "They look how I feel."

"How do you feel?"

"Past it. Stoned. I'm full of morphine. Officially and medically high."

"I brought nightdresses, make-up, washing things, the cassette player and some tapes."

"Let's have the Stones."

Hannah found a Stones tape, put it on quietly, began unpacking and putting away.

"What time is it?" said Bibi.

"About eleven."

"Thanks for coming."

She was silent for some minutes, drifting. Hannah crossed to the window, looked into the street below. Sex shops, chemists, cheap cafés. She stuck her head out to escape from the hospital smell of ether and immersed herself in the smell of hot tar from the road menders beneath, with an overtone of petrol fumes and stale fat frying. The rumble of traffic was a comforting physical presence. Hannah loved London, even the dirt. But she missed David. Would now and then David be better than nothing? Seeing him only when he could spare the time, when he wasn't with the children. So many of her days would be spent without an adult companion; so much of his involvement would be away from her. For years she would have only part of him...

"What are you thinking about?" said Bibi in a more normal voice.

"David," said Hannah.

"You still haven't heard from him?"

"No."

"He came to visit me last week."

Hannah sat down beside the bed. Bibi didn't go on; Hannah wouldn't ask. "When does Nicholas get back?" she asked instead. "And what were you doing out on your own anyway? Didn't the nurse come?"

"I cancelled her." Bibi's ravaged face was a vision of innocence.

"What are you up to?" said Hannah. "Don't think you can fool me."

"Leave it, Hannah," said Bibi.

"I certainly won't. Where were you going?"

"Out. By myself. I didn't take my pain pills last night or this morning. I wanted to be conscious for once. But when I was walking it hurt too much and I fainted. Will you ring my mother, Hannah?"

"What do you want me to tell her?"

"Just say I'm in hospital and ask her to come."

Hannah hesitated, wondering if Bibi was rambling. "Are you sure?"

"I want my mother to know. I think I'm dying, Hannah."

"I hope not," said Hannah.

"I can't concentrate. Too full of dope." Bibi's voice drifted away. Hannah hurried to the door and found a nurse.

"Public telephone down the hall," she said, and smiled widely, teeth white and gums pink against her Jamaican skin.

Search through bag, address book, dial. Ring ring ring ring.

"Beatrice? Hannah Dodgson here."

"Hello, Hannah," said a voice full of apprehension. "Is it Bibi?"

"She's at St Mary's, Paddington, the private ward. She'd like you to come and see her."

"She's conscious, then."

"Oh yes."

"I'll come at once." Pulling herself to courtesy: "How are you, my dear? It's been ages since we met."

"I'm very well," said Hannah, guilty. "See you soon, then."

"Yes. Tell her I'll start immediately. Thank you for letting me know. Is Nicholas still in Germany?"

"He'll be back any time."

Hannah was beginning to have a sense of doomed urgency.

Bibi was alert when she returned to her room. "Was she there?"

"Yes. She's coming straight away."

"Good. Don't leave me, Hannah. It's beginning to hurt again. Talk to me."

"Caroline's still going out with Oscar," said Hannah. "There was a photograph of them in the *Express* this morning."

"What did Caroline wear?"

"It wasn't the kind of photograph you can see clothes in, just heads." Hannah smiled. "Funny. She and I are both taking your leavings – David and Oscar."

Bibi turned slowly, her eyes searching for Hannah's, and she tried for a smile. "Don't think of David as a leaving. Think of him as sampled and thoroughly recommended." Pause. "Do you know what the nurse told me? The Princess of Wales is going to have her baby in this hospital. Next month. Perhaps in this very room, Hannah."

"Oh."

"In this room, imagine." Her face puckered in muzzy pain. "Would you tell the Sister it's hurting? Please?"

Bibi was dozing. Her mother arrived first; close behind, Nicholas. It was time for Hannah to go. She was at the door and Bibi's voice halted her. "Hannah? Are you going, Hannah?"

"Yes."

"I want to tell you something." Her hand stretched out in a feeble reaching gesture. Hannah stood near the bed, took her hand. "The Princess can't possibly have her baby here," said Bibi.

"Why not?"

"Look at those bloody curtains. They're hideous."

"I cooked the lunch," Karen announced proudly. "Hamburgers and baked beans. How's Bibi?"

"Very ill."

"Is she dying?"

"I'm not sure. She's very sleepy from the drugs." Hannah's eyes were swollen with tears and John patted her, awkward, not liking her hurt.

"I've entered a competition," he said. "For a Granada. We could win a Granada. A spot-the-ball competition."

"Shut up," said Karen. "Not now. Do you want some tea, Mummy?" Hannah sat and drank the tea, looking at Karen, so young and pretty even with her ridiculous pit-pony hairstyle growing out from punk and sticking up at the front, stiffened with sugar and water.

When Bibi died there would be no measuring the loss.

"David rang," said Karen. "He left his telephone number. He'll be in Wales till the day after tomorrow."

The telephone rang. Let it be David, thought Hannah. John answered.

"It's Granny Crester-Fyfe."

Say I'm out, Hannah pantomimed, too late. "Hello, Jane."

"I wish you'd call me Mother," said Jane, fretfully. "Have you a cold? Why are you snuffling?"

"I'm crying. Bibi's in hospital."

"That girl. Racketing about. And her poor mother, perfectly normal, living in Rottingdean."

"I can't talk now."

"Why?"

"I'm going to Wales." As soon as she said it, it became true. "Goodbye." She put the receiver down on a plaintive question.

"This is very sudden, surely?" said Brian, every inch the well-kept man; cavalry twill trousers, handmade shoes, a Harris tweed jacket. Children's cases, sag-bags, cassette players were heaped on the Eaton Square pavement. "Why are you in a clapped-out van with Zabriskie Cleaners on the side? Why aren't you in the Renault?"

"It wouldn't start."

"Bet it hasn't been serviced."

Karen moved anxiously between them and Hannah made an effort to smile. "Bibi's ill, Daddy."

Brian raised his eyebrows. The tan suited him. He looked sleek and well maintained, like a chauffeur-tended Jaguar. "Cancer, isn't it?"

"Yes."

"She never looked after herself properly. I expect she ate too many saturated fats."

"They don't cause cancer," said Hannah, remembering Brian's hypochondriacal garbling of popular medical theories. But Brian, even radiant with money, was blurred in her view. She imagined Bibi, head turning jerkily on her hospital pillow.

"So you're driving this old thing to Wales."

"Aberystwyth."

"Better take the A44. Knowing you and maps, you'll get lost otherwise. Check the oil and tyre-pressure before you start."

"OK."

"Poor Bibi," said Brian. "Any chance she'll recover?"

"Not much."

"When'll you be back from Wales?"

"Day after tomorrow."

Bark bark went the spaniels, winding John into a maypole with their leads.

"Good photograph of you in the *Sun*," said Brian.

"I didn't see it."

"Six months ago now. At the Law Courts. You're looking good, Hannah. Bit puffy around the eyes."

"Tears."

"So I guessed. You'll want to be off, then. Come on, kids, get moving."

The van rattled her bones. The heater was broken, the bodywork draughty. She followed the road signs automatically. A40, A34, A44. She didn't think about David and his welcome. She took him for granted. Her mind was a jumble of people and events. Miss Thirkettle, Marjorie, the barmitzvah man; dinner at the Cummins and the hospital room where even now Nicholas would be sitting by a sleeping Bibi, probably flossing his teeth. Mrs Harris, Nigel, Pendlebury fitting in a last doughnut before his evening cocoa; Mr Patel missing his van if he happened to drop into the office. Felicity Wakefield cramming for the O levels she would certainly fail. Caroline copulating with Oscar.

Darkened Wales and the road was winding, unexpected. She had to slow down; the van didn't find hills easy. She stopped at a tripper's café that was just about to close for the night and drank a cup of tea. The café had a telephone and she dialled David's number. After ten rings he answered. "David Bowen speaking."

Pip pip pip. The ten pence piece wouldn't go in at first. "This is Hannah."

"Where are you?"

"Near Rhayader. Driving to Aberystwyth."

"I'll stay up for you."

The last part of the journey passed quickly; she occupied her mind with plans for Zabriskie Cleaners. Persuade Mr Patel to invest enough to modernise the equipment. Organise training schemes for supervisors – soon there would be too much to do herself. Sweet-talk Nicholas into doing layout for a brochure and flysheets.

Once in the town David's directions weren't hard to follow. She drove along the seafront, turned right up the hill and crawled by the row of terraced houses looking for number 43. Exactly half the number of Bibi's hospital room. If she was still in it.

She stopped the van, got out, stretched the ache from her body, rang the doorbell marked Bowen, and stood waiting, washed in the seaweed air.

The door opened. David stood there. He looked very unlike Brian.

"I think Bibi's dying," said Hannah.

"Come and get warm," said David, and put his arm round her shoulder.

9

The following morning, Hannah was thirty-six.